The Nursing Home Murder

Dame Ngaio Marsh was born in New Zealand in 1895 and died in February 1982. She wrote over 30 detective novels and many of her stories have theatrical settings, for Ngaio Marsh's real passion was the theatre. She was both actress and producer and almost single-handedly revived the New Zealand public's interest in the theatre. It was for this work that the received what she called her 'damery' in 1966.

NGAIO MARSH

THE NURSING HOME MURDER

HarperCollins*Publishers*

HarperCollins*Publishers*
77-85 Fulham Palace Road
Hammersmith, London W6 8JB

This paperback edition published 1999
1

First published in Great Britain by
Geoffrey Bles 1935

Copyright Ngaio Marsh 1935

ISBN 978 0 00 794466 8

Printed in Great Britain by
Clays Ltd, St Ives plc

Contents

CHAPTER I

10 Downing Street

Friday, the fifth. Afternoon.

The Home Secretary, with an air of finality, laid down the papers from which he had been reading and glanced round the table. He was struck, not for the first time, by the owlish solemnity of the other members of the Cabinet. "Really," he thought, "we look for all the world like a Cabinet Meeting in a cinema. We are too good to be true." As if to confirm this impression, the Prime Minister flung himself back in his chair, laid the palms of his hands on the table, and cleared his throat.

"Well, gentlemen," he said portentously, "there we have it."

"Strong!" said the Foreign Secretary. He folded his arms and stared at the ceiling.

"Drastic!" added the Lord Chancellor. "I venture to think—drastic."

"But in my opinion," the Postmaster-General said, "neither too strong nor too drastic." He fidgeted with his tie and became almost human. "Damn it all," he said irritably, "we've got to do something."

There was a pause. The Home Secretary drew in his breath sharply.

"Well," repeated the Prime Minister, "we have talked a great deal, gentlemen, and now we've heard the proposed Bill. We have all the facts. To put it briefly, we are perfectly well aware of the activities of these anarchistic personages. We know what they are about and we know they mean to take definite action. We are agreed that the importance of the matter can hardly be overstated. The reports from the F.O., the Secret Service and the C.I.D. are sufficiently conclusive. We have to deal with a definite menace and a growing menace. It's a bad business. This Bill"—he made a gesture towards the Home Secretary—"may be drastic. Does anyone think it too drastic? Should it be modified?"

"No," said the Postmaster-General. "No."

"I agree," said the Attorney-General.

"Has it occurred to you," asked the Lord Chancellor, looking across the table to the Home Secretary, "that you yourself, Sir Derek, have most cause to hesitate?"

The others looked at him. The Home Secretary smiled faintly.

"As sponsor for this Bill," continued the Lord Chancellor, "you will get a lot of limelight. We know what these people are capable of doing. Assassination is a word that occurs rather frequently in the reports." The Home Secretary's smile broadened a little. "I think I do not exaggerate if I say their attention will be focused on yourself. Have you considered this possibility, my dear fellow?"

"I quite appreciate your point," answered the Home Secretary. "The Bill is my child—I'll not disclaim parentship and I'll look after myself."

"I think the Home Secretary should be given proper protection," said the Chancellor of the Exchequer.

"Certainly," agreed the Prime Minister warmly. "We owe it to the country. Her valuable assets must be guarded. The Home Secretary is an extremely valuable asset."

Sir Derek made a curious grimace.

"I can assure you," he said, "that I'm in no hurry to play the hero's part in a theatrical assassination. On the other hand, I really don't feel there is any necessity for me to walk down to the House surrounded by policemen dressed up as private secretaries and journalists."

"I met Roderick Alleyn of the C.I.D. yesterday," said the Prime Minister ponderously, "and discussed this business quite unofficially with him. He's had these gentry under his eye for some time. He's the last man on earth to exaggerate a position of this sort. He considers that the Minister who introduces a Bill to deal with them will be in real danger from the organisation. I strongly urge you to let the Yard take any measures it thinks necessary for your protection."

"Very well," said Sir Derek. He moved uneasily in his chair and passed his hand over his face. "I take it," he added wearily, "that the Cabinet approves the introduction of the Bill?"

They fell to discussing again the suggested measures. Their behaviour was weirdly solemn. They used parliamentary phrases and politicians' gestures. It was as though they had so saturated themselves with professional behaviourism that they had lost the knack of being natural. The Home Secretary sat with his eyes fixed on the papers before him, as though sunk in a profound and unwilling meditation.

At last the Prime Minister put the matter to the vote—did the Cabinet consider the introduction of the Home Secretary's Bill advisable? It did.

"Well," said the Prime Minister, "that is as far as we need go."

The Home Secretary groaned slightly.

. They all turned to him. His face was extremely white and he was leaning forward over the table.

"O'Callaghan!" exclaimed the Postmaster-General. "What's the matter? You're ill?"

"It's all right. Pain. Pass off in a moment."

"Brandy," said the Prime Minister and stretched out his hand to a bell.

"Water," whispered Sir Derek. "Just water." When it came he drank it greedily and then mopped his face.

"Better," he told them presently, "I'm sorry."

They looked uncomfortable and concerned. The Lord Chancellor hovered uncertainly over him. The others eyed him with that horrified ineptitude with which we observe sudden illness in our fellow men.

"I must apologise," said Sir Derek. "I've had one or two bouts like this lately. Appendix, I imagine. I'll have to get vetted. It's an infernal bore for myself and everyone else. I want to stave it off until after this business if I can." He drew himself up in his chair, paused a moment, and then got slowly to his feet.

"Everything settled?" he asked.

"Yes, yes. Won't you lie down for a little?" suggested the Prime Minister.

"Thank you so much, P.M.—no, I'll go home, I think. If someone could tell my chauffeur——" A secretary was summoned. O'Callaghan turned to the door. The Postmaster-General made as if to take his arm. Sir Derek nodded his thanks, but walked out independently. In the hall the secretary took his coat from the butler and helped him into it.

11

"Shall I come out to the car, Sir Derek?"

"No, thank you, my boy. I'm my own man again." With a word of farewell to the Prime Minister he went out alone.

"He looks devilish ill," said the Prime Minister irritably. "I hope to heaven it's not serious."

"It'll be damned awkward if it is," said the Postmaster-General. "Poor old O'Callaghan," he added hurriedly.

In his car the Home Secretary looked out of the window drearily. They turned out of Downing Street into Whitehall. It was a cold, gusty evening. The faces of the people in the streets looked pinched and their clothes drab and uneventful. Their heads were bent to the wind. A thin rain was driving fitfully across the window-pane. He wondered if he was going to be very ill. He was overwhelmed with melancholy. Perhaps he would die of this thing that seized him with such devastating agony. That would save the anarchists and the C.I.D. a lot of trouble. It would also save him a lot of trouble. Did he really care tuppence about his Bill or about the machinations of people who wanted to revolutionise the system of British government? Did he care about anything or anybody? He was conscious only of a pallid indifference and an overwhelming inertia. He was going to be ill.

At the top of Constitution Hill his car was held up by a traffic jam. A taxi drew up close beside it. He could see that there was a fare inside, but no more than that. The driver looked several times at O'Callaghan's chauffeur and called out something which his man answered gruffly. O'Callaghan had the feeling that the person inside the taxi stared in at his window. He was being watched. He had experienced this sensation many times lately. He thought, with a sort of amusement, of the Prime Minister's anxiety. He pulled a cord and the inside of the car was flooded with light.

"Give them a good view while I'm about it," he thought grimly.

To his surprise the windows of the taxi were lit up as if in answer. He peered across, shading the pane with his hand. The taxi's fare was a solitary man in a dinner-jacket. He sat with his hands resting on the knob of a stick. His silk hat was worn at a slight angle, revealing a clear-cut and singularly handsome profile. It was an intelligent and well-bred face, with a straight nose, firm mouth and dark eyes. The man did not turn his head, and while Sir Derek O'Callaghan still watched him, the ranks of cars moved on and the taxi was left behind.

"That's someone I know," thought O'Callaghan with a kind of languid surprise. He tried for a moment to place this individual, but it was too much bother. He gave it up. In a few minutes his chauffeur pulled up outside his own house in Catherine Street and opened the door of the car.

The Home Secretary got out slowly and toiled up the steps. His butler let him in. While he was still in the hall his wife came downstairs. He stood and contemplated her without speaking.

"Well, Derek," she said.

"Hallo, Cicely."

She stood at the foot of the stairs and watched him composedly.

"You're late," she observed after a moment.

"Am I? I suppose I am. Those fellows jawed and jawed. Do you mind if I don't change? I'm tired."

"Of course not. There's only Ruth dining."

He grimaced.

"I really can't help it if your sister likes to see you occasionally," remarked Lady O'Callaghan tranquilly.

"All right," said her husband wearily. "All right."

He glanced at her inimically and thought how tiresomely good-looking she was. Always so perfectly groomed, so admirably gowned, so maddeningly remote. Their very embraces were masked in a chilly patina of good form. Occasionally he had the feeling that she rather disliked him, but as a rule he had no feeling about her at all. He supposed he had married her in a brief wave of enthusiasm for polar exploration. There had been no children. Just as well since there was a taint of insanity in his own family. He supposed he was all right himself. His wife would have brought out any traces of it, he reflected sardonically. Cicely was an acid test for normality.

She walked away from him towards the drawing-room. At the door she paused for a moment to ask:

"Have you been worried at all by that pain to-day?"

"Oh, yes," said O'Callaghan.

"What a bore it is," she murmured vaguely, and went into the drawing-room.

He looked after her for a moment and then crossed the little hall and entered his own study, a companionable room with a good fireplace, a practical desk and deep square-angled chairs. Cedar logs blazed in the grate and a tray with glasses and a decanter of his particular sherry waited near his particular chair.

She certainly saw to it that he was adequately looked after.

He poured himself out a glass of sherry and opened his afternoon post. It was abysmally dull. His secretary had dealt with the bulk of his letters and evidently considered that these were all personal. Most of them were so marked. One writer begged for money, another for preferment, a third for information. A typewritten envelope had already been opened by his secretary. It contained an anonymous and threatening message and was merely the latest of a long series of such communications. He picked up the last letter, glanced at the envelope, raised his eyebrows and then frowned. He finished his sherry and poured out another glass before he opened the letter and read it.

It was from Jane Harden.

From Jane. He might have known he wouldn't hear the end of that business in a hurry. He might have known he was a fool to suppose she would let him go without making difficulties. That week-end in Cornwall—it had been pleasant enough but before it was over he'd known he was in for trouble. Damn it all, women were never fair—never. They talked about leading their own lives, said they wanted to get their experience like men, and then broke all the rules of the game. He glanced again over the letter. She reminded him that she had "given herself" to him (what nonsense that was. She'd wanted it as much as he had!), that their families had been neighbours in Dorset for generations before her father went bankrupt. He flinched away from the imputation of disloyalty which, since he was a tolerably honest and conservative man, made him profoundly uncomfortable. She said he'd treated her as though she was a suburban pick-up. He wished fretfully that she had been. She wrote that she was going to a post in a private nursing-home. Would he write to her at the Nurses' Club? Up to this point the letter had apparently been written with a certain amount of self-control, but from then onwards O'Callaghan saw, with something like horror, that Jane's emotions had run away with her pen. She loved him but what had she left to offer him? she asked. Must they both forget? She was fighting for her soul and nothing was too desperate. There was a devil tearing at her soul and if she lost him it would get her. She added again that she loved him and that if he persisted in ignoring her she would do something terrible. With a sudden petulant gesture he crumpled up the sheet of paper and threw it on the fire.

"Blast!" he said. "Blast! Blast! Blast!"

14

There was a light tap on the door, which opened far enough to disclose a large nose, a vague mouth, a receding chin, and a gigantic earring.

"Affairs of state, Derry?" asked a coy voice. "Affairs of state?"

"Oh, come in, Ruth," said Sir Derek O'Callaghan.

CHAPTER II

Introduces a Patent Medicine

Friday, the fifth. Evening.

During the following week the Home Secretary followed his usual routine. He had become more or less accustomed to the attacks of pain. If anything they occurred more often and with increasing severity. He told himself that the day after he had introduced his Bill, he would consult a doctor. Meanwhile he took three tablets of aspirin whenever the pain threatened to become unendurable, and grew more and more dispirited and wretched. The memory of Jane Harden's letter lurked at the back of his thoughts, like a bad taste in the conscience.

His sister Ruth, an advanced hypochondriac, with the persistence of a missionary, continually pressed upon him strange boluses, pills and draughts. She made a practice of calling on him after dinner armed with chemists' parcels and a store of maddening condolences and counsels. On Friday night he retreated to his study, begging his wife to tell Ruth, if she appeared, that he was extremely busy, and not to be interrupted. His wife looked at him for a moment.

"I shall ask Nash," she said, "to say we are both out."

He paused and then said uncomfortably:

"I don't think I quite like——"

"I too," said his wife, "find myself bored by Ruth."

"Still, Cicely—after all she is exceedingly kind. Perhaps it would be better——"

"You will see her then?"

"No, damn it, I won't."

"Very well, Derek. I'll tell Nash. Has your pain been worrying you lately?"

"Quite a lot, thank you."

"That, of course, is why you are irritable. I think you are foolish not to see a doctor."

"I think I told you I would call in John Phillips as soon as this Bill was through."

"It's for you to decide, of course. Shall I ask Nash to take your coffee into the study?"

"If you please."

"Yes." She had a curiously remote way of saying "Yes," as though it was a sort of bored comment on everything he uttered.

"Good night, Derek. I am going up early and won't disturb you."

"Good night, Cicely."

She stepped towards him and waited. By some mischance his kiss fell upon her lips instead of her cheek. He almost felt he ought to apologise. However, she merely repeated "Good night" and he went off to his study.

Here his secretary Ronald Jameson awaited him. Jameson, just down from Oxford, was an eager but not too tiresomely earnest young man. He did his work well, and was intelligent. Normally, O'Callaghan found him tolerable and even likeable. To-night, the sight of his secretary irritated and depressed him.

"Well, Ronald?"

He sank down into his chair, and reached for a cigar.

"Sir John Phillips has rung up, sir, and would like to come and see you this evening if you are free."

"Phillips? Has anyone been talking about me to Phillips? What does he want? Is it a professional visit?"

"I don't think so, sir. Sir John didn't mention your—indisposition."

"Ring him up and say I'll be delighted. Anything else?"

"These letters. There's another of the threatening variety. I do wish, sir, that you'd let me talk to Scotland Yard."

"No. Anything else?"

"Only one, marked personal. It's on your desk."

"Give it to me, will you?"

Jameson brought the letter and handed it to him. He looked at it and experienced the sensation of going down in a lift. It was from Jane Harden. O'Callaghan let his arm swing down by the side of his chair. The letter hung from his fingers. He remained

17

staring at the fire, the unlighted cigar between his lips.

Ronald Jameson waited uncomfortably. At last he produced his lighter and advanced it towards O'Callaghan's cigar.

"Thank you," said O'Callaghan absently.

"Is there anything I can do, sir?"

"No, thank you."

Jameson hesitated, looked uneasily at his employer's white face, reflected that Sir John Phillips still awaited his message, and left the room.

For some time after the door had shut behind his secretary O'Callaghan sat and stared at the fire. At last, with an enormous effort, he forced himself to read through the letter. Jane Harden had written a frantic, bitter arraignment, rather than an appeal. She said she felt like killing herself. A little further on, she added that if an opportunity presented itself she would not hesitate to kill him: "Don't cross my path. I'm warning you for my own sake, not for yours. I mean it, Derek, for you and all men like you are better out of the way. This is my final word.—Jane Harden."

O'Callaghan had a swift mental picture of the letter as it would appear in the columns of the penny Press. Rather to his surprise O'Callaghan heard his wife speak to the secretary in the hall outside. Something in the quality of her voice arrested his attention. He listened.

"—something seems to be worrying him."

"I think so too, Lady O'Callaghan," Jameson murmured.

"—any idea—any letters?" The voice faded away.

"To-night—seemed to upset—of course this Bill——"

O'Callaghan got up and strode across the room. He flung open the door.

His wife and Ronald Jameson stood facing each other with something of the air of conspirators. As he opened the door they turned their faces towards him. Jameson's became very red and he looked swiftly from husband to wife. Lady O'Callaghan merely regarded Sir Derek placidly. He felt himself trembling with anger.

"Hitherto," he said to Jameson, "I have seen no reason to suppose you did not understand the essentially confidential nature of your job. Apparently I have been mistaken."

"I'm—I'm terribly sorry, Sir Derek—it was only because——"

"You have no business to discuss my letters with anyone. With *anyone*. You understand?"

"Yes, sir."

"Please don't be absurd, Derek," said his wife. "I asked Mr. Jameson a question that he could not avoid answering. We are both very worried about you."

O'Callaghan jerked his head. Jameson made a miserable little bow and turned away. At the door of his own room he paused, murmured "I'm extremely sorry, sir," and disappeared.

"Really, Derek," said Lady O'Callaghan, "I think you are unreasonable. I merely asked that unfortunate youth if you had received any letter that might account for your otherwise rather unaccountable behaviour. He said a letter in this evening's mail seemed to upset you. What was this letter, Derek? Was it another threat from these people—these anarchists or whatever they are?"

He was not so angry that he did not hear an unusual note in her voice.

"Such threats are an intolerable impertinence," she said hastily. "I cannot understand why you do not deal with these people."

"The letter had nothing whatever to do with them, and my "unaccountable behaviour," as you call it, has nothing to do with the letter. I am unwell and I'm worried. It may satisfy you to hear that John Phillips is coming in this evening."

"I'm delighted to hear it."

The front-door bell sounded. They looked at each other questioningly.

"Ruth?" murmured Lady O'Callaghan.

"I'm off," he said quickly. Suddenly he felt more friendly towards her. "You'd better bolt, Cicely," he said.

She moved swiftly into his study and he followed her. They heard Nash come out and open the door. They listened, almost in sympathy with each other.

"Sir Derek and my lady are not at home, madam."

"But there's a light in the study!"

They exchanged horrified glances.

"Perhaps Mr. Jameson——" said Nash.

"Just the man I want to see."

They heard Nash bleating in dismay and the sound of Miss Ruth O'Callaghan's umbrella being rammed home in the ship's bucket. With one accord they walked over to the fireplace. Lady O'Callaghan lit a cigarette.

The door opened, and Ruth came in. They had a brief glimpse

of Nash's agonised countenance and then were overwhelmed in embraces.

"*There* you are, darlings. Nash said you were out."

"We're only 'not at home,' Ruth darling," said Lady O'Callaghan, very tranquilly. "Derek expects his doctor. It was too stupid of Nash not to realise you were different."

"Ah-ha," said Ruth, with really terrifying gaiety, "you don't defeat your old sister like that. Now, Derry darling, I've come especially to see you, and I shall be very cross and dreadfully hurt if you don't do exactly what I tell you."

She rummaged in an enormous handbag, and fetched up out of its depths the familiar sealed white parcel.

"Really, Ruth, I can *not* swallow every patent medicine that commends itself to your attention."

"I don't want you to do that, darling. I know you think your old sister's a silly-billy"—she squinted playfully at him—"but she knows what's good for her big, famous brother. Cicely, he'll listen to you. Please, please, persuade him to take just one of these teeny little powders. They're too marvellous. You've only to read the letters——"

With eager, clumsy fingers she undid the wrapping and disclosed a round green box decorated with the picture of a naked gentleman, standing in front of something that looked like an electric shock.

"There are six powders altogether," she told them excitedly, "but after the first, you feel a *marked* improvement. 'Fulvita-volts'. Hundreds of letters, Derry, from physicians, surgeons, politicians—*lots* of politicians, Derry. They all swear by it. Their symptoms were precisely the same as yours. Honestly."

She looked pathetically eager. She was so awkward and vehement with her thick hands, her watery eyes, and her enormous nose.

"You don't know what my symptoms are, Ruth."

"Indeed I do. Violent abdominal seizures. Cicely—do read it all."

Lady O'Callaghan took the box and looked at one of the folded cachets.

"I'll give him one to-night, Ruth," she promised, exactly as though she was humouring an excitable child.

"That's topping!" Ruth had a peculiar trick of using unreal slang. "I'm most awfully bucked. And in the morning all those horrid pains will have *flown* away." She made a sort of blundering, ineffectual gestue. She beamed at them.

"And now, old girl, I'm afraid you'll have to fly away yourself," said O'Callaghan with a desperate effort to answer roguishness with brotherly playfulness. "I think I hear Phillips arriving."

"Come along, Ruth," said his wife. "We must make ourselves scarce. Good night again, Derek."

Ruth laid a gnarled finger on her lips and tiptoed elaborately to the door. There she turned and blew him a kiss.

He heard them greet Sir John Phillips briefly and go upstairs. In his relief at being rid of his sister, O'Callaghan felt a wave of good-fellowship for John Phillips. Phillips was an old friend. It would be a relief to tell him how ill he felt—to learn how ill he really was. Perhaps Phillips would give him something that would help him along for the time being. He already felt a little better. Very likely it was a trifling thing after all. Phillips would know. He turned to the door with an air of pleased expectancy. Nash opened the door and came in.

"Sir John Phillips, sir."

Phillips entered the room.

He was an extremely tall man with an habitual stoop. His eyes, full-lidded and of a peculiarly light grey, were piercingly bright. No one ever saw him without his single eye-glass and there was a rumour that he wore it ribbonless while he operated. His nose was a beak and his under lip jutted out aggressively. He was unmarried, and unmoved, so it was said, by the general tendency among his women patients to fall extravagantly in love with him. Perhaps next to actors medical men profit most by the possession of that curious quality that people call "personality". Sir John Phillips was, very definitely, a personage. His rudeness was more glamorously famous than his brilliant ability.

O'Callaghan moved towards him, his hand extended.

"Phillips!" he said, "I'm delighted to see you."

Phillips ignored the hand and stood stockstill until the door had closed behind Nash. Then he spoke.

"You will be less delighted when you hear my business," he said.

"Why—what on earth's the matter with you?"

"I can scarcely trust myself to speak to you."

"What the devil do you mean?"

"Precisely what I say. I've discovered your are a blackguard and

21

I've come to tell you so."

O'Callaghan stared at him in silence.

"Apparently you are serious," he said at last. "May I ask if you intend merely to call me names and then walk out? Or am I to be given an explanation?"

"I'll give you your explanation. In two words. Jane Harden."

There was a long silence. The two men stared at each other. At last O'Callaghan turned away. A kind of mulish huffiness in his expression made him look ridiculous and unlikeable.

"What about Jane Harden?" he said at last.

"Only this. She's a nurse at my hospital. For a very long time her happiness has been an important thing for me. I have asked her to marry me. She has refused, over and over again. To-day she told me why. It seems you made capital out of a friendship with her father and out of her present poverty. You played the 'old family friend' combined with the distinguished philanderer."

"I don't know what you're talking about."

"Don't lie, O'Callaghan!"

"Look here——"

"I know the facts."

"What sort of tale have you listened to?"

"One that brought me here to-night angrier than I ever remember myself before. I know the precise history of your—your friendship with her. You amused yourself, evidently. I dislike overstatement but I believe it would be no overstatement if I said, as I do say, that you've ruined Jane's life for her."

"Damn' sentimental twaddle!" said O'Callaghan breathlessly. "She's a modern young woman and she knows how to enjoy herself."

"That's a complete misrepresentation." Phillips had turned exceedingly white, but he spoke evenly. "If, by the phrase 'a modern young woman', you mean a 'loose woman' you must know yourself it's a lie. This is the only episode of the sort in her life. She loved you and you let her suppose she was loved in return."

"Nothing of the sort. She gave me no reason to suppose she attached more importance to the thing than I did myself. You say she's in love with me. If it's true I'm sorry. I don't think it's true. What does she want? It's not——" O'Callaghan stopped short and looked frightened. "It's not that she's going to have a child?"

"Oh, no. She has no actual claim on you. No legal claim.

22

Evidently you don't recognise moral obligations."

"I've sent her £300. What more will she want?"

"I'm so near hitting you, O'Callaghan, I think I'd better go."

"You can go to hell if you like. What's the matter with you? If you don't want to marry her there's an alternative. It ought to be quite simple—I had no difficulty."

"You swine!" shouted Phillips. "My God——" He stopped short. His lips moved tremblingly. When he spoke again it was more quietly. "You'd do well to keep clear of me," he said. "I assure you that if the opportunity presented itself I should have no hesitation—none—in putting you out of the way."

Something in O'Callaghan's face made him pause. The Home Secretary was looking beyond him, towards the door.

"Excuse me, sir," said Nash quietly. He crossed the room with a tray holding glasses and a decanter. He put the tray down noiselessly and returned to the door.

"Is there anything further, sir?" asked Nash.

"Sir John Phillips is leaving. Will you show him out?"

"Certainly, sir."

Without another word Phillips turned on his heel and left the room.

"Good night, Nash," said O'Callaghan.

"Good night, sir," said Nash softly. He followed Sir John Phillips out and closed the door.

O'Callaghan gave a sharp cry of pain. He stumbled towards his chair and bent over it, leaning on the arm. For a minute or two he hung on, doubled up with pain. Then he managed to get into the chair, and in a little while poured out half a tumbler of whisky. He noticed Ruth's patent medicine lying on the table beside him. With a tremulous hand he shook one of the powders into the glass and gulped it down with the whisky.

CHAPTER III

Sequel to a Scene in the House

Thursday, the eleventh. Afternoon.

The Home Secretary paused and looked round the House. The sea of faces was blurred and nightmarish. They were playing that trick on him that he had noticed before. They would swim together like cells under a microscope and then one face would come out clearly and stare at him. He thought: "I may just manage it—only one more paragraph", and raised the paper. The type swirled and eddied, and then settled down. He heard his own voice. He must speak up.

"In view of the extraordinary propaganda——"

They were making too much noise.

"Mr. Speaker——"

A disgusting feeling of nausea, a kind of vapourish tightness behind his nose.

"Mr. Speaker——"

He looked up again. A mistake. The sea of faces jerked up and revolved very quickly. A tiny voice, somewhere up in the attic, was calling: "He's fainted."

He did not feel himself pitch forward across the desk. Nor did he hear a voice from the back benches that called out: "You'll be worse than that before you've finished with your bloody Bill."

"Who's his doctor—anyone know?"

"Yes—I do. It's bound to be Sir John Phillips—they're old friends."

"Phillips? He runs that nursing-home in Brook Street, doesn't he?"

"I've no idea."

24

"Somebody must ring Lady O'Callaghan."

"I will if you like. I know her."

"Is he coming round?"

"Doesn't look like it. Tillotley went to see about the ambulance."

"Here he is. Did you fix up for an ambulance, Tillotley?"

"It's coming. Where are you sending him?"

"Cuthbert's gone to ring up his wife."

"God, he looks bad!"

"Did you hear that fellow yell out from the back benches?"

"Yes. Who was it?"

"I don't know. I say, do you think there's anything fishy about this?"

"Oh, rot!"

"Here's Dr. Wendover—I didn't know he was in the House." They stood back from O'Callaghan. A little tubby man, Communist member for a North Country constituency, came through the group of men and knelt down.

"Open those windows, will you?" he said.

He loosened O'Callaghan's clothes. The others eyed him respectfully. After a minute or two he looked round.

"Who's his medical man?" he asked.

"Cuthbert thinks it's Sir John Phillips. He's ringing his wife now."

"Phillips is a surgeon. It's a surgical case."

"What's the trouble, Dr. Wendover?"

"Looks like an acute appendix. There's no time to be lost. You'd better ring the Brook Street Private Hospital. Is the ambulance there? Can't wait for his wife."

From the doorway somebody said: "The men from the ambulance."

"Good. Here's your patient."

Two men came in carrying a stretcher. O'Callaghan was got on to it, covered up, and carried out. Cuthbert hurried in.

"Yes," he said, "it's Phillips. She wants him taken to Phillips's nursing-home."

"He's going there," said little Dr. Wendover, and walked out after the ambulance men.

O'Callaghan climbed up, sickeningly, from nowhere into semi-consciousness. Grandiloquent images slid rapidly downwards.

His wife's face came near and then receded. Somebody groaned close to him. Somebody was in bed beside him, groaning.

"Is the pain very bad?" said a voice.

He himself was in pain.

"Bad," he said solemnly.

"The doctor will be here soon. He'll give you something to take it away."

He now knew it was he who had groaned.

Cicely's face came close.

"The doctor's coming, Derek."

He closed his eyes to show he had understood.

"Poor old Derry, poor old boy."

"I'll just leave you with him for a minute, Lady O'Callaghan. If you want me, will you ring? I think I hear Sir John." A door closed.

"This pain's very bad," said O'Callaghan clearly.

The two women exchanged glances. Lady O'Callaghan drew up a chair to the bed and sat down.

"It won't be for long, Derek," she said quietly. "It's your appendix, you know."

"Oh."

Ruth had begun to whisper.

"What's Ruth say?"

"Never mind me, Derry-boy. It's just silly old Ruthie."

He muttered something, shut his eyes, and seemed to fall asleep.

"Cicely darling, I know you laugh at my ideas, but listen. As soon as I heard about Derry I went and saw Harold Sage. He's the *brilliant* young chemist I told you about. I explained *exactly* what was the matter and he gave me something that he says will relieve the pain *at once* and can do no harm at all. It's an invention of his own. In a few months all the hospitals will use it."

She began a search in her handbag.

"Suggest it to Sir John if you like, Ruth. Of course nothing can be done without his knowledge."

"Doctors are so bigoted. I *know*, my dear. The things Harold has told me——!"

"You seem to be very friendly with this young man."

"He interests me enormously, Cicely."

"Really?"

The nurse came back.

"Sir John would like to see you for a moment, Lady O'Callaghan."

"Thank you. I'll come."

Left alone with her brother, Ruth dabbed at his hand. He opened his eyes.

"Oh, God, Ruth," he said, "I'm in such pain."

"Just hold on for one moment, Derry. I'll make it better."

She had found the little package. There was a tumbler of water by the bedside.

In a few minutes Phillips came back with the nurse.

"Sir John is going to make an examination," said Nurse Graham quietly to Ruth. "If you wouldn't mind joining Lady O'Callaghan for a moment."

"I shan't keep you long," said Phillips and opened the door.

Ruth, with a distracted and guilty look at her brother, gathered herself up and blundered out of the room.

O'Callaghan had relapsed into unconsciousness. Nurse Graham uncovered the abdomen and Phillips with his long inquisitive fingers pressed it there—and there—and there. His eyes were closed and his brain seemed to be in his hands.

"That will do," he said suddenly. "It looks like peritonitis. He's in a bad way. I've warned them we may need the theatre." The nurse covered the patient and in answer to a nod from Phillips fetched the two women. As soon as they came in, Phillips turned to Lady O'Callaghan but did not look at her. "The operation should be performed immediately," he said. "Will you allow me to try to get hold of Somerset Black?"

"But you, Sir John, won't you do it yourself?"

Phillips walked over to the window and stared out.

"You wish me to operate?" he said at last.

"Of course I do. I know that sometimes surgeons dislike operating on their friends, but unless you feel—I do hope—I beg you to do it."

"Very well."

He returned to the patient.

"Nurse," he said, "tell them to get Dr. Thoms. He's in the hospital and has been warned that an operation may be necessary. Ring up Dr. Grey and arrange for the anæsthetic—I'll speak to him myself. Tell the theatre sister I'll operate as soon as they are ready. Now, Lady O'Callaghan, if you don't mind leaving the patient, Nurse will show you where you can wait."

The nurse opened the door and the others moved away from the bed. At the threshold they were arrested by a kind of stifled cry. They turned and looked back to the bed. Derek O'Callaghan had opened his eyes and was staring as if hypnotised at Phillips.

"Don't——" he said. "Don't—let——"

His lips moved convulsively. A curious whining sound came from them. For a moment or two he struggled for speech and then suddenly his head fell back.

"Come along, Lady O'Callaghan," said the nurse gently. "He doesn't know what he is saying, you know."

In the anteroom of the theatre two nurses and a sister prepared for the operation.

"Now you mustn't forget," said Sister Marigold, who was also the matron of the hospital, "that Sir John likes his instruments left on the tray. He does *not* like them handed to him."

She covered a tray of instruments and Jane Harden carried it into the theatre.

"It's a big responsibility," said the sister chattily, "for a surgeon, in a case of this sort. It would be a terrible catastrophe for the country if anything happened to Sir Derek O'Callaghan. The only strong man in the Government, in my opinion."

Nurse Banks, an older woman than her superior, looked up from the sterilising apparatus.

"The biggest tyrant of the lot," she remarked surprisingly.

"Nurse! What did you say?"

"My politics are not Sir Derek O'Callaghan's, Matron, and I don't care who knows it."

Jane Harden returned from the theatre. Sister Marigold cast an indignant glance at Nurse Banks and said briefly:

"Did you look at the hyoscine solution, Nurse, and the anti-gas ampoule?"

"Yes, Matron."

"Gracious, child, you look very white. Are you all right?"

"Quite, thank you," answered Jane. She busied herself with tins of sterilised dressings. After another glance at her, the matron returned to the attack on Nurse Banks.

"Of course, Nurse, we all know you are a Bolshie. Still, you can't deny greatness when you see it. Now Sir Derek is my idea of a big—a *really* big man."

"And for that reason he's the more devilish," announced Banks with remarkable venom. "He's done murderous things since he's been in office. Look at his Casual Labour Bill of last year. He's directly responsible for every death from under-nourishment that has occurred during the last ten months. He's the enemy of the proletariat. If I had my way he'd be treated as a common murderer or else as a homicidal maniac. He ought to be certified. There is insanity in his blood. Everybody knows his father was dotty. That's what I think of your Derek O'Callaghan with a title bought with blood-money," said Banks, making a great clatter with sterilised bowls.

"Then perhaps"—Sister Marigold's voice was ominously quiet—"perhaps you'll explain what you're doing working for Sir John Phillips. Perhaps his title was bought with blood-money too."

"As long as this rotten system stands, we've got to live," declared Banks ambiguously, "but it won't be for ever and I'll be the first to declare myself when the time comes. O'Callaghan will have to go and all his blood-sucking bourgeois party with him. It would be a fine thing for the people if he went now. There, Matron!"

"It would be a better thing if you went yourself, Nurse Banks, and if I had another theatre nurse free, go you would. I'm ashamed of you. You talk about a patient like that—what are you thinking of?"

"I can't help it if my blood boils."

"There's a great deal too much blood, boiling or not, in your conversation."

With the air of one silenced but not defeated, Banks set out a table with hypodermic appliances and wheeled it into the theatre.

"Really, Nurse Harden," said Sister Marigold, "I'm ashamed of that woman. The vindictiveness! She ought not to be here. One might almost think she would——" Matron paused, unable to articulate the enormity of her thought.

"No such—thing," said Jane. "I'd be more likely to do him harm than she."

"And that's an outside chance," declared matron more genially. "I must say, Nurse Harden, you're the best theatre nurse I've had for a long time. A real compliment, my dear, because I'm very particular. Are we ready? Yes. And here come the doctors."

Jane put her hands behind her back and stood to attention.

Sister Marigold assumed an air of efficient repose. Nurse Banks appeared for a moment in the doorway, seemed to recollect something, and returned to the theatre.

Sir John Phillips came in followed by Thoms, his assistant, and the anæsthetist. Thoms was fat, scarlet-faced and industriously facetious. Dr. Roberts was a thin, sandy-haired man, with a deprecating manner. He took off his spectacles and polished them.

"Ready, Matron?" asked Phillips.

"Quite ready, Sir John."

"Dr. Roberts will give the anæsthetic. Dr. Grey is engaged. We were lucky to get you, Roberts, at such short notice."

"I'm delighted to come," said Roberts. "I've been doing a good deal of Grey's work lately. It is always an honour, and an interesting experience, to work under you, Sir John."

He spoke with a curious formality as if he considered each sentence and then offered it to the person he addressed.

"If I may I'll just take a look at the anæsthetising-room before we begin."

"Certainly."

The truculent Banks reappeared.

"Nurse Banks," said the matron, "go with Dr. Roberts to the anæsthetising-room, please."

Dr. Roberts blinked at Banks, and followed her out.

Sir John went into the theatre and crossed to a small table, enamelled white, on which were various appliances concerned with the business of giving hypodermic injections. There were three syringes, each in a little dish of sterile water. Two were of the usual size known to the layman. The third was so large as to suggest it was intended for veterinary rather than human needs. The small syringes held twenty-five minims each, the larger at least six times as much. An ampoule, a bottle, a small bowl and a measure-glass also stood on the table. The bottle was marked: 'Hyoscine solution 0.25 per cent. Five minims contains $^1/_{100}$ a grain.' The ampoule was marked: 'Gas-Gangrene Antitoxin (concentrated).' The bowl contained sterile water.

Phillips produced from his pocket a small hypodermic case from which he took a tiny tube labelled: 'Hyoscine gr. $^1/_{100}$.' The tube being completely covered by its label, it was difficult to see the contents. He removed the cork, examined the inside closely, laid down the tube and took another, similarly labelled, from his case. His fingers worked uncertainly, as though his mind was on something else. At last he took one of the smaller syringes, filled it with sterile water, and squirted its contents into the measure-glass. Then he dropped in the hyoscine, stirred it with the needle of the syringe, and finally, pulling back the piston, sucked the solution into the syringe.

Thoms came into the theatre.

"We ought to get washed up, sir," he said.

He glanced at the table.

"Hallo!" he shouted. "*Two* tubes! You're doing him proud."

"One was empty." Phillips picked them up automatically and put them back in his case.

Thoms looked at the syringe.

"You use a lot of water, don't you?" he observed.

"I do," said Phillips shortly. Taking the syringe with him, he walked out of the theatre into the anæsthetic-room. Thoms, wearing that air of brisk abstraction which people assume when they are determined to ignore a snub, remained staring at the table. He joined the others a few minutes later in the anteroom. Phillips returned from the anæsthetic-room.

Jane Harden and Sister Marigold helped the two surgeons to turn themselves into pieces of sterilized machinery. In a little while the anteroom was an austere arrangement in white, steel, and rubber-brown. There is something slightly repellent as well as something beautiful in absolute white. It is the negation of colour, the expression of coldness, the emblem of death. There is less sensuous pleasure in white than in any of the colours, and more suggestion of the macabre. A surgeon in his white robe, the warmth of his hands hidden by sleek chilly rubber, the animal vigour of his hair covered by a white cap, is more like a symbol in modern sculpture than a human being. To the layman he is translated, a priest in sacramental robes, a terrifying and subtly fascinating figure.

"Seen this new show at the Palladium?" asked Thoms. "Blast this glove! Give me another, Matron."

"No," said Sir John Phillips.

"There's a one-act play. Anteroom to a theatre in a private hospital. Famous surgeon has to operate on a man who ruined him and seduced his wife. Problem—does he stick a knife into the patient? Grand Guignol stuff. Awful rot, I thought it."

Phillips turned slowly and stared at him. Jane Harden uttered a

31

little stifled cry.

"What's that, Nurse?" asked Thoms. "Have you seen it? Here, give me the glove."

"No, sir," murmured Jane, "I haven't seen it."

"Jolly well acted it was, and someone had put them right about technical matters, but, of course, the situation was altogether too far-fetched. I'll just go and see——" He walked out, still talking, into the theatre, and after a minute or two called to the matron, who followed him.

"Jane," said Phillips.

"Yes?"

"This—this is a queer business."

"Nemesis, perhaps," said Jane Harden.

"What do you mean?"

"Oh, nothing," she said drearily. "Only it is rather like a Greek play, don't you think? 'Fate delivers our enemy into our hands.' Mr. Thoms would think the situation very far-fetched."

Phillips washed his hands slowly in a basin of sterilised water. "I knew nothing of this illness," he said. "It's the merest chance that I was here at this hour. I'd only just got in from St. Jude's. I tried to get out of it, but his wife insisted. Evidently she has no idea we—quarrelled."

"She could hardly know *why* you quarrelled, could she?"

"I'd give anything to be out of it—anything."

"And I. How do you think I feel?"

He squeezed the water off his gloves and turned towards her, holding his hands out in front of him. He looked a grotesque and somehow pathetic figure.

"Jane," he whispered, "won't you change your mind? I love you so much."

"No," she said. "No. I loathe him. I never want to see him again, but as long as he's alive I can't marry you."

"I don't understand you," he said heavily.

"I don't understand myself," answered Jane, "so how should you?"

"I shall go on—I shall ask you again and again."

"It's no good. I suppose I'm queer, but as long as he's there I— I'm in pawn."

"It's insane—after his treatment of you. He's—he's discarded you, Jane."

She laughed harshly.

"Oh, yes. It's quite according to Victorian tradition. I'm a 'ruined girl', you know!"

"Well, stick to the Victorian tradition and let me make an honest woman of you."

"Look here," said Jane suddenly. "I'll try and be an honest woman *with* you. I mean I'll try and explain what's inexplicable and pretty humiliating. I told him I wanted to live my own life, experience everything, all that sort of chat. I deceived myself as well as him. In the back of my mind I knew I was simply a fool who had lost her head as well as her heart. Then, when it happened, I realised just how little it meant to him and just how much it meant to me. I knew I ought to keep up the game, shake hands and part friends, and all that. Well—I couldn't. My pride wanted to, but—I couldn't. It's all too grimly commonplace. I 'loved and hated' him at the same time. I wanted to keep him, knew I hadn't a chance, and longed to hurt him. I wrote to him and told him so. It's a nightmare and it's still going on. There! Don't ask me to talk about it again. Leave me alone to get over it as best I may."

"Couldn't I help?"

"No. Someone's coming—be careful."

Thoms and Roberts returned and washed up. Roberts went away to give the anæsthetic. Phillips stood and watched his assistant.

"How did your play end?" he asked suddenly.

"What? Oh. Back to the conversation we first thought of. It ended in doubt. You were left to wonder if the patient died under the anæsthetic, or if the surgeon did him in. As a matter of fact, under the circumstances, no one could have found out. Are you thinking of trying it out on the Home Secretary, sir? I thought you were a pal of his?"

The mask over Phillips's face creased as though he were smiling. "Given the circumstances," he said, "I suppose it might be a temptation."

He heard a movement behind him and turned to see Nurse Banks regarding him fixedly from the door into the theatre. Sister Marigold appeared behind her, said: "If you please, Nurse," in a frigid voice, and came through the door.

"Oh, Matron," said Phillips abruptly, "I have given an injection of hyoscine, as usual. If we find peritonitis, as I think we shall, I shall also inject serum."

"I remembered the hyoscine, of course, Sir John. The stock solution had been put out, but I saw you had prepared your own injection."

"Yes, we won't need the stock solution. Always use my own tablets—like to be sure of the correct dosage. Are we all ready?"

He went into the theatre.

"Well," said Sister Marigold, "I'm sure the stock solution is good enough for most people."

"You can't be too careful, Matron," Thoms assured her genially. "Hyoscine's a ticklish drug, you know."

The sickly reek of ether began to drift into the room.

"I must say I don't quite understand why Sir John is so keen on giving hyoscine.'

"It saves anæsthetic and it has a soothing effect after the operation. I give it myself," added Thoms importantly.

"What is the usual dose, sir?" asked Nurse Banks abruptly.

"From a hundredth to a two-hundredth of a grain, Nurse."

"As little as that!"

"Oh, yes. I can't tell you the minimum lethal dose—varies with different cases. A quarter-grain would do anyone in."

"A quarter of a grain," said Nurse Banks thoughtfully. "Fancy!"

CHAPTER IV

Post-operative

Thursday, the eleventh. Late afternoon.

Sir John waited in the theatre for his patient.

The matron, Jane and Nurse Banks came in with Thoms. They stood near the table, a group of robed and expressionless automata. They were silent. The sound of wheels. A trolley appeared with Dr. Roberts and the special nurse walking behind it. Dr. Roberts held the anæsthetic mask over the patient's face. On the trolley lay the figure of the Home Secretary. As they lifted it on the table the head spoke suddenly and inconsequently.

"Not to-day, not to-day, not to-day, damn' the bloody thing," it said very rapidly.

The special nurse went away.

The reek of ether rose up like incense round the table. Dr. Roberts wheeled forward his anæsthetising apparatus, an object that, with its cylinders of compressed gases carried in an iron framework, resembled a gigantic cruet. A low screen was fixed across the patient's chest to shut off the anæsthetist. Thoms looked at the patient curiously.

"He's a striking-looking chap, isn't he?" he remarked lightly. "Curious head. What do you make of it, Roberts? You're a bit of a dog at that sort of thing, aren't you? Read your book the other day. There's insanity somewhere in the racial make-up here, isn't there? Wasn't his old man bats?"

Roberts looked scandalised.

"That is so," he said stiffly, "but one would hardly expect to find evidence of racial insanity clearly defined in the facial structure, Mr. Thoms."

35

The sister arranged the sterile coverings over the abdomen. With the head screened, the patient was no longer an individual. A subject for operation lay on the table—that was all.

Sir John took up a scalpel and made the first incision.

"Peritonitis, all right," said Thoms presently.

"Hal-lo!" he added a little later. "Ruptured abscess. He's made a job of it."

"Accounts for the attacks of pain," Phillips grunted.

"Of course, sir. Wonder he kept going so long—look there."

"Nasty mess," said Phillips. "Good God, Matron, are you deaf? I said forceps."

Sister Marigold bridled slightly and gave a genteel cough. There was silence for some time. Sir John's fingers worked, nervously, inquisitively, and with a kind of delicate assurance.

"The pulse is weak, Sir John," said Roberts suddenly.

"Oh? Look at this, Thoms."

"I don't like this pulse."

"What's the matter, Roberts? Pulse?"

"Yes. It's rather weak. I don't like his looks. Get me an injection of camphor, will you, Nurse?"

Nurse Banks filled the second small hypodermic syringe and brought it to him.

"Give it, Nurse, at once, please."

She did so.

"Serum," grunted Phillips.

"Serum, Nurse Harden," murmured the sister.

Jane crossed to the table of apparatus. There was a little delay.

"Well—well, where is it?" asked Phillips impatiently.

"Nurse!" called Thoms angrily. "What are you doing?"

"I'm sorry—but——"

"It's the large syringe," said Nurse Banks.

"Very well," said Jane faintly.

She bent over the table.

Phillips finished sewing up the incision.

"Nurse," repeated Thoms, "*will* you bring me that syringe? What's the matter with you?"

An agitated drop appeared on the end of his nose. Sister Marigold cast an expert glance at it and wiped it off with a piece of gauze.

Jane came back uncertainly, holding the tray. Phillips straightened his back and stood looking at the wound. Thoms put on the dressing and then gave the injection.

"Well," he said, "that's that. Very nasty case. I suppose he's neglected it."

"I believe so," answered Phillips slowly, "I saw him the other evening and I had no idea he was ill—no idea of it."

"How's the condition now, Roberts?" asked Thoms.

"Not too brilliant."

"Well—take him to bed," said Phillips.

"And take that tray away," added Thoms irritably to Jane who still stood at his elbow.

She turned her head and looked into Phillips's eyes. He seemed to avoid her gaze and moved away. She turned towards the other table. Her steps grew more uncertain. She stopped, swayed a little, and fell forward on the tiled floor.

"Good God, what's the girl up to now?" shouted Thoms.

Phillips strode across the theatre and stood staring down at her.

"Fainted," he said behind his mask. He looked at his blood-stained gloves, pulled them off and knelt beside her. Sister Marigold "Tut-tut-tutted" like a scandalised hen and rang a bell. Nurse Banks glanced across and then stolidly helped Thoms to cover the patient and lift him back on the trolley. Dr. Roberts did not even look up. He had bent over the patient in an attitude of the most intense concentration. Two nurses came in.

"Nurse Harden's fainted," said the matron briefly.

They managed to get Jane to her feet. She opened her eyes and looked vaguely at them. Between them they half carried her out of the theatre.

The patient was wheeled away.

Phillips walked off into the anteroom followed by Thoms.

"Well, sir," remarked Thoms cheerfully, "I think the usual state of things has been reversed. You are the fierce member of the party as a rule, but to-day you're a perfect sucking-dove and I damned that poor girl to heaps. I'm sorry about it. Suppose she was feeling groggy all through the op."

"I suppose so," said Phillips, turning on a tap.

"I'm sorry about it. She's a nice girl and a good nurse. Attractive. Wonder if she's engaged."

"No."

"Not?"

"No."

Thoms paused, towel in hand, and stared curiously at his

37

senior. Sir John washed up sedately and methodically.

"Unpleasant game, operating on your friends, isn't it?" ventured Thoms, after a pause. "And such a distinguished friend, too. Jove, there are lots of Bolshie-minded gentlemen that wouldn't be overwhelmed with grief if O'Callaghan faded out! I can see it's hit you up a bit, sir. I've never before seen the faintest tremor in your hands."

"My dear Thoms, there's nothing the matter with my hands."

"Oh—I'm sorry."

"Nothing to be sorry about." He took off his gown and cap and brushed his hair. "You're quite right," he said suddenly, "I didn't enjoy the operation."

Thoms grinned good-naturedly and then looked sympathetic. The door opened and Dr. Roberts came in.

"I just looked in to report, Sir John," he began. "The patient's condition is rather disquieting. The camphor injection helped matters at the time but the pulse is still unsatisfactory." He glanced nervously from one surgeon to the other and polished his glasses. "I must confess I feel rather anxious," he said. "It's—it's such an important case."

"All cases are important," said Phillips.

"Of course, Sir John. What I meant to convey was my possible over-anxiety, occasioned by the illustriousness of the patient."

"You speak like your books, Roberts," said Thoms facetiously.

"However," continued Roberts with a doubtful glance at the fat little man. "However, I *am* anxious."

"I'll come and look at him," answered Phillips. "I can understand your concern. Thoms, you'd better come along with us."

"I won't be a minute, sir."

"There's something about his condition that one doesn't quite expect," Roberts said. He went into details. Phillips listened attentively. Thoms darted a complacent glance at the mirror.

"I'm ready," he told them.

He turned to Roberts.

"That's a rum-looking old stethoscope you sport, Roberts," he said jovially.

Roberts looked at it rather proudly. It was an old-fashioned straight instrument of wood with a thick stem, decorated by a row of notches cut down each quadrant.

"I wouldn't part with that for the latest and best thing on the market, Mr. Thoms," said Roberts.

"It looks like a tally-stick. What are the notches in aid of?"

Roberts looked self-conscious. He glanced deprecatingly at Phillips.

"I'm afraid you'll set me down as a very vain individual," he said shyly.

"Come on," said Thoms. "Spill the beans! Are they all the people you've killed or are they your millionaire patients?"

"Not that—no. As a matter of fact, it is a sort of tally. They represent cases of severe heart disease to whom I have given anæsthetic successfully."

Thoms roared with laughter and Roberts blushed like a schoolboy.

"Are you ready?" asked Phillips coldly.

They all went out together.

In the theatre Sister Marigold, Nurse Banks, and a nurse who had appeared to "scally", cleaned up and prepared for another operation, an urgent bronchoscopy, to be performed by a throat specialist. Jane had been taken off to the nurses' quarters.

"Two urgent ops. in one evening!" exclaimed the matron importantly; "we *are* busy. What's the time, Nurse?"

"Six thirty-five," said Banks.

"Whatever was the matter with Harden, Matron?" asked the scally.

"I'm sure I don't know, Nurse," rejoined Sister Marigold.

"I do," said Nurse Banks grimly.

Sister Marigold cast upon her a glance in which curiosity struggled with dignity. Dignity triumphed. Fortunately the scally was not so handicapped.

"Well, Banks," she said, "come clean. Why *did* she faint?"

"She knew the patient."

"What! Knew Sir Derek O'Callaghan? Harden?"

"Oh, yes! Their people were neighbours down in Dorset, don't you know," aped Banks with what she imagined to be the accent of landed proprietorship.

Sister Marigold's starch seemed to crackle disapproval.

"Nurse Harden comes of a very nice family," she said pointedly to the scally.

"Oh, most fraytefully nayce," jeered Banks. "Yes, she knew O'Callaghan all right. I happened to say, about a month ago it was, that he was probably the most completely unscrupulous of the Tories and she didn't half flare up. Then she told me."

"Thank you, Nurse Banks, that will do," said Matron icily. "The theatre is not the place for politics. I think we are ready now. I want a word with the doctor about this case."

She rustled out of the theatre.

"You've got a nerve, Banks," said the scally. "Fancy talking like that about Sir Derek. I think he looks lovely in his photos."

"You think because he's got a face like Conrad Veidt he's a suitable leader of the people—a man to make laws. Typical bourgeois ignorance and stupidity! However, he's probably the last of his species and he'll be the first to go when the Dawn breaks."

"Whatever are you talking about?"

"I know what I'm talking about."

"Well, I'm sure I don't. What Dawn?"

"The Dawn of the Proletariat Day."

"What's that? No, don't lose your hair, Banks. I'd like to know."

"You will know," said Banks. "Very shortly."

Upon which the throat specialist appeared and inquired if they were all ready for him. In ten minutes' time the figure of a child was wheeled into the theatre and once again the fumes of the anæsthetic rose like incense about the table. In another ten minutes the child was taken away. Nurse Banks and the scally began to clear up again. The throat specialist whistled as he washed up in the anteroom. He thrust his head in at the door, remarked: "No rest for the wicked, Nurse," and took himself off.

The two women worked in silence for a little while. Nurse Banks seemed preoccupied and rather morose.

"Hallo," said the scally, "there's Pips growling on the stairs." ('Pips' was hospital slang for Sir John Phillips.) "*And* Thomcat. Wonder how he is now. Sir Derek, I mean."

Nurse Banks did not answer.

"I don't believe you care."

"Oh, I'm quite interested."

The voices grew louder but neither of the two nurses could hear what was said. They stood very still, listening intently.

Presently there seemed to be some kind of movement. A woman's voice joined in the conversation.

"Who's that?" asked the scally.

"Sounds like Marigold," said Banks. "God, that woman

40

infuriates me!"

"Ssh! What's it all about, I wonder?"

Sir John Phillips's voice sounded clearly above the others.
"I'd better attend to that," it said.

"Pip sounds absolutely *rampant*," breathed the scally.

"Yes," said Thoms clearly. "Yes."

A sound of footsteps. Then suddenly the door into the theatre
opened and O'Callaghan's special nurse burst into the room.

"Isn't it frightful!" she said. "Oh, isn't it frightful!"

"What? What's the matter with you?"

"He's dead—Sir Derek O'Callaghan's dead!"

"Nurse!" The scally gazed at her speechless.

"It really is awful," said Nurse Graham. "Lady O'Callaghan is
there now—she wanted to be left alone with him. I felt I simply
must tell somebody."

There was a dead silence, and then, prompted perhaps by some
kind of mental telepathy, they both turned and stared at Banks.

The older woman's head was tipped back. She held her arms
stiffly at her sides. Her eyes shone and her lips worked
convulsively.

"Banks!" said the scally, "Banks! How can you behave like
that? I believe you're glad he's gone!"

"If I hadn't cast off the worn-out shackles of religion," said
Banks, "I should say 'Praise the Lord for He hath cast down our
Enemy'."

"You disgusting old horror," said the special, and went out of
the theatre.

CHAPTER V

Lady O'Callaghan Insists

Friday, the twelfth: Afternoon.

"Lady O'Callaghan, I'm terribly sorry to bother, but may I speak to you for a moment?"

Ronald Jameson paused and looked apologetically at the widow of his late employer. She was very handsome in black. Her hair—he could never make up his mind whether it was a warm white or a white blonde—looked as though it had been ironed into place. Her hands, thin and elegant, hung relaxed against the matt surface of her dress. Her pale blue eyes under their heavy lids regarded him with a kind of polite detachment.

"Yes," she said vaguely. "Come into my room, Mr. Jameson."

He followed her into that place of frozen elegance. She sat down leisurely, her back to the light.

"Yes," she repeated. "Sit down, Mr. Jameson."

Ronald said: "Thank you so much," nervously, and sat on the most uncomfortable chair.

"I've just come back from the House," he began. "The Prime Minister saw me in his room. He is terribly distressed about—about yesterday. He wished me to tell you that—that he is entirely at your service should there be anything——"

"So kind of him," she said.

"Of course, he is also very much troubled about the Bill—Sir Derek's Anarchy Bill, you know. The business arising from it has to go forward, you see, and this tragedy has complicated matters." He paused again.

"I see—yes."

"It's a question of Sir Derek's private notes. They can do

42

nothing without them. I said that the matter would have to wait until after the—until after tomorrow; but the Prime Minister thinks the whole business is so urgent that he ought to see them immediately. I believe they are in the desk in the study, but of course, before I could do anything about it, I felt I must have your permission."

She took so long to answer that he felt quite alarmed. At last, looking at her hands which lay delicately clasped on her lap, she said: "This Bill. Will it deal with the persons who killed him?"

He was so completely dumbfounded by this amazing inquiry that he could think of nothing to say. He was a young man with a good deal of *savoir-faire*, but evidently her extraordinary assumption took him unawares.

"I'm afraid I don't—do you mean—surely, Lady O'Callaghan, you can't believe——" He could get no further with it.

"Oh, yes," she said tranquilly, "I'm iuite sure they killed him."

"But—who?"

"These people. Anarchists, aren't they? They threatened to kill my husband. I believe they have done so. I understand his Bill was designed to suppress such persons. Please do anything you can to help it to go forward."

"Thank you," said Ronald idiotically.

"Yes. Is that all, Mr. Jameson?"

"But, Lady O'Callaghan—please—have you thought— honestly, you have simply amazed me. It's a terrible idea. Surely the doctors' report is clear! Sir Derek had acute peritonitis."

"Sir John Phillips said the operation was successful. He was poisoned."

"By peritonitis and a ruptured abscess. Really, I can't think anything else. How could he be deliberately poisoned?"

"One of the letters threatened poison. The one he had last Monday, it was."

"But many leading politicians get letters of that sort. Nothing ever happens. Forgive me, Lady O'Callaghan, but I'm sure you are utterly wrong. How *could* they have poisoned him? It's—it's impossible. I do beg you not to distress yourself." He glanced uncomfortably at her placid face. "I'm sure you are quite mistaken," ended Ronald wildly.

"Let us go into his room," she murmured and, without another word, led the way into O'Callaghan's study.

They unlocked the desk and she sat and watched, while Ronald went through the papers in the top pigeon-holes.

"The drawers on the left," he explained to her, "were used for private correspondence—I did not have anything to do with them."

"They will have to be opened. I will do that."

"Of course. Here is one of the threatening letters—several—I think all of them. I wanted to show them to Chief Detective-Inspector Alleyn at the Yard. Sir Derek wouldn't allow me to do so."

"Let me see them."

He gave her the bundle of letters and returned to the pigeon-holes.

"Here are his notes," he said presently. She did not answer, and he glanced up and was astonished to surprise in her face an expression of some sort of an emotion. She looked venomous.

"Here is the letter I spoke of," she said. "You will see that they threaten to poison him."

"Yes. I see."

"You still do not believe me, Mr. Jameson?"

"I'm sorry. I'm afraid I don't."

"I shall insist upon an inquiry."

"An inquiry? Oh Lord!" said Ronald involuntarily. "I mean—I wouldn't, really, Lady O'Callaghan. It's—we've no grounds for it."

"Are you taking these notes to the Prime Minister to-day?"

"Yes."

"Will you tell him, if you please, what I propose to do? You may discuss it with him. In the meantime I shall go through the private letters. Have you the keys of those drawers?"

Ronald took a bunch of keys from the desk, and with an air of reluctance put them in her hand.

"When is your appointment?"

"For three o'clock."

"It is now only half-past two. Please come and see me before you leave."

As he left her she was fitting a key to the bottom drawer.

To anybody who had the curiosity to watch him—Nash, the butler, for instance—Ronald Jameson would have appeared to be very much upset. He went up to his bedroom, wandered aimlessly about, smoked three cigarettes, and finally sat on the bed, staring in a sort of trance at a wood-engraving that hung above his dressing-table. At last he looked at his watch, went downstairs, got his hat and umbrella and returned to the study.

He found Lady O'Callaghan seated at the desk with a neatly arranged pile of letters in front of her. She did not turn her head when he came in. She simply stared very fixedly at a paper she held in her hand. It struck him that she had sat like that for some time—while he himself had done much the same thing upstairs in his room. Her face was always pale—she did not use rouge—but he thought now that it was deadly white. There was a thin ridge, like a taut thread, linking her nostrils with the corners of her mouth.

"Come here," she said quietly.

He went and stood by the desk.

"You told me that night, a week ago, I think, that my husband had received a letter that seemed to upset him. Was this the letter?"

He glanced at it and then looked away.

"I did not see the letter," he stammered. "Only the envelope."

"Is that the envelope?"

"I—I think so. I can't be sure."

"Read it."

With an expression of extreme distaste he read the letter. It was Jane Harden's.

"If an opportunity presented itself," Jane had written, "I would not hesitate to kill you."

Ronald put it down on the desk.

"Now read this."

The second letter was from Sir John Phillips. Phillips had written it at fever-heat on the night he got home from his interview with O'Callaghan, and had posted it before he had time to cool down.

I gather you're going to cut your losses and evade what, to any decent man, would be a responsibility. You talked of sending Jane a cheque. She will, of course, either tear it up or return it. I cannot force your hand, for that would do still more harm to a lady who is already deeply wronged. I warn you, however, to keep clear of me. I've a certain devil in me that I thought was scotched, but you have brought it to life again, and I think I could very easily kill you. This may sound like hyperbole; as a matter of fact it is meiosis.

"Have you seen that before?" asked Lady O'Callaghan.

"Never," said Ronald.

"You notice the signature? It was written by the man who operated on my husband."

"Yes."

"Who is this woman—Jane Harden?"

"Honestly, I have no idea, Lady O'Callaghan."

"No? A nurse, evidently. Look at the address, Mr. Jameson."

"Good God," said Ronald. "It's—it's the nursing-home."

"Yes. We sent him to a strange place for his operation."

"But——"

"Will you please take these letters with you?"

"But, Lady O'Callaghan, I can't possibly show them to the P.M.—the Prime Minister—really!"

"Then I shall have to do so myself. Of course, there must be an inquest." .

"Forgive me, but in the shock of reading these letters and—and realising their inferences, have you considered the effect any publicity would have on yourself?"

"What do you mean? What shock? Do you suppose I did not know he had mistresses?"

"I've no idea, I'm sure," said poor Ronald unhappily.

"Of course I knew," she said composedly. "That seems to me to have nothing to do with the point we are discussing. I knew he had been murdered. I thought at first that these other people——" She made a slight gesture towards the neat little pile on the desk. "Now I find he had bitter enemies nearer to him than that." Her hand closed over the letters on her knee. "He has been murdered. Probably by this nurse or by Sir John Phillips; possibly by both of them in collaboration. I shall demand an inquest."

"An inquest! You know, I doubt very much if you would be given permission."

"To whom does one apply?"

"One can't just order an inquest," Ronald said evasively.

"Who can do so, Mr. Jameson?"

"The—well, the coroner for the district, I imagine."

"Or the police?"

Ronald winced.

46

"I suppose so—yes."

"Yes. Thank you, Mr. Jameson."

Ronald, in a panic, took himself off to the House.

Lady O'Callaghan put a jade paper-weight on the little heap of letters and opened the telephone directory. The number she wanted was printed in large letters on a front page. She dialled it, and was answered immediately.

"Is that New Scotland Yard?" she asked, pitching her voice in a sort of serene falsetto. "It is Lady O'Callaghan speaking. My husband was Sir Derek O'Callaghan, the late Home Secretary. I want to speak to someone in authority, in reference to the death of my husband. No, not on the telephone. Perhaps someone would call? Immediately, if possible. Thank you."

She hung up the receiver and leant back in her chair. Then she rang for Nash, who came in looking like a Stilton in mourning.

"Nash," she said, "an officer from Scotland Yard is calling in ten minutes. It is in reference to the funeral. I wish to speak to him myself. If Miss O'Callaghan calls, will you tell her I am unable to see her? Show the officer in here when he comes."

"Very good, m'lady," breathed Nash and withdrew.

Cicely O'Callaghan then went to the room where her husband lay, awaiting his last journey down Whitehall. She was an Anglo-Catholic, so candles burned, small golden plumes, at the head and foot of the coffin. The room, a large one, was massed heavily with flowers. It smelt like a tropical island, but was very cold. A nun from the church that the O'Callaghans attended knelt at a little distance from the coffin. She did not look up when Lady O'Callaghan came in.

The wife knelt beside her for a moment, crossed herself with a thin vague movement of her hand, and then rose and contemplated her husband.

Derek O'Callaghan looked impressive. The heavy eyebrows, black hair, jutting nose and thin wide mouth were striking accents in the absolute pallor of his face. His hands, stiffly crossed, obediently fixed a crucifix to the hard curve of his breast. His wife, only a little less pale than he, stared at him. It would have been impossible to guess her thoughts. She simply looked in the direction of the dead face. In the distance a door opened and shut. She turned away from the bier, and walked out of the room.

In the hall Nash waited gloomily, while a tall, thickly built man handed him hat and umbrella.

"Inspector Fox, my lady."

"Will you come in here?"

She took the inspector into the study. Nash had lit the fire, and she held her thin hands towards it.

"Please sit down," she murmured. They sat facing each other. Inspector Fox regarded her with respectful attention.

"I asked you to come and see me," she began very quietly, "because I believe my husband to have been murdered."

Fox did not speak for a moment. He sat stockily, very still, looking gravely before him.

"I'm sorry to hear that, Lady O'Callaghan," he said at last. "It sounds rather serious."

Apparently she had met her match in understatement.

"Of course, I should not have called you in unless I had material evidence to put before you. I believe the police are aware of the activities of those persons against whom my husband's Anarchy Bill was directed?"

"We know a good deal about them."

"Yes. My husband had received many threatening letters which were believed to come from these people. I wished him to let the police see the letters, but he refused."

"We were informed of the matter from another source," said Fox.

"The Prime Minister, perhaps?"

Fox regarded her placidly, but did not reply.

"I have the letters here," she continued, after a moment, "and would like you to read them." She took them from the desk and gave them to him.

Fox took a spectacle case from an inner pocket and put on a pair of gold-rimmed glasses. He looked extremely respectable.

He read the letters through stolidly, laying them down neatly one on top of the other. When the last was finished, he clasped his enormous hands together and said:

"Yes. That's the sort of things these people write."

"Now, will you read these?"

She gave him the letters from Sir John Phillips and Jane Harden. He read them carefully, in exactly the same way.

"Sir John Phillips is the surgeon who operated upon my husband. I understand the other letter is from a nurse in the hospital."

"Is that so, Lady O'Callaghan?" said Fox politely.

"My husband had peritonitis but I believe he died of poisoning. I believe he was poisoned."

"In view of these letters? These two, or the others?"

"I do not know. I am inclined to regard the personal ones as being more important. They definitely threaten his life."

"Yes. Very vindictive, they seem to be."

"I wish to have an inquest."

"I see," said Fox. "Now that's quite a serious matter, Lady O'Callaghan."

A faint redness appeared in her cheeks. Another woman would possibly have screamed in his face.

"Of course it is serious," she said.

"I mean, if you understand me, that before an order is made for an inquest, the coroner who makes it has to be certain of one or two points. What about the death certificate, for instance?"

"What do you mean?"

"Well, was one signed?"

"Yes."

"By Sir John Phillips?"

"I don't know. Possibly. Mr. Thoms, the assistant surgeon, may have signed it."

"Yes. Well, now, Mr. Thoms is a well-known surgeon. Sir Derek was a distinguished patient. He would take every care before he signed. I think that would be considered sufficiently conclusive by the coroner."

"But these threats! I am convinced he was murdered. I shall demand an inquest."

Fox stared gravely into the fire.

"Perhaps," he said, rather ponderously, "perhaps you would like me to ring up the coroner and put the case before him."

"Certainly, if you will."

"It would be better if you could tell him, definitely, who signed the certificate."

"Mr. Jameson, my husband's secretary, may know. He had an appointment with the Prime Minister at three."

"It's fifteen minutes to four."

"I shall ring up the House," she said, and did.

She got Ronald at last and asked her question.

"It was Mr. Thoms?" she said into the telephone. Ronald's voice quacked audibly in the room. "Yes. Thank you. Have you discussed the matter? I see. No, I think not, Mr. Jameson; I am communicating directly with the police."

She hung up the receiver and informed Fox that Thoms had signed the certificate.

Inspector Fox then rang up the coroner. He held a long and muffled conversation. The coroner talked a great deal and appeared to be agitated. Lady O'Callaghan listened. Her fingers drummed bonily on the arm of her chair. For her, it was a terrific gesture. At last Fox rang off.

"It's as I thought," he said. "He says he cannot interfere."

"Then I shall go direct to the Prime Minister."

He got rather ponderously to his feet.

"I don't think I'd do that, Lady O'Callaghan—at least not yet. If you'll allow me to I'd like to talk it over with my superior, Chief Detective-Inspector Alleyn."

"Alleyn? I think I've heard of him. Isn't he—" She paused. Cicely O'Callaghan had nearly dropped a brick. She had been about to say "Isn't he a gentleman?" She must have been really very much perturbed to come within hail of such a *gaffe*. Inspector Fox answered her very simply.

"Yes," he said, "he's rather well known. He's a very highly educated man. Quite a different type from me, you might say."

Again a faint pink tinged her cheeks.

"I'm grateful to you for the trouble you are taking," she told him.

"It's all in the day's work," said Fox. "If you'll excuse me, Lady O'Callaghan, I'll get along. I'll speak to the chief at once. If you're agreeable, I'll show him the correspondence."

"Yes."

"Thank you very much. I'll wish you good afternoon."

"Will you have something to drink before you go?"

"No, thank you. Very kind of you, I'm sure." He tramped to the door, turned and made a little bow.

"I hope you'll allow me to offer my sympathy," he said. "It's a great loss to the nation."

"Thank you."

"Good afternoon, Lady O'Callaghan."

"Good afternoon, Inspector."

So Inspector Fox went to the Yard to see Alleyn.

CHAPTER VI

Chief Detective-Inspector Alleyn

Friday, the twelfth. Afternoon and evening.

"Hallo, Brer Fox," said Alleyn, looking up from his desk. "Where've you been in your new bowler?"

"Paying a call on the Snow Queen," replied Fox with unexpected imaginativeness. "And when I say 'Snow Queen' I don't mean cocaine, either."

"No? Then what do you mean? Sit down and have a smoke. You look perturbed."

"Well, I am," said Fox heavily. He produced a pipe and blew down it, staring solemnly at his superior. "I've been to see the wife of the late Home Secretary," he said.

"What? You *are* coming on."

"Look here, chief. She says it's murder."

"She says what's murder?"

"Him. Sir Derek O'Callaghan."

Alleyn put his pipe down and swung round slowly in his chair.

"Oh!" he said. He raised one eyebrow to an excruciating height and twisted his mouth sideways. This trick invested his handsome face with a kind of impish fastidiousness.

"What sort of woman is she?" he asked.

"A very cold fishy sort of lady," answered Fox. "A Snow Queen, in fact. Not the hysterical sort, if that's what you mean."

"She was a Rattisbon. All the Rattisbons are a bit frosty. I was at school with her brother—who was, of course, called 'Ratsbane'. I speak like Mr. Gossip, don't I? A very churlish fellow, he was. Well, let's have the whole story."

Fox told him the whole story, dwelling a little on the letters.

"I see," said Alleyn. "And she's hell-bent on an inquest?"

"That she is. If we won't do anything, she's going to the Prime Minister. He's a friend of yours, isn't he, sir?"

"I know the old creature, yes. As a matter of fact, he summoned me to the presence on another matter about a fortnight ago and we had an Oppenheimian conversation about anarchists. He was very perturbed and asked me if I didn't consider O'Callaghan would be in personal danger if he pushed the Bill. Well, one never knows, and I said so. Some bright young Communist might bowl a bomb. As a matter of cold fact, I greatly doubt it. They do a certain amount of mischief, they're an almighty nuisance, but as murderers I've no real faith in the British anarchist. Anarchist! The word is *vieux jeu*."

"I suppose that's French?"

"Quite right, Fox. I always said you had a flair for languages."

"I'm teaching myself with the gramophone. All the same, sir, these anarchists are no joke."

"Of course they're not. The P.M., as I believe the member for Little Squidgemere calls him, thought O'Callaghan ought to have police protection. I quite agreed. I couldn't very well do anything else. O'Callaghan pooh-poohed the idea. As you know, we were looking after him in our unassuming way. On the afternoon of the Cabinet Meeting, when they decided to introduce the Bill, I went along to Downing Street myself. I'd got wind of that insufferable nuisance Nicholas Kakaroff, and found him standing about in the street, dressed up as something rather ridiculous—a photographer, I think. He made off, with all his infra-red rays and what not, as soon as he saw me. I took a taxi and followed O'Callaghan home. We were alongside each other at one moment. He turned up the lights in his car and I returned the compliment."

"His servants are all right, aren't they?" asked Fox.

"Oh, yes; we went as far as that. But, of course, we couldn't do much without O'Callaghan's permission or knowledge."

"No. I think her ladyship suspects the surgeon or the girl."

" 'The Surgeon or the Girl'—it sounds like a talkie. Sir John Phillips is a very able man and handy, so I understand, with the knife. She thinks he dug it into an unlawful spot, because O'Callaghan had been interfering with his girl—is that it?"

"She thinks Sir Derek was poisoned, otherwise that seems to be the general idea, but of course his letter isn't very explicit."

"Have you got the letters?"

"Yes. Here they are."

Alleyn read them carefully.

"You know, Fox, hundreds of people write letters like these without planning murder."

"Isn't that what I tried to tell her!"

"My poor Foxkin! See if you can find the Press report of his death."

Fox produced a paper.

"I brought it with me," he said.

"You think of everything. Here we are. He died an hour after the operation was over. The anæsthetist was worried—peritonitis—ruptured abscess—'unwilling to run aside from the gigantic task'—he'd neglected his tummy, evidently. It sounds straightforward enough, and yet—"

Alleyn took the tip of his straight nose between his thumb and finger and pulled it thoughtfully.

"Oh, lord!" he said sadly. "I'll have to go and see the lady."

Fox looked relieved.

"If there's anything in it," he reflected, "it'll be a hell of a big case. What you call"—he paused self-consciously—"a *cause célèbre.*"

"It will indeed," said Alleyn, who never made too much fun of anybody. "I wonder if she would see me this evening?"

"I'm certain she would, sir."

"I'll ask."

Alleyn rang up the house in Catherine Street. "Is that Lady O'Callaghan's house? Is it her butler speaking? Chief Inspector Alleyn, Scotland Yard, here. Will you ask her ladyship if I may call on her to-night at any time that would suit her? Inspector Alleyn, yes. Thank you."

He stared absent-mindedly at Fox while he waited for the reply.

"At nine o'clock. Thank you so much."

He hung up the receiver.

"I'm for it," he said.

After Fox had gone Alleyn sat and gazed at the opposite wall for twenty minutes. Then he rang up the divisional surgeon and talked to him about the human appendix, peritonitis and anæsthetics. Then he went to his flat near Coventry Street, bathed, changed into a dinner-jacket, dined, and read the first scene in *Hamlet*, to which he was partial. By that time it was twenty to nine. He decided to walk to Catherine Street. His servant, Vassily [see *A Man Lay Dead*], helped him into his overcoat.

"Vassily," said Alleyn, "do you ever see anything of your disreputable pals—The Pan-Soviet Brotherhood, or whatever they were—nowadays?"

"No, sir. Not now am I such a foolish old rascal. I am one bite too shy."

"So I should hope, you old donkey. You don't happen to remember hearing any gossip about Nicholas Kakaroff?"

Vassily crossed himself lavishly from right to left.

"*Hospodi bozhe moy!* He is one of the most worst of them," he said energetically. "A bad fellow. Before the Soviet he was young and anysing but conserff-a-tiff. After the Soviet he was older and always up to no-goods. The Soviet pleased him no better than the Romanoffs. So sometimes he was killing officials, and at last he has heated up Russia for himself too much, so has come to England."

"Where he seems to have been given the usual hearty welcome. Yes, I knew all that, Vassily. Thank you. Don't wait up. Good night."

"Good night, sir," Vassily laid his hand on Alleyn's sleeve. "Please, sir," he said, "have no business with Nikolai Alexaivich—he is a very bad rascal."

"Well, you ought to know," Alleyn remarked lightly, and went out smiling to himself.

At Catherine Street he was received by Nash, who stared like a boiled owl at the inspector. Nash, who carried in his head a sort of social ladder, had quietly decided that police officers of all ranks were to be graded with piano-tuners. Chief Detective-Inspector Alleyn did not conform, in appearance or in manner, to this classification. Nash performed a reluctant mental somersault.

"Lady O'Callaghan?" asked Alleyn.

"Her ladyship is expecting you, sir." Alleyn gave him his hat and overcoat. Nash said: "Thank you, sir," and waddled off towards the study. Alleyn followed him. Nash opened the door.

"Mr. Alleyn, m'lady," he said. Obviously the degrading titles were better omitted.

Alleyn walked in.

Cicely O'Callaghan sat before the fire in her husband's armchair. As Alleyn came in she rose to her feet and looked serenely at him.

"How do you do?" she said.

"How do you do? I am extremely sorry to bother you, Lady

O'Callaghan."

He thought: "Golly, she *is* like Ratsbane!"

"But I wished to see you. It is good of you to come so promptly."

"Not a bit." This was an exceedingly polite introduction to a murder story.

"Do sit down. I suppose the man who came here this afternoon has told you my reason for communicating with the police?"

"I believe Inspector Fox gave me a full account of your conversation."

"Yes. I am convinced that my husband was murdered—probably poisoned."

"I am sorry that in addition to your grief you should suffer the pain occasioned by such a suspicion," said Alleyn, and wondered how long they were to make speeches at each other.

"Thank you. Do you agree with me that the circumstances warrant an inquest?"

"I think I should like to hear a little more about them. I have read the letters."

"Surely they in themselves are enough to arouse anybody's suspicion?"

"Lady O'Callaghan, it is extremely unusual for a person contemplating homicide to write such letters. I do not say it is unknown, but it *is* very unusual. I expect Fox told you that."

"I believe he said something of the sort. My point is this: I do not think the murderer contemplated homicide when writing the letter. I do think that a person capable of writing such a letter would also be capable of seizing the opportunity when it presented itself."

"So it *is* Phillips and the girl she's after," thought Alleyn.

"I see your point, of course," he said slowly.

"There is another incident which I did not go into with—Inspector Fox. Before my husband's operation I was in his room with him. He did not realise where he was or what had happened to him. I tried to explain about the appendix. Then Sir John Phillips came into the room. When my husband saw him he exclaimed: "Don't—don't let——" and then he collapsed. He seemed terrified by the presence of Sir John Phillips and I am certain that he tried to say: 'Don't let him touch me'. I must tell you that a week before this Sir John called on my husband. I hoped that it was for a consultation about his pain, which was then very severe. Next morning I asked my husband if Sir John

55

had examined him. He evaded my question, and seemed very much upset. I had met Sir John in the hall and had thought his manner most unusual. His letter was written that same night, evidently as a result of the interview."

"You definitely connect Sir John's letter with the other, signed Jane Harden?"

"Yes. She is a nurse in the hospital where my husband was a patient. After your man left, this afternoon, I rang up the hospital and under pretext of wishing to thank the nurses concerned in the case, I found out their names. She was actually present in the operating theatre and I dare say assisted Sir John."

She drawled all this out in her serene, high-pitched voice, exactly as though she was reading aloud.

"Forgive me," said Alleyn, "but did you know anything about this business? I hope you will understand that I only ask because——"

"Because you wonder if I am prejudiced?"

"Exactly."

"I knew my husband was unfaithful to me from time to time. I also believed these incidents to be more or less casual encounters."

"You were unaware of this Miss Harden's existence?"

"Quite."

Alleyn was silent for a little while. Then he rose to his feet.

"I think, with you, that there should be an inquest," he told her.

She made a slight movement and the heavy folds of her dress stirred. It was as though she had suddenly gone tense all over. When she spoke, however, it was with her customary equanimity.

"You have, I am sure, made a very wise decision."

"I'm afraid we shall have difficulty with the coroner. Naturally he is rather chary about starting such an alarming hare. It will be impossible to keep the thing even moderately quiet. The papers already have wind of these threatening letters from Sir Derek's political enemies."

He watched her closely, but beyond a faint expression of distaste, could find no evidence of any sort of emotion.

"That will be rather disagreeable," she murmured.

"I am afraid so. Is there anything else that you would like to discuss?"

"I was going to suggest that you speak to Mr. Ronald Jameson, my husband's secretary. He will, I think, confirm what I have said about Sir Derek's reaction to these letters."

"If you wish it, I will see him. Of course, if the post-mortem shows that poison has been given, it will then be my duty to make very exhaustive inquiries."

"Of course," she agreed.

Evidently she had made up her mind Alleyn should see Jameson, because she sent for him then and there. Ronald came in looking very perturbed and uneasy.

"This is my husband's secretary—Mr. Jameson, Mr. Alleyn."

"How do you do, sir?" said Ronald. "You won't have the foggiest recollection of me, I'm afraid, but we have met before."

"I've a filthy memory," declared Chief Inspector Alleyn.

"It was at Nigel Bathgate's."

"Oh, yes." Alleyn was polite, but non-committal.

"Really?" murmured Lady O'Callaghan. "Yes, I thought too that perhaps I had seen you—that your face——" She seemed uncertain how to go on.

"People often find they are familiar with the faces of the police," said Alleyn gravely.

"It's not that, sir," Ronald turned to Lady O'Callaghan. "Mr. Alleyn is in some of Mr. Rattisbon's photos in the study at Karnelly."

"Ratsbane's cricketing groups," thought Alleyn. "Oh, Lord!"

"Oh," said Lady O'Callaghan. "Yes." She stared rather blankly at him.

"Mr. Jameson," Alleyn began, "I believe Lady O'Callaghan wants me to speak to you about an incident that took place here a week before Sir Derek's operation."

Ronald jumped and glanced nervously at the lady.

"I have spoken to Mr. Alleyn about my suspicions. He agrees that there should be an inquest."

"Really, sir? Look here—I mean, of course, you know best, but, well—it's—it's a pretty ghastly thought, isn't it?"

"You remember the evening my husband had the letter signed Jane Harden?"

"Yes," said Ronald very reluctantly.

"You remember that you told me the letter seemed to upset him very much?"

"Yes—but——"

"And when he overheard you speaking of it he was quite unreasonably angry?"

57

"I don't think *unreasonably*, Lady O'Callaghan," Ronald protested. "Sir Derek was quite right. I should not have mentioned his correspondence. I had never done so before."

"Why did you do so then?" she asked him.

"Really," thought Alleyn, "she might be an Attorney-General."

"Because—well, because it seemed to upset him so much." Ronald saw the fence too late and crashed into it.

"Yes," said Lady O'Callaghan.

"Would you describe him as being alarmed?" Alleyn asked.

"Well—more sort of disturbed and distressed. After all, sir, it *was* an unpleasant letter to get."

Ronald seemed to be in a perfect agony of embarrassment.

"Certainly," Alleyn agreed. "You were not present, were you, at any time during the interview between Sir Derek and Sir John Phillips?"

"No. I—no, I wasn't."

"What were you going to say? Was anyone else there?"

"Nash, the butler, took in the tray."

"Has he spoken to you on the subject?" asked Alleyn casually.

"Er—yes. Servants' gossip. I rather snubbed him, sir."

"What did he say before you'd snubbed him?"

"He's an awful old woman—Nash. He seemed to think Sir John had used some sort of threatening expression. Honestly, sir, he's a fearful ass."

"I see. I think that's all, Lady O'Callaghan. Perhaps the apprehensive Nash will make an appearance when I go."

She rang the bell.

"He should have come in with the tray by this time," she said vaguely.

When Nash appeared it was with the tray, which he set down delicately.

"Mr. Alleyn, will you——?"

"No thank you so much. I must be off. Good-bye, Lady O'Callaghan. I'll ring you up if I may."

"Yes. Thank you. Good-bye."

Nash opened the door and followed Alleyn into the hall. Jameson made as if to see the inspector out.

"Oh—Mr. Jameson," said Lady O'Callaghan. He hesitated and then returned to the study, closing the door.

As he took his hat and coat from the butler Alleyn paused and looked directly at him.

"Perhaps you realise why I am here?" he said.

"Not altogether, sir," murmured Nash composedly.

"It is in connection with Sir Derek's death." Nash bowed very slightly.

"If I ask you a question," Alleyn continued, "you must understand there is no obligation to answer if you don't want to. I particularly do not wish the matter mentioned in or out of the servants' hall. You understand?"

"Certainly, sir," said Nash quietly.

"I believe I can depend on you. How long have you been with Sir Derek?"

"Twenty years, sir. I was footman to his father."

"Yes. Did you hear Sir John Phillips say anything to your master the last time he came here?"

"Yes, sir."

"What was it?"

" 'If the opportunity presented itself, I should have no hesitation in putting you out of the way'. Those were the exact words, sir."

"I see. Have you told anyone about this?"

"Mr. Jameson, sir. I considered it my duty. No one in the hall has any idea of the incident, sir."

"What did Mr. Jameson think about it?"

"He appeared to attach no importance to it, sir."

"No? Thank you, Nash."

"Thank you very much, sir. Shall I get you a taxi, sir?"

"No, I'll walk. Good night."

"Good evening, sir."

Nash opened the door and Alleyn went out into the street. He paused for a moment to light a cigarette. He had taken a few steps along the pavement when he heard something that made him pause and turn.

Ronald Jameson had come out of the house and hurried after him, bareheaded.

"Please, forgive me, sir," he said hurriedly, "but I felt I must have another word with you. It was rather difficult with Lady O'Callaghan present. About these ideas of hers. I'm certain there's nothing in it. Sir Derek was a man of the world and—and, of course, he had his relaxations. She seems very cold and all that, but I believe she was frightfully jealous and she wants to punish this girl. I'm sure that's all it is."

"Oh. Why should she want to punish Sir John Phillips as well as Miss Harden?"

"Oh, Lord knows. You can't tell with women, sir, can you?"

"I haven't tried," said Alleyn.

"I expect you think it frightful cheek, my butting in like this, but, you see, I—well, Sir Derek was rather a marvellous person to me, and I simply loathe the idea of everything being dragged out and made public. It's a ghastly thought."

Something of Ronald's semi-diplomatic air of winning tactfulness still appeared in his rather dishevelled manner. He gazed with anxious deference into Alleyn's sardonic face. The inspector cocked an eyebrow.

"And yet," he said, "I imagine, if Sir Derek was actually killed, you would rather the murderer didn't get off scot-free?"

"Yes, but, you know, I'm sure he wasn't. Those two letters didn't mean anything—I thought so at—" Ronald stopped short.

"Were you about to say 'at the time'?" inquired Alleyn.

"I meant at the time Lady O'Callaghan found them."

"Where were the letters kept, Mr. Jameson?"

"In his private drawer," said Ronald with a very red face.

"And the keys?"

"Er—oh, usually in the desk."

"I see. Well, we must pursue the subject no more until we discover whether Sir Derek was murdered."

"I'm absolutely certain there's nothing in it, sir."

"I hope you are right. Good night."

"Thank you so much, sir," said Ronald, all eager and charming. "Good night."

Alleyn swung his stick up, turned on his heel, and walked away. Ronald gazed after the long, elegant figure for some seconds. His fingers fidgeted with his tie. Then he looked up at the windows of the house, slightly shrugged his shoulders, and ran up the steps and through the door.

Alleyn heard the door slam. As he turned out of Catherine Street towards Buckingham Gate he began to whistle Ophelia's song:

He is dead and gone, lady,
He is dead and gone;
At his head a grass-green turf.
At his heels a stone.

CHAPTER VII

Post-Mortem

Monday, the fifteenth. Afternoon.

"Everybody talks to me about "P.M's'," complained Chief Detective-Inspector Alleyn to Inspector Fox on Monday afternoon, "and I never know whether they mean post-mortem or Prime Minister. Really, it's very difficult when you happen to be involved with both."

"It must be," said Fox dryly. "How's the case going?"

"It's too young to be called a case. So far it's only a naughty thought. As you know, Lady O'Callaghan urged the inquest and threatened to appeal to the P.M. However, the coroner ordered the inquest, which opened on Saturday a.m. and was adjourned for a P.M. which has been going on during the week-end p.m. and a.m. You see how tricky it all is?"

"I can see you're worried, chief."

"When you call me "chief", Fox, I feel like a cross between an Indian brave and one of those men with jaws and cigars in gangster films."

"Okay, chief," said Fox imperturbably. "It's a big job, this," he added sombrely.

"It is," said Alleyn. "I don't mind admitting I was nervous over the inquest. I should have looked remarkably silly if it had gone the other way and no P.M. had been ordered."

"It might very easily have happened. Phillips did his best to put the kybosh on a post-mortem."

"You thought so?"

"Well—didn't you?"

"Yes, I suppose so. Oh, yes."

"Of course," said Fox slowly, "an innocent man in his position would have been anxious for a P.M."

"Not if he thought someone else had done the trick."

"Oh," Fox ruminated. "That's the big idea, is it, sir?"

"It's only one idea—possibly a silly one. What did you think of the matron's contribution to the evidence? Sister Marigold?"

"Couldn't make her out at all and that's a fact. She seemed to welcome the inquest. She obviously resented any hint of criticism against Sir John Phillips."

"She made one or two very acid remarks about the other nurse—Nurse Banks."

"Yes. Now, that struck me as rum, too, sir. No suggestion of anything as regards the Harden girl, but when Nurse Banks was mentioned——"

"She bridled like a Persian," said Alleyn. "I know—'rum's' the word, Fox."

"The medical witnesses are always a bit trying in a case like this," reflected Inspector Fox. "On the defensive, as you might say. They all pull together."

"Now that's exactly what I thought they did *not* do. I've just read over the shorthand report of the inquest and the thing that struck me all of a heap was that the hospital gang seemed to be playing a sort of tig-in-the-dark game. Or rather tug-of-war in the dark. They wanted to pull together, but didn't know which way to pull. Here's the report. Let us go over it, shall we? Where's your pipe?"

They lit up. Alleyn shoved a carbon copy of the verbatim report on the inquest across to his subordinate.

"First you get straight-out evidence on the operation. Phillips said Sir Derek O'Callaghan, suffering from a ruptured abscess of the appendix, was admitted to the Brook Street hospital. He examined the patient, advised an immediate operation, which, at Lady O'Callaghan's request, he undertook to perform himself. Peritonitis was found. The anæsthetist was Dr. Roberts, engaged for the job because the usual man was unavailable. Phillips says Roberts used all possible care and he can find no fault in that department. Thoms, the assistant, agrees. So do Sister Marigold and the two nurses. Before he began, Phillips injected hyoscine, his usual procedure for all operations. For this injection he used tablets he brought with him, saying that he preferred them to the solution in the theatre, as hyoscine is an extremely tricky drug.

"All care taken, no responsibility accepted." one feels moved to remark. He prepared the syringe himself. At the end of the operation a concoction prettily named "*Concentrated Gas-Gangrene Antitoxin*", used in cases of peritonitis, was injected. The serum, together with a large syringe, was laid out by Nurse Banks before the operation. It was a commercial preparation kept in an ampoule from which she simply filled the syringe. Nurse Harden fetched the syringe and gave it to Thoms, who injected the stuff. Meanwhile Roberts, the anæesthetist, had got all hot and hectic about the patient's heart and had asked for an injection of camphor, which was prepared and given by the elder nurse. They then tacked up the tear in the tummy and away went the patient. He died an hour later, presumably, one longs to say, of heart-failure, but my medical friends tell me that's as good as saying 'he died of dying'. So we can only murmur humbly 'he died as the result of an operation which, apart from this little incident, was a howling success.' "

"Well," said Fox, "so far they all agree."

"Yes, but did you notice that where it came to the bit about Jane Harden fetching the syringe with the anti-gas, as they call it for short, they all went rather warily. She herself looked pretty sick when the coroner asked her about it. Here it is:

" 'The Coroner: I understand you brought the syringe containing the anti-gas, to Dr. Thoms?

" 'Nurse Harden (after a pause): Yes.

" 'The Coroner: There was no unusual delay, or anything of that sort?

" 'Nurse Harden: I—I did hesitate a moment. The syringe was already full and I paused to make sure it was the right one.

" 'The Coroner: Did you not expect to find it prepared?

" 'Nurse Harden: I was not sure. I—I wasn't well, and for a moment I hesitated and then Nurse Banks said it was the large syringe and I brought it to Dr. Thoms."

" 'Sir John Phillips, recalled, said that the delay was of no significance. Nurse Harden was unwell and had subsequently fainted.

" 'The Coroner: I understand you were personally acquainted with the deceased?

" 'Nurse Harden: Yes.' "

Alleyn laid down the report.

"That's the incident," he said. "It's all perfectly natural, but I smelt high tension among the expert witnesses, whenever it was mentioned."

He waited for a moment and then said slowly:

"That incident would never have come out if it hadn't been for Thoms."

"I noticed that, sir. Mr. Thoms let it out during his evidence and then looked as if he wished he hadn't."

"Yes," said Alleyn dryly.

Fox eyed him cautiously and then went on:

"That girl must have been in a pretty good fatigue—in the light of what we know, I mean. There was this man to whom she'd been writing—the man she'd gone off with, as far as we can tell. She'd reckoned on some sort of permanent understanding, anyway, according to her letter, and when there was nothing doing she'd said she'd like to kill him and—there he was."

"Very dramatic," said Alleyn. "The same line of chat, with a difference, may be applied to Sir John Phillips."

"That's so," admitted Fox. "They may have been in collusion."

"I'm entirely against any sort of speculation until we get the analyst's report, Fox. I have not interviewed any of these people. As you know, I thought it best to start no hares before the inquest. I wanted the inquest to be as colourless as possible. The post-mortem may be a wash-out, in which case we'll want to fade away with the minimum amount of publicity."

"That's right," said Fox heavily.

"We're only noting any points of interest in the evidence that may come in handy for future reference. Exhibit A—Nurse Harden and the anti-gas. Exhibit B—curious behaviour of Nurse Banks while giving evidence. The woman closely resembled a chestnut on the hob. She might have spontaneously combusted at any moment. However, she didn't, more's the pity perhaps, but I think she managed to fill the minds of the jury with strange surmises. It struck me that she hadn't exactly hero-worshipped the late Home Secretary. There was more than a suspicion of a snort in her references to him."

"Bolshie-minded, perhaps," ruminated Fox.

"Dare say. She looks like that."

"He may have carried on with her too."

"Oh, Fox! She does *not* look like that."

"People take very strange fancies sometimes, sir."

"How true that is. No speculations, Foxkin."

"All right, sir, all right. What about Exhibit C?"

"Exhibit C, *In re* above. Heavy restraint of the matron, Sister Marigold, when Banks was mentioned. Marigold seemed to me to seethe with suppressed information. 'Wild horses wouldn't get me to tell, but, my oath, if wild horses could——?' "

"And Sir John himself?"

"*Agitato ma non troppo*, and unnaturally *ppp*. This abbreviation business is insidious. Sir John was so anxious to let everybody know he had prepared the hyoscine injection, wasn't he?"

"Very straightforward of him, I thought," remarked Fox doubtfully.

"Oh," said Alleyn vaguely, "so did I. As honest as the day." Fox regarded him suspiciously.

"Lady O'Callaghan gave her evidence well," he said.

"Admirably. But, oh, lummie, how we did hover on the brink of those letters. I'd warned the coroner, who had, of course, read them and thought they were sufficient grounds for a postmortem. However, he agreed it was better they should not come out. He was very coy about the whole thing anyway, and would have repressed pints of hyoscine——"

"Hyoscine!" shouted Fox. "Aha—you are thinking of hyoscine!"

"Don't shriek at me like that; I nearly bit my pipe stem in half. I'm not thinking particularly of hyoscine. I was about to remark that I was in deadly fear Lady O'Callaghan would drag in the letters. I'd warned her, advised her, implored her not to, but she's not a Ratsbane for nothing, and you never know."

"And Thoms?"

"Thoms took the line that the whole show was unnecessary, but he gave his evidence well, appeared to have nothing to conceal apart from his regret over divulging the fainting episode, an seemed to resent the slightest criticism of Phillips."

"Yes," Fox agreed, "I noticed that. Roberts took much the same line. That's what I mean about the experts sticking together."

"Oh quite. They wanted to pull together but I'm pretty certain they were not all agreed. I did rather feel that they were uneasy about Nurse Harden's delay over the anti-gas syringe, and that there was something about Nurse Banks that both Sister Marigold and Jane Harden shied away from."

"There were three injections altogether," said Fox thoughtfully. He held up as many short fingers. "The hyoscine, prepared and injected by Phillips; the camphor, prepared and injected by Nurse Banks; and the anti-gas, prepared by Nurse Banks and injected by Mr. Thoms."

"Sounds like a petrol station. Well, there it is. If his tummy turns up a natural, we can forget all about it. If dirty weather sets in, it'll be with a vengeance. Do you like cocktail metaphors?"

"I've been talking to Inspector Boys about the political side," said Fox. "He's got all the Kakaroff crowd taped out and he doesn't think there's much in it."

"Nor do I. Since the Krasinky lot were roped in they've piped down considerably [see *A Man Lay Dead*]. Still, you never know with these people. They may mean business. If that Bill goes through next week, it'll larn 'em. I hope there's no nonsense at the funeral to-morrow. We're making elaborate enough arrangements for burying the poor chap—shutting the stable door with a gold padlock. They might possibly choose the moment to celebrate at the funeral, but, no, I don't think they were in on the murder. I'm inclined to think they would have staged something more spectacular—a suitable echo to the Yugoslavia affair. Hyoscine doesn't sound their cup of tea at all."

"Why hyoscine?" asked Fox with massive innocence.

"You old devil," said Alleyn, "I refuse to discuss the case with you. Go and catch pickpockets."

"Sorry, sir."

"And if anything comes of this P.M. business, you can jolly well deal with Lady O'Callaghan yourself. That makes you blanch. What's the time?"

"Three o'clock, sir. The results of the post-mortem ought to come in fairly soon."

"I suppose so. Our famous pathologist is going to ring me up himself as soon as he has informed the coroner."

Alleyn got up and walked about the room hunching up one shoulder and whistling under his breath. The desk telephone rang. Fox answered it.

"It's a Miss O'Callaghan asking for you," he said stolidly.

"Miss——? Who the devil——? Oh, all right. *Now* what's in the wind, do you suppose?"

"Send her up," said Fox to the telephone. "I'd better push off, sir," he added.

"I suppose you had. This is all very rum—very rum indeed."

Fox departed. Alleyn knocked out his pipe, opened the window, and sat behind the desk. A woman's voice sounded in the passage outside. The door was opened by a police-constable, who said: "Miss O'Callaghan, sir," and withdrew.

Ruth O'Callaghan walked into the room. She appeared to be dressed in a series of unrelated lengths of material. Her eye-glasses were canted over the top angle of her enormous nose. Her handbag and umbrella, wedded by an unhappy confusion of cords and leather thongs, dangled from a gaunt wrist. Her face, exclusive of the nose, was pale. She seemed to be grievously agitated.

Alleyn rose and waited politely.

"Oh!" said Ruth, catching sight of him. "Oh!" She came towards him at a kind of gallop and held out the hand that was encumbered with the umbrella and handbag. Alleyn shook it.

"How do you do?" he murmured.

"So good of you to see me," Ruth began. "I know how busy you must be. The statistics of crime are so appalling. Too kind."

"I am making no arrests this afternoon," said Alleyn gravely.

She gazed at him dubiously and then broke into a sort of whooping laugh.

"Oh, no, no, no," said Ruth. "That's very funny—no, of course, I didn't suppose——" She stopped laughing abruptly and looked disconcertingly lugubrious.

"No," she repeated. "But it *is* kind, all the same, when I expect you think I'm a jolly old nuisance of an interfering woman."

"Do sit down," said Alleyn gently, and pulled forward a chair. Ruth shut up rather like a two-foot rule. He pushed the chair under her and returned to his own. She leant forward, resting her elbows on his desk and gazed earnestly at him.

"Mr. Alleyn," Ruth began, "what is this dreadful, dreadful suspicion about my brother's death?"

"At the moment, Miss O'Callaghan, it can scarcely be called a suspicion."

"I don't understand. I've been talking to my sister-in-law. She said some dreadful things to me—terrible—appalling. She says my brother was——" Ruth drew in her breath noisily and on the crest of the intake uttered the word "murdered."

"Lady O'Callaghan attaches a certain amount of importance to threatening letters which were sent to Sir Derek. You have heard of these letters, I expect."

"You mean from those horrible anarchist people? Of course, I know they behaved very badly, but Derry—my brother, you know—always said they wouldn't do anything, and I'm quite certain he was right. Nobody else could have any reason for wishing him harm." ("She hasn't heard about the other letters, then," thought Alleyn.) "Everybody adored him, simply adored him, dear old boy. Mr. Alleyn, I've come to *beg* you not to go on with the case. The inquest was bad enough, but the other—the— you know what I mean. I can't endure the thought of it. Please— please, Mr. Alleyn——" She fumbled desperately in the bag and produced a colossal handkerchief.

"I'm so sorry," said Alleyn. "I know it's a beastly idea, but just think a little. Does it matter so much what they do to our bodies when we've finished with them? I can't think so. It seems to me that the impulse to shrink from such things is based on a fallacy. Perhaps it is impertinent of me to speak so frankly." Ruth gurgled and shook her head dolefully. "Well then, suppose there was no post-mortem, what about your feelings then? There would always be an unscotched suspicion whenever you thought of your brother."

"He was ill. It was his illness. If only he had followed my advice! Mr. Alleyn, I have a friend, a brilliant young chemist, a rising man. I consulted him about my brother and he— generously and nobly—gave me a wonderful remedy, "Fulvita- volts", that would have cured my brother. I *begged* him to take it. It *would* have cured him; I know it would. My friend assured me of it and he *knows*. He said——" She broke off abruptly and darted a curiously frightened glance at Alleyn. "My brother always laughed at me," she added quickly.

"And he refused to try this 'Fulvitavolts'?"

"Yes—at least—yes, he did. I left the tablets there but, of course—he just laughed. My sister-in-law is not very——" Here Ruth floundered unhappily. "I'm sure he didn't take them."

"I see. People are generally very conservative about medicine."

"Yes, *aren't* they?" agreed Ruth eagerly and then stopped again and blew her nose.

"The lack of interest shown in chemical research must be very discouraging to a young man like your friend," Alleyn went on. "I know a brilliant fellow—only twenty-five—who has already——" He stopped and bent towards her. "I suppose we can't possibly be speaking of the same person?"

Ruth beamed at him through her tears.

"Oh, no," she assured him.

"Now, how do you know, Miss O'Callaghan?" said Alleyn gaily. "I'm a very great believer in coincidence. My man is James Graham."

"No, no." She hesitated again, oddly, and then in another burst of confidence: "I'm talking about Harold Sage. Perhaps you've heard of him too? He's getting quite famous. He's—he's practically thirty."

"The name seems to strike a chord," lied Alleyn thoughtfully. The desk telephone rang.

"Will you excuse me?" he asked her, and took off the receiver.

"Hallo? Yes, speaking. Yes. Yes. I see. Thank very much. I'm engaged at the moment, but if I may I'll come round and see you to-morrow? Right." He hung up the receiver. Ruth had just got to her feet.

"I mustn't keep you, Mr. Alleyn. Only before I go—please, please let me beg you to go no further with these investigations. I've—I've got a reason—I mean I'm so sure Derry died naturally. It is all so dreadful. If I could be sure you were satisfied——" She made an ineffectual movement with her hands, a clumsy gesture of entreaty. "Tell me you'll go no further!" begged Ruth.

"I am extremely sorry," said Alleyn formally, "but that would be impossible. The post-mortem has already been held. That message gave me the result."

She stood gaping at him, her mouth half open, her big hands clutching at her bag.

"But what—what is it? What do they say?"

"Your brother died of an overdose of a dangerous drug," said Alleyn.

She stared at him in utter dismay and then, without another word, turned and blundered out of the room.

Alleyn wrote the name 'Harold Sage' in a minute notebook that he carried. Having done so, he stared at it with an air of incredulity, sighed, shut up his book and went to find Fox.

CHAPTER VIII

Hyoscine

Tuesday, the sixteenth. Afternoon.

On the following afternoon, five days after his death, Derek O'Callaghan was buried with a great deal of pomp and ceremony. Alleyn was right about the funeral—there was no demonstration from the late Home Secretary's obscure opponents, and the long procession streamed slowly down Whitehall without disturbance. Meanwhile the inquest had been resumed and concluded. After hearing the pathologist's and the analyst's reports, the jury returned a verdict of murder against "a person or persons unknown". Alleyn had had a few words in private with the pathologist before the inquest opened.

"Well," said the great man, "there wasn't much doubt about the hyoscine. The usual dose is a hundredth to a two-hundredth of a grain. My calculations, based on traces of hyoscine found in the organs, show that more than a quarter of a grain had been given. The minimum lethal dose would be something very much less."

"I see," said Alleyn slowly.

"Did you expect hyoscine, Alleyn?"

"It was on the *tapis*. I wish to heaven you hadn't found it."

"Yes. Unpleasant business."

"Do they ever put hyoscine in patent medicines?"

"Oh, yes. Had Sir Derek taken patent medicines?"

"I don't know. It's possible."

"The dosage would be too small to enter into the picture."

"If he swallowed an entire packet?"

The pathologist shrugged his shoulders. "Would he take an entire packet?" Alleyn did not answer. "I can see you've got

70

something in mind," said the pathologist, who knew him.

"Sir John Phillips injected hyoscine. Suppose O'Callaghan had taken a patent medicine containing the drug?" Alleyn suggested.

"The average injection, as I have said, is about, say, a hundredth of a grain. The amount in patent medicines would be very much less. The two together, even if he had taken quantities of his rot-gut, could scarcely constitute a lethal dose—unless, of course, O'Callaghan had an idiosyncrasy for hyoscine, and even if there was an idiosyncrasy for hyoscine, it wouldn't account for the amount we found. If you want my private opinion, for what it is worth, I consider the man was murdered."

"Thank you for all the trouble you have taken," said Alleyn glumly. "I shan't wait to hear the verdict; it's a foregone conclusion. Fox can grace the court for me. There's one other point. Were you able to find the marks of the injections?"

"Yes."

"How many were there?"

"Three."

"Three. That tallies. Damn!"

"It's not conclusive, Alleyn. There might be a fourth injected where we couldn't see it. Inside the ear, under the hair, or even into the exact spot where one of the others was given."

"I see. Oh, well, I must bustle away and solve the murder."

"Let me know if there's anything further I can do."

"Thank you, I will. Good-bye."

Alleyn went out, changed his mind and stuck his head round the door.

"If I send you a pill or two, will you have them dissected for me?"

"Analysed?"

"If you'd rather. Good-bye."

Alleyn took a taxi to the Brook Street home. He asked a lugubrious individual in a chastened sort of uniform if Sir John Phillips was in the hospital. Sir John had not yet come in. When would he be in? The lugubrious individual was afraid he "reely couldn't say."

"Please find someone who can say," said Alleyn. "And when he's free give Sir John this card."

He was invited to wait in one of those extraordinary drawing-rooms that can only be found in expensive private hospitals in the West End of London. Thick carpet, subfusc curtains of pseudo-empire pattern and gilt-legged chairs combined to disseminate the atmosphere of a mausoleum. Chief Inspector Alleyn and a marble woman whose salient features were picked out embarrassingly in gilt stared coldly at each other. A nurse came in starchily, glanced in doubt at Alleyn, and went out again. A clock, flaunted aloft by a defiant bronze-nude, swung its pendulum industriously to and fro for twenty minutes. A man's voice sounded somewhere and in a moment the door opened and Phillips came in.

He was, as usual, immaculate, a very model for a fashionable surgeon, with his effective ugliness, his eye-glass, his air of professional cleanliness, pointed by the faint reek of ether. Alleyn wondered if the extreme pallor of his face was habitual.

"Inspector Alleyn?" he said. "I am sorry to have kept you waiting."

"Not a bit, sir," said Alleyn. "I must apologise for bothering you, but I felt you would like to know the report of the post-mortem as soon as it came through."

Phillips went back to the door and shut it quietly. His face was turned away from his visitor as he spoke.

"Thank you. I shall be relieved to hear it."

"I'm afraid 'relieved' is scarcely the word."

"No?"

Phillips faced round slowly.

"No," said Alleyn. "They have found strongly marked traces of hyoscine in the organs. He must have had at least a quarter of a grain."

"*A quarter of a grain!*" He moved his eyebrows and his glass fell to the floor. He looked extraordinarily shocked and astonished. "Impossible!" he said sharply. He stooped and picked up his monocle.

"There has been no mistake," said Alleyn quietly.

Phillips glanced at him in silence.

"I beg your pardon, Inspector," he said at last. "Of course, you have made certain of your facts, but—hyoscine—it's incredible."

"You understand that I shall be forced to make exhaustive inquiries."

"I—I suppose so."

"In a case of this sort the police feel more than usually helpless. We must delve into highly technical matters. I will be quite frank with you, Sir John. Sir Derek died of the effects of a lethal dose of hyoscine. Unless it can be proved that he took the drug himself,

72

we are faced with a very serious situation. Naturally I shall have to go into the history of his operation. There are many questions which I should like to put to you. I need not remind you that you are under no compulsion to answer them."

Phillips took his time in replying to this. Then he said courteously:

"Of course, I quite understand. I shall be glad to tell you anything that will help—anxious to do so. I owe it to myself. O'Callaghan came here as my patient. I operated on him. Naturally I shall be one of the possible suspects."

"I hope we shall dispose of your claims to that position very early in the game. Now, first of all—Sir Derek O'Callaghan, as you told us at the inquest, had been given hyoscine."

"Certainly. One-hundredth of a grain was injected prior to the operation."

"Exactly. You approved of this injection, of course?"

"I gave it," said Phillips evenly.

"So you did. I'm afraid I know absolutely nothing about the properties of this drug. Is it always used in cases of peritonitis?"

"It had nothing to do with peritonitis. It is always my practice to give an injection of hyoscine before operating. It reduces the amount of anæsthetic necessary and the patient is more comfortable afterwards."

"It is much more generally used nowadays than, say, twenty years ago?"

"Oh, yes."

"Do you mind telling me just how, and at what stage of the proceedings, it is given? This was not stated specifically at the inquest I think."

"It was given in the anæsthetising-room immediately before the operation and after the patient was under the anæsthetic. A hypodermic syringe was used."

"Prepared, I imagine, by the nurse in charge of the theatre?"

"In this instance, no. I thought this was all perfectly clear, Inspector. I prepared the injection myself."

"Yes, of course—how stupid I am!" Alleyn exclaimed. "That makes it much simpler for me. What exactly did you do? Dip the syringe in a blue bottle and suck up a dram?"

"Not quite." Phillips smiled for the first time and produced a cigarette-case. "Shall we sit down?" he said. "And will you smoke?"

"Do you mind if I have one of my own? Good cigarettes are wasted on me."

They sat on two incredibly uncomfortable chairs under the right elbow of the marble woman.

"As regards the actual solution," said Phillips, "I used a tablet of a hundredth of a grain. This I dissolved in twenty-five minims of distilled water. There was a stock solution of hyoscine in the theatre which I did not use."

"Less reliable or something?"

"It's no doubt perfectly reliable, but hyoscine is a drug that should be used with extreme care. By preparing it myself I am sure of the correct dosage. In most theatres nowadays, it's put out in ampoules. I shall see," added Phillips grimly, "that this procedure is followed here in future."

"In this instance you went through the customary routine?"

"I did."

"Were you alone when you prepared the syringe?"

"There may have been a nurse in the theatre—I don't remember." He paused and then added: "Thoms came in just as I finished."

"Did he go out with you?"

"I really don't know. I rather think he returned to the ante-room a few moments later. I left him in the theatre. I went to the anæsthetic-room and gave the injection."

"Of course, you have no doubt in your own mind about the dosage?"

"I know quite well what you are thinking, Inspector Alleyn. It is a perfectly reasonable suspicion. I am absolutely assured that I dissolved one tablet and one tablet only. I filled the syringe with distilled water, squirted it into a measuring-glass, shook one tablet into my hand, saw that it *was* a single tablet, and dropped it into the glass."

Phillips leant back, looked steadily into Alleyn's eyes, and thrust his hands into his pockets. "I am prepared to swear to that," he said.

"It's perfectly clear, sir," said Alleyn, "and although I had to consider the possibility of a mistake, I realise that even if you had dropped two tablets into the water it would have only meant a dosage of a fiftieth of a grain. Probably the entire contents of the tube would not be a quarter of a grain—the amount estimated."

For the first time Phillips hesitated. "They are packed in tubes of twenty," he said at last, "so an entire tube would contain a fifth of a grain of hyoscine." He felt in his coat pocket and produced a hypodermic case which he handed to Alleyn.

"The actual tube is still in there. I have since used one tablet."

Alleyn opened the case and took out a glass tube completely covered by its paper label. He pulled out the tiny cork and looked in.

"May I?" he asked, and shook out the contents into his hand. There were eighteen tablets.

"That settles it," he said cheerfully. "Do you mind if I take these for analysis? Purely a matter of routine, as one says in crime fiction."

"Do," said Phillips, looking rather bored.

Alleyn took an envelope from his pocket, put the tablets back into the tube, the tube into the envelope, and the envelope into his pocket.

"Thank you so much," he said. "You've been extremely courteous. You've no idea how scared we are of experts at the Yard."

"Indeed?"

"Yes, indeed. This must have been a distressing business for you."

"Very."

"I believe Sir Derek was a personal friend."

"I knew him personally—yes."

"Had you seen much of him recently?"

Phillips did not answer immediately. Then, looking straight in front of him, he said: "What do you call recently?"

"Well—a fortnight or so."

"I called at his house on the Friday evening before the operation."

"A professional call?"

"No."

"Did you think he was heading for a serious illness then?"

"I did not know there was anything the matter with him."

"He did not mention a patent medicine?"

"No," said Phillips sharply. "What is this about patent medicines?"

"Merely a point that arises."

"If there is any question of his taking a drug," said Phillips more cordially, "it should be gone into most thoroughly."

"That is my view," Alleyn answered coolly.

"He may," Phillips went on, "have had an idiosyncrasy for hyoscine and if he had been taking it——"

"Exactly."

The two men seemed to have changed positions. It was the surgeon who now made the advances. Alleyn was polite and withdrawn.

"Is there any evidence that O'Callaghan had taken a patent medicine?"

"It's possible."

"Damn fool!" ejaculated Phillips.

"Strange he didn't tell you he was ill on the Friday."

"He—I—we discussed another matter altogether."

"Would you care to tell me what it was?"

"It was purely personal."

"Sir John," said Alleyn mildly, "I think I should let you know at once that I have seen your letter to Sir Derek."

Phillips's head jerked up as though he had come suddenly face to face with a threatening obstacle. He did not speak for perhaps half a minute and then he said very softly:

"Do you enjoy reading other people's private correspondence?"

"About as much as you enjoy glaring into a septic abdomen, I should think," rejoined Alleyn. "It has a technical interest."

"I suppose you've spoken to the butler?"

"Would you like to give me your own explanation of the business?"

"No," said Phillips. "No."

"Speaking unofficially—a thing I am far too prone to do—I am extremely sorry for you, Sir John."

Phillips looked at him.

"Do you know, I think I believe you," he said. "Is there anything else?"

"No, I've kept you quite long enough. Would it be an awful bore for everyone if I had a word with the nurses who attended the case?"

"I don't think they can tell you very much further."

"Probably not, but I think I ought to see them unless they are all heavily engaged in operations."

"The theatre is not in use at the moment. The matron and the nurse who assists her—Nurse Banks—will be free."

"Splendid. What about Sir Derek's personal nurse and the other one from the theatre—Nurse Harden, wasn't it?"

"I will find out," said Phillips. "Do you mind waiting?"

"Not at all," murmured Alleyn with an involuntary glance at

76

the marble woman. "May I see them one by one—it will be less violently embarrassing for all of us?"

"You do not impress me," rejoined Phillips, "as a person who suffers from shyness, but no doubt you would rather sleuth in secret. You shall see them one by one."

"Thank you."

Alleyn waited only a few minutes after Sir John left him and then the door reopened to admit Sister Marigold in whose countenance gentility, curiosity and resentment were exquisitely reflected.

"How do you do, Matron?" said Alleyn.

"Good afternoon," said Sister Marigold.

"Won't you sit down? Here? Or under the statue?"

"Thank you very much, I'm sure." She sat with a rustle, and eyed the inspector guardedly.

"Perhaps Sir John has told you the report on the post-mortem?" Alleyn suggested.

"It's terrible. Such a loss, as I say, to the country."

"Unthinkable. One of the really strong men in the right party," said Alleyn with low cunning.

"Just what I said when it happened."

"Now look here, Matron, will you take mercy on a wretched ignorant policeman and help me out of the awful fog I'm wallowing in? Here's this man, perhaps the foremost statesman of his time, lying dead with a quarter of a grain of hyoscine inside him, and here am I, an abysmally incompetent layman, with the terrific task before me of finding out how it got there. What the devil am I to do about it, Matron?"

He smiled very charmingly into her competent spectacles. Her very veil seemed to lose starch.

"Well, really," said Sister Marigold, "I'm sure it's all very trying for everybody."

"Exactly. You yourself must have had a great shock."

"Well, I did. Of course, in the ordinary way we nurses become accustomed to the sad side of things. People think us dreadfully hard-hearted sometimes."

"You won't get me to believe that. Of course, this discovery—"

"That's what makes it so dreadful, Mr.—er—I never could have believed it, never. Such a thing has never happened in the whole of my experience. And for it to be after an operation in my own theatre! Nobody could have taken more care. Nothing went

77

wrong."

"Now you've hit the nail right on the head!" exclaimed Alleyn, gazing at her as if she was a sort of sibyl. "I felt assured of that. You know as well as I do, Matron, that Sir Derek was a man with many bitter enemies. I may tell you in confidence that at the Yard we know where to look. We are in close touch with the Secret Service"—he noted with satisfaction the glint of intrigue in her eye—"and we are pretty sure how the land lies. In our midst—in our very midst, Matron—are secret agents, secret societies, powers of evil known to the Yard but unsuspected by the general public. Mercifully so." He stopped short, folded his arms, and wondered how much of this the woman would swallow. Apparently the whole dose.

"Fancy!" breathed Sister Marigold. "Just fancy!"

"Well—that's the position," said Alleyn grandly, throwing himself back in his chair. "But here's my difficulty. Before we can fire point-blank we've got to clear away the other possibilities. Suppose we made an arrest now—what would be the defence? An attempt would be made to throw suspicion on innocent persons, on the very people who fought to save Sir Derek's life, on the surgeon who operated, and on his assistants."

"But that's terrible!"

"Nevertheless it is what would happen. Now to meet that position I must have the actual history of Sir Derek's operation, in all its details, at my fingers' ends. That is why I have laid my cards on the table, Matron, and that is why I have come to you."

Sister Marigold stared at him so long that he wondered nervously if he had been inartistic. However, when she did speak, it was with the greatest air of earnestness.

"I shall consider it my duty," she said, "to give you what help I can."

Alleyn thought it better not to shake hands with her. He merely said with quiet reverence:

"Thank you, Matron, you have made a wise decision. Now to come down to tin tacks. I understand Sir John performed the operation assisted by Mr. Thoms and with Dr. Roberts as anæsthetist. Sir John gave the hyoscine injection and prepared it himself."

"Yes. Sir John always does that. As I always say, he's so conscientious."

"Splendid, isn't it? And Mr Thoms gave the anti-gas injection.

Nurse Harden brought it to him, didn't she?"

"Yes, she did. Poor Harden, she was dreadfully upset. Sir Derek was a great friend of her own family, a very old Dorsetshire family, Mr.—er——"

"Really? Strange coincidence. She fainted afterwards, didn't she, poor girl?"

"Yes. But I assure you she did her work all through the op., quite as usual—really." Sister Marigold's voice trailed away doubtfully.

"Someone said something about a delay over the anti-gas injection."

"It was only for a moment. She told me afterwards she was so faint she had to pause before she brought it across."

"Yes, I see. Frightfully bad luck. Nurse Banks gave the camphor injection, didn't she?"

"She did." Sister Marigold's thin lips closed in a whippy line.

"And prepared the serum?"

"That is so."

"I suppose I'll have to see her. Between you and me and the Marble Lady, Matron, she rather alarms me."

"H'm!" said Sister Marigold. "Really? Fancy!"

"Still, it *is* my duty and I *must*. Is she on the premises?"

"Nurse Banks is leaving us to-morrow. I believe she is in the hospital this afternoon."

"Leaving you, is she? Does she frighten you too, Matron?" Sister Marigold pursed her lips.

"She is not a type I care to have nursing for me," she said. "As I say, personal feelings should not interfere with a nurse's work, much less political opinions."

"I *thought* she looked as if she was suffering from High Ideals," Alleyn remarked.

"Call them high ideals! Beastly Bolshevik nonsense," said Sister Marigold vigorously. "She had the impertinence to tell me, in my own theatre, that she would be glad if the patient—" She stopped short and looked extremely uncomfortable. "Not, of course, that she meant anything. Still, as I say——"

"Yes, quite. They'd say anything, some of these people. Of course with those views she'd loathe the very sight of O'Callaghan."

"How she dared!" fumed Sister Marigold.

"Tell me about it," said Alleyn winningly.

After a little hesitation she did.

CHAPTER IX

Three Nurses

Tuesday, the sixteenth. Afternoon.

The unbosoming of Sister Marigold was almost an epic. Once the floodgates of her wrath were opened the spate of disclosure flowed turbulently. Alleyn decided that in the Marigold's eye Banks was a murderess. Derek O'Callaghan's nurse had told Sister Marigold of Banks's triumph at the news of his death. The theatre scally had lost her head and told everybody. At first, prompted no doubt by her anxiety to stifle the breath of scandal in her hospital, Sister Marigold had determined to say as little as possible about the unspeakable Banks. Alleyn's hints that Phillips, his assistants, even she herself, would come under suspicion had evidently decided her to speak. She now said that Banks was obviously an agent of Sir Derek's political enemies. Alleyn let her talk and talk, and contrived to remain brilliantly non-committal. He discovered that she had an excellent memory, and, by dint of careful questioning, he arrived at the procession of events during, and immediately before, the operation. It appeared that the only members of the party who had been alone in the theatre were Phillips, herself, Thoms, and possibly one of the nurses. Mr. Thoms, she thought, had come out of the theatre into the anteroom a few moments after Sir John had prepared his syringe. When she had told him everything two or three times over, Alleyn said that he was a brute to keep her so long and could he see the private nurse and the scally. He asked her not to mention the result of the post-mortem. The scally came first. She was alarmed and inclined to shy off his questions, but quietened down presently and stuck to her story of Banks's indecent rejoicing. She said Banks was always dinning

Soviet teaching into the other nurses. She added nervously that Banks was a good nurse and would never forget her duty to a patient. She described the impedimenta that were put out on a side table before the operation—a full bottle of hyoscine solution, an ampoule of anti-gas serum, syringes, a bowl of distilled water. She was quite sure the bottle of hyoscine solution had been full. She believed that a small amount had since been used. She hadn't looked at it immediately after the operation. This tallied with information already given by the matron. The scally herself had put all the things away and had cleaned the outsides of all the jars carefully. Matron was so particular. "No use looking for prints on this job," thought Alleyn with a sigh. He thanked her and let her go.

Nurse Graham, O'Callaghan's special, was then sent into the room. She came in quietly, smiled at Alleyn and stood with her hands behind her back waiting. She had blue eyes, set far apart, a wide humorous mouth, slightly prominent teeth and a neat figure. She had an air of repose and efficiency which pleased the inspector.

"Do sit down, won't you?" Alleyn invited her. She sat down comfortably and didn't fidget.

"You nursed Sir Derek, didn't you?" he began.

"Yes."

"How long was it from the time he was admitted until the operation?"

"Nearly an hour, I think. He came in soon after I went on duty at five o'clock. The operation was at a quarter to six."

"Yes. Look here, Nurse Graham, will you tell me the whole story of that hour as though you were writing it down in detail?"

She looked gravely at him for a moment or two.

"I'll try," she said at last. Alleyn took out a notebook and with an uneasy glance at it she began: "Soon after I came on duty a message came up that he was on his way and I was to 'special' him. I met the stretcher, put him to bed, and prepared him for the operation."

"Did you give him an injection of any sort?"

"No. The usual injection of morphia and atropine was not given. Sir John's injection of hyoscine took its place."

"I see. Well, nurse?"

"While that was being done Lady O'Callaghan and Sir Derek's sister arrived and when the preparation was over they went into his room. He was semi-conscious. Am I doing this properly?"

"Admirably. Please go on."

"Well, let me think. I was in the room with them at first. Lady O'Callaghan was very good—quiet, and didn't upset the patient. Miss O'Callaghan was rather distressed. They sat down by the bed. I went out to speak to Sir John. When I came back they were talking together. Sir Derek was lying with his eyes closed, but he opened them for a moment and groaned. I think he was conscious just then and he seemed very uncomfortable. Lady O'Callaghan came out and spoke for a minute to Sir John. Then we all returned and Sir John made an examination. The patient seemed much easier, but I thought that now he was quite unconscious, more deeply so than he had been since he came in. Sir John diagnosed ruptured appendix abscess and offered to get Mr. Somerset Black to operate immediately. Lady O'Callaghan begged him to do it himself and he finally said he would. I took Lady O'Callaghan and Miss O'Callaghan out."

Nurse Graham paused and looked very earnestly at the inspector.

"Was there any further incident before they left the room?" Alleyn asked.

"You mean—? There was something else, but please, Inspector Alleyn, do not attach too much importance to it. The patient, I am sure, did not realise in the least what he said."

"What did he say?"

"He opened his eyes and said "Don't—don't let——" and then relapsed again."

"Did you get any idea of what he was trying to say?"

"It might have been anything."

"At what was he looking?"

"He looked at Sir John, who was nearest the bed."

"How would you describe his look? Appealing? Entreating? What?"

"N-no. He—he seemed frightened. It might have been anything. He looked rather like a patient who had been given a drug—morphia, for instance. It's a kind of frowning stare—I have often noticed it appear when the drug is beginning to take effect."

"And yet you tell me he had not had anything of the sort."

"I gave him nothing," Nurse Graham said.

"There's a curious inflexion in your voice, Nurse. *You* gave him nothing? Now of what are you thinking?"

She moved uneasily and her face became rather pink.

"I have said nothing about this to anybody," she told him. "It seemed to me a dangerous thing to speak of what was—was—not absolute fact."

"Quite right. Don't you think, though, that you should tell me? Nurse Graham, Sir Derek O'Callaghan was murdered." He watched her closely. She seemed both startled and shocked. She gave a quick look as if she hoped she had mistaken what he'd said. After a moment he went on:

"He was given a lethal dose of hyoscine. At least four people come under the possibility of suspicion. The very incident you are shying away from might be the one to save an innocent person. I am too old a hand to jump at asinine conclusions. Do you really think you can do any good by keeping me in the dark?"

"Perhaps not."

"Let me help you. You think, don't you, that someone had given O'Callaghan something—a drug of some sort?"

"It looked like it, and yet it was too soon for a drug to act."

"What happened when you returned to your patient? What did you find?"

"You are—very acute," she said. "When I went back I tidied the room. The patient seemed to be asleep. I lifted his eyelid and he was quite unconscious. The pupil was not contracted. I knew then that he could not have had morphia. Then I saw under a chair by the bed a small piece of white paper. I picked it up and noticed that it had broken pieces of sealing-wax on it. It was certainly not there when Sir Derek was admitted."

"Have you kept it?"

"I—yes, I have. I wondered then if he had been given anything, and when the room was done out I put the paper into a drawer in his dressing-table. It will still be there."

"I'll look at it later on if I may. Who had sat in the chair?"

"Miss O'Callaghan," she said uneasily.

"And Miss O'Callaghan was alone with the patient for—how long? Three minutes? Five minutes?"

"Quite five, I should think."

"Notice anything else? Had he had a drink of water, do you think?"

"The glass on the bedside table had been used."

"You are a model witness. I suppose this glass has also been cleaned? Yes. A hospital is a poor hunting-ground for the likes of me. Now don't worry too much about this. It may be quite beside the point. In any case it would have been criminal to withhold it. Consciousness of having done the right thing brings, I understand, solace to the troubled breast."

"I can't say it does to mine."

"Nonsense. Now will you be very kind and get your scrap of paper for me? Bring Nurse Banks back with you, and don't mention homicide. By the way, what did you think about her reception of the glad tidings—I gather she looked upon them as glad?"

"She's an ass," answered Nurse Graham unexpectedly, "but she's no murderer."

"What did she say exactly?"

"Oh, something out of the Bible about praising the Lord for He hath cast down our enemies."

"Good lack!" apostrophised Alleyn. "What an old—I beg your pardon, Nurse. Ask the lady to come here, will you? And if you hear me scream come in and rescue me. I've no desire to die at the feet of that marble goddess there—who is she, by the way—Anæsthesia?"

"I've no idea, Inspector," said Nurse Graham with a sudden broad smile. She went out briskly and returned in a few minutes to give him a small square of white paper such as chemists use in wrapping up prescriptions. Fragments of red sealing-wax remained on the margins and the creases suggested that it had contained a round box. Alleyn put it in his pocket-book.

"Nurse Banks is waiting," remarked Nurse Graham.

"Loose her," said Alleyn. "Good-bye, Nurse."

"Good-bye, Inspector."

Miss Banks made a somewhat truculent entrance. She refused a chair and stood uncomfortably erect, just inside the door. Alleyn remained politely on his feet.

"Perhaps Nurse Graham has told you of my business here?" he suggested.

"She said something about Scotland Yard," sniffed Banks. "I didn't know what she was talking about."

"I am investigating the circumstances of Sir Derek O'Callaghan's death."

"I said all there was to say about it at that inquest."

Alleyn decided that finesse was not indicated.

"You didn't mention it was murder," he remarked.

For a moment he thought she looked frightened. Then she said woodenly:

"Is it?"

"Yes. What do you think of that?"

"How do you know?"

"The post-mortem revealed indications of at least a quarter of a grain of hyoscine."

"A quarter of a grain!" exclaimed Banks. He was reminded of Phillips. Neither of these two had ejaculated 'Hyoscine!' as one might have expected, but had exclaimed at the amount.

"Wouldn't you have expected that to kill him?" he asked.

"Oh, yes. Mr. Thoms said——" She stopped short.

"What did Mr. Thoms say?"

"Heard him say before the op. that a quarter-grain would be a fatal dose."

"How did the subject arise?"

"Don't remember."

"I understand you prepared and gave the camphor injection and prepared the anti-gas injection."

"Yes. I didn't put hyoscine in either if that's what you're thinking."

"No doubt there will be some means of proving that," said Alleyn smoothly. "I shall have the matter investigated, of course."

"You'd better," snorted Banks.

"Sir John prepared and gave the hyoscine."

"Well, what if he did? Sir John Phillips wouldn't poison his worst enemy in the theatre. Too much the little surgeon."

"I'm glad you think so," said Alleyn mildly.

Banks was silent.

"I hear you look upon the affair as a dispensation of Providence," he added.

"I am an agnostic. I said 'if'."

" 'If'?"

"If I wasn't, I would."

"Oh," said Alleyn. "It's cryptic, but I get you. Can you tell me which members of the party were alone in the theatre before the operation?"

"No, I can't."

"Do try. Do you remember if you were?"

"No. Phillips was. Thoms was."

"When?"

"Just before they washed up. We were in the anteroom. Phillips came in first and that little fool followed him."

"Meaning Mr. Thoms?"

"I said so, didn't I?"

"Are you going to hear Nicholas Kakaroff speak to-night?" This was a shot in the dark. Kakaroff was to address a large meeting of Soviet sympathisers. The Yard would think it worth while to put in an amiable appearance. Nurse Banks threw up her chin and glared at him.

"I shall be proud to be there," she said loudly.

"That's the spirit!" cried Alleyn.

Inspired perhaps by fiery recollections of former meetings, Nurse Banks suddenly came out strong with a speech.

"You may stand there with a smile on your lips," she stormed, "but you won't smile for long. I know your type—the gentleman policeman—the latest development of the capitalist system. You've got where you are by influence while better men do bigger work for a slave's pittance. You'll go, and all others like you, when the Dawn breaks. You think I killed Derek O'Callaghan. I didn't, but I'll tell you this much—I should be proud—proud, do you hear, if I had."

She reeled all this out with remarkable fluency, as though it was a preposterous recitation. Alleyn had a swift picture of her covering her friends' suburban tea-parties with exquisite confusion. Small wonder the other nurses fought shy of her.

"Do you know, Nurse," he said, "until the Dawn does break I rather think I'd pipe down a bit if I were you. Unless you really fancy the martyr's crown, you're talking like a remarkably silly woman. You had as good a chance as anyone else of pumping hyoscine into the deceased. You're now shrieking your motive into my capitalist face. I'm not threatening you. No, you'd better not say anything more at the moment, but when the mantle of Mr. Kakaroff is laid aside you may think it advisable to make a statement. Until then, Nurse Banks, if you'll forgive me the suggestion, I should really pipe down. Will you tell Nurse Harden I'm ready?"

He opened the door for her. She stood for a moment staring above his head. Then she walked to the door, paused, and looked directly at him.

"I'll tell you this much," she said. "Neither Phillips nor Harden did it. Phillips is a conscientious surgeon and Harden is a conscientious nurse. They are hidebound by their professional code, both of them."

With this emphatic assertion she left him. Alleyn screwed his face sideways and opened his notebook. Here, in an incredibly fine and upright hand he wrote "Thoms—conversation about hyoscine," and after a moment's hesitation "P and H—hidebound by their professional code, says the B."

He wrote busily, shut his little book, glanced up and gave a start of surprise. Jane Harden had come in so quietly that he had not heard her. There she stood, her fingers twisted together, staring at the inspector. He had thought at the inquest that she was very good-looking. Now, with the white veil behind it, the extreme pallor of her face was less emphatic. She was beautiful, with that peculiar beauty that covers delicate bone. The contour of the forehead and cheek-bones, the little hollows of the temples, and the fine-drawn arches of the eyes had the quality of a Holbein drawing. The eyes themselves were a very dark grey, the nose absolutely straight, and the mouth, rather too small, with drooping corners, was at once sensuous and obstinate.

"I beg your pardon," said Alleyn; "I did not hear you come in. Please sit down."

He pulled forward the nearest of the preposterous chairs, turning it towards the window. The afternoon had darkened and a chilly sort of gloom masked the ceiling and corners of the room. Jane Harden sat down and clasped the knobs of the chair-arms with long fingers that even the exigencies of nursing had not reddened.

"I expect you know why I'm here?" said Alleyn.

"What was the—is the post-mortem finished?" She spoke quite evenly, but with a kind of breathlessness.

"Yes. He was murdered. Hyoscine."

She seemed to stiffen and become uncannily still.

"So the hunt is up," added Alleyn calmly.

"Hyoscine," she whispered. "Hyoscine. How much?"

"At least a quarter of a grain. Sir John injected a hundredth, he tells me. Therefore someone else gave the patient a little more than a fifth of a grain—six twenty-fifths, to be exact. It may have been more, of course. I don't know if the post-mortem can be relied upon to account for every particle."

"I don't know either," said Jane.

"There are one or two questions I must ask you."

"Yes?"

"I'm afraid this is all very distressing for you. You knew Sir Derek personally, I believe?"

"Yes."

"I'm terribly sorry to have to bother you. Let's get it over as soon as possible. As regards the anti-gas injection. At the close of the operation Sir John or Mr. Thoms asked for it. Sister Marigold told you to get it. You went to a side table, where you found the syringe. Was it ready—prepared for use?"

"Yes."

"At the inquest it appeared that you delayed a little while. Why was this?"

"There were two syringes. I felt faint and could not think, for a moment, which was the right one. Then Banks said: "The large syringe", and I brought it."

"You did not hesitate because you thought there might be something wrong with the large syringe?"

This suggestion seemed to startle her very much. She moved her hands nervously and gave a soft exclamation.

"Oh! No. No—Why should I think that?"

"Nurse Banks prepared this syringe, didn't she?"

"Yes," said Jane.

Alleyn was silent for a minute. He got up and walked across to the window. From where she sat his profile looked black, like a silhouette with blurred edges. He stared out at the darkening roofs. Something about a movement of his shoulders suggested a kind of distaste. He shoved his hands down into his trouser pockets and swung round, facing the room. He looked shadowy, but larger than life against the yellowish window-pane.

"How well did you know Sir Derek?" he asked suddenly. His voice sounded oddly flat in the thickly furnished room.

"Quite well," she said after another pause.

"Intimately?"

"I don't know what you mean."

"Well—did you meet often—as friends, shall I say?"

She stared at his darkened face. Her own, lit by the sallow light from the window, looked thin and secret.

"Sometimes."

"Recently?"

"No. I can't see what my acquaintanceship with him has to do with the matter."

"Why did you faint?"

"I was—I wasn't well; I'm run down."

"It had nothing to do with the identity of the patient? It wasn't because Sir Derek was so ill?"

"Naturally that distressed me."

"Have you ever written to him?"

She seemed to shrink back into the chair as though he had actually hurt her.

"You need not answer any of these questions if you think it better not to," he announced. "Still, I shall, of course, go to other people for the information."

"*I* have done nothing to hurt *him*," she said loudly.

"No. But have you ever written to him? That was my question, you know."

She took a long time to answer this. At last she murmured: "Oh yes."

"How often?"

"I don't know——

"Recently?"

"Fairly recently."

"Threatening letters?"

"She moved her head from side to side as though the increasing dusk held a menace.

"No," said Jane.

He saw now that she looked at him with terror in her eyes. It was a glance to which he had become accustomed, but since in his way he was a sensitive man, never quite reconciled.

"I think it would be better," he pronounced slowly, "if you told me the whole story. There is no need, is there, for me to tell you that you are one of the people whom I must take into consideration? Your presence in the operating theatre brings you into the picture. Naturally I want an explanation."

"I should have thought my—distress—would have given you that," she whispered, and in that half-light he saw her pallor change to a painful red. "You see, I loved him," added Jane.

"I think I understand that part of it," he said abruptly. "I am extremely sorry that these beastly circumstances oblige me to pry into such very painful matters. Try to think of me as a sort of automaton, unpleasant but quite impersonal. Can you do that, do you think?"

"I suppose I must try."

"Thank you. First of all—was there anything beyond ordinary friendship between you and O'Callaghan?"

She made a slight movement.

"Not—" She paused and then said: "Not really."

"Were you going to say 'Not now'? I think there had been. You say you wrote to him. Perhaps your letters terminated a phase of your friendship?"

She seemed to consider this and then answered uneasily: "The second did."

He thought: "Two letters. I wonder what happened to the other?"

Aloud, he said: "Now, as I understand it, you had known Sir. Derek for some time—an old family friendship. Recently this friendship changed to a more intimate association. When was this?"

"Last June—three months ago."

"And it went on—for how long?"

Her hands moved to her face. As if ashamed of this pitiful gesture she snatched them away, and raising her voice, said clearly: "Three days."

"I see," said Alleyn gently. "Was that the last time you saw him?"

"Yes—until the operation."

"Had there been any quarrel?"

"No."

"None?"

"No." She tilted her head back and began to speak rapidly. "It was a mutual agreement. People make such a fuss about sex. It's only a normal physical experience, like hunger or thirst. The sensible thing is to satisfy it in a perfectly reasonable and natural way. That's what we did. There was no need to meet again. We had had our experience."

"My poor child!" Alleyn ejaculated.

"What do you mean?"

"You reel it all off as if you'd learnt it out of a textbook. 'First Steps in Sex'. 'O Brave New World', as Miranda and Mr. Huxley would say! And it didn't work out according to the receipt?"

"Yes, it did."

"Then why did you write those letters?"

90

Her mouth opened. She looked pitifully ludicrous and, for a moment, not at all pretty.

"You've seen them—you've—"

"I'm afraid so," said Alleyn.

She gave a curious dry sob and put her hands up to the neck of her uniform as though it choked her.

"You see," Alleyn continued, "it would be better to tell me the truth, really it would."

She began to weep very bitterly.

"I can't help it. I'm sorry. It's been so awful—I can't help it."

Alleyn swung round to the light again.

"It's all right," he said to the window-pane. "Don't mind about me—only an automaton, remember."

She seemed to pull herself together quickly. He heard a stifled sob or two and a rustle as if she had made a violent movement of some sort.

"Better," she murmured presently. When he turned back to the room she was sitting there, staring at him, as though there had been no break in their conversation.

"There's not much more," he began—very businesslike and pleasant. "Nobody accuses you of anything. I simply want to check up on the operation. You did not see Sir Derek from June until he was brought into the theatre. Very well. Beyond these two letters you did not communicate with him in any way whatever? All right. Now the only place where you step into the picture is where you fetched the syringe containing the anti-gas concoction. You delayed. You were faint. You are positive you brought the right syringe?"

"Oh, yes. It was much bigger than the others."

"Good enough. I'll look at it presently if I may. Now I understand that the jar, bottle, or pot containing the serum——"

"It was an ampoule," said Jane.

"So it was—and the pipkin, cruse, or pottle containing hyoscine were on the table. Could you, feeling all faint and bothered, have possibly sucked up hyoscine by mistake?"

"But, don't you understand, it was ready!" she said impatiently.

"So I am told, but I've got to make sure, you know. You are positive, for instance, that you didn't squirt out the contents and refill the syringe?"

"Of course—positive." She spoke with more assurance and less agitation than he had expected.

"You remember getting the syringe? You were not so groggy that you did it more or less blindly?"

That seemed to get home. She looked frightened again.

"I—I was very faint, but I *know*, I *know* I made no mistake."

"Right. Anyone watch you?"

He watched her himself, closely. The light was now very dim, but her face was still lit from the window behind him.

"They—may—have. I didn't notice."

"I understand Mr. Thoms complained of the delay. Perhaps he turned to see what you were doing?"

"He's always watching—I beg your pardon; that's got nothing to do with it."

"What were you going to say?"

"Only that Mr. Thoms has rather an offensive trick of staring."

"Did you happen to notice, before the operation, how much of the hyoscine solution there was in the bottle?"

She thought for some time.

"I think it was full," she said.

"Has it been used since?"

"Once, I believe."

"Good."

He moved away from the window briskly, found the light switch and snapped it down. Jane rose to her feet. Her hands shook and her face was a little marked with tears.

"That's all," said Alleyn brightly. "Cheer up, Nurse Harden."

"I'll try."

She hesitated a moment after he had opened the door, looked as if she wanted to say something further, but finally, without another word, left the room.

After she had gone Alleyn stood stock-still and stared at the opposite wall.

At last, catching sight of himself in an ornate mirror, he made a wry face at his own reflection.

"Oh, damn the doings," said Alleyn.

CHAPTER X

Thoms in the Theatre

Tuesday, the sixteenth. Afternoon.

It was Mr. Thoms who took Alleyn into the theatre. After Jane left him the inspector had wandered into the hall and run into the plump little surgeon. Alleyn had explained who he was, and Thoms instantly assumed an expression of intense seriousness that made him look rather like a clown pulling a mock-tragic face.

"I say!" he exclaimed. "You're not here about Sir Derek O'Callaghan's business, are you?"

"That's it, Mr. Thoms," Alleyn rejoined wearily. "The man was murdered."

Thoms began to babble excitedly. Alleyn held up a long hand.

"Hyoscine. At least a quarter of a grain. Wilful murder," he said briefly.

"Lor'!" ejaculated Thoms.

"Lor' it is. I've been badgering nurses and now I want to see the theatre of operations. It never struck me till just then what a localised implication that phrase has."

"See the theatre?" said Thoms. "Yes. Of course. Look here. It's not in use now. Sir John's gone out. I'll show you round if you like."

"Thank you so much," said Alleyn.

Thoms talked excitedly as he led the way. "It's the most amazing thing I ever heard. Damn' nasty business, too. I hope to God you don't think I pumped hyoscine into the man. Thought you police chaps must have something up your sleeves when you pushed the inquest. Yes. Well, here we are. This is an anteroom to the theatre, where we wash and dress ourselves up for the business. Along there's the anæsthetising-room. Here's the theatre."

He butted open the swing-doors.

"Wait a bit," said Alleyn. "Let's get a sort of picture of the proceedings, may we? Before the operation you and the other medical men foregathered in here."

"That's it. Sir John and I came in here together. Dr Roberts came in for a moment and then went off to the anæsthetising-room, where the patient was brought to him."

"Anyone else in here during that time?"

"With Phillips and me, you mean? Oh, yes—the matron, Sister Marigold, you know. She does theatre sister. It's only a small hospital, and she rather fancies herself at the job, does old Marigold. Then, let me see, the other two nurses were dodging about. Thingummy, the Bolshie one, and that pretty girl that did a faint—Harden."

"What did you all talk about?"

"*Talk* about?" echoed Thoms. He had a curious trick of gaping at the simplest question as though much taken aback. His eyes popped and his mouth fell open. He then gave a short and, to Alleyn, tiresome guffaw. "What did we *talk* about?" he repeated. "Well, let's see. Oh, I asked Sir John if he had seen the show at the Palladium this week and——" He stopped short and again his eyes bolted.

"Well—what about it?" asked Alleyn patiently.

"He said he hadn't," said Thoms. He looked ridiculously uncomfortable, as though he had nearly said something frightfully improper.

"I missed the Palladium this week," Alleyn remarked. "It's particularly good, I hear."

"Oh," Thoms mumbled, "not bad. Rather rot really."

He seemed extraordinarily embarrassed.

"And had Sir John seen the show?" asked Alleyn lightly.

"Er—no, no, he hadn't."

"Did you discuss any particular part of it?"

"No. Only mentioned the show—nothing particular."

There was a long pause during which Thoms whistled under his breath.

"During this time," said Alleyn at last, "was any one member of the theatre party alone?"

"In here?"

"In here."

"Let me think," begged Thoms. Alleyn let him think. "No—no. As far as I remember, we were all here. Then one of the nurses showed Roberts to the anæsthetising-room. That left Sir John and the other two nurses and myself. I went with Marigold into the theatre to look round. That left Sir John and the other nurse—the pretty one—in this room. They were here when I got back. Then Roberts and I washed up while Sir John went into the theatre to fix his hyoscine injection. He always does that and gives it himself. Rum idea. We usually leave all that game to the anæsthetist. Of course, in this instance everything had been very hurried. The patient had not been given the usual morphia and atropine injection. Well, let's see. The females were dodging about, I suppose. I remember the—what's-her-name—the Banks woman asked me why Sir John didn't use the stock solution."

"Why didn't he?"

"Oh—well, because he wanted to be sure of the dosage, I suppose."

"And then?"

"I went into the theatre."

"Where you joined Phillips?"

"Yes. He'd just put the hyoscine tablet into the water, I think."

"Did you notice the little bottle—how many tablets were left? I simply want to check up, you understand."

"Of course. Well, it's a tube; you can't see the number of tablets unless you peer into it, and then you can only guess, but, of course, there would be nineteen, because it was a new lot."

"How do you know that, Mr Thoms?"

"Well, as a matter of fact, I saw he had two tubes and said something about it, and he said one of them was empty, so he'd opened another."

"What happened to the empty one?"

"Eh? Search me. Chucked it away, I suppose. I say—er—look here, what *is* your name?"

"Alleyn."

"Oh. Well, look here, Alleyn, you're not attaching any importance to the second tube, are you? Because you jolly well needn't. It's all perfectly simple. Phillips uses a hypodermic case which holds two of these little phials. He'd obviously used the last tablet on a previous case without realising it was the last. Very easy thing to do."

"I see that. All this business is merely by way of checking up."

"Yes, but——"

"For my own sake I've got to account for every movement of the game, Mr. Thoms. It's all frightfully muddling and I've got to try to learn it like a lesson. Do you remember anything that was said just then?"

"Well,—well, I chaffed him about the two tubes—said he was doing Sir Derek proud, and then I—I remarked that he used a lot of water."

"Did this seem to upset him at all?"

"Oh, Lord—no. I mean,—Sir John always stands a bit on his dignity. I mean, he rather shut me up. He hasn't got what I call a sense of humour."

"Really? Did you go out together?"

"Yes. I went into the anteroom and Sir John into the anæsthetic-room to give the injection. I went first."

"Sure, Mr. Thoms?"

"Oh, yes," said Thoms, opening his eyes very wide. "Why?"

"I only want to get the order of events. Now let's look at the theatre, shall we?"

Once again Thoms butted the swing-doors with his compact little stern, and this time Inspector Alleyn followed him through.

The theatre was scrupulously, monstrously immaculate—a place of tiles and chromium and white enamel. Thoms turned on a switch and for a moment an enormous high-powered cluster of lights poured down its truncated conical glare on the blank surface of the table. The theatre instantly became alive and expectant. He snapped it off and in its stead an insignificant wall bracket came to life over a side table on rubber castors.

"Is this how it was for the operation?" asked Alleyn. "Everything in its right place?"

"Er—yes, I think so. Yes."

"Which way did the patient lie?"

"Head here. Eastward position, eh? Ha ha!"

"I see. There would be a trolley alongside the table, perhaps?"

"It would be wheeled away as soon as the patient was taken off it."

"That's the side table, over by the windows, where the syringes were set out?"

"That's it."

"Can you show me just where you all stood at the time each of the injections was given? Wait a bit—I'll make a sort of plan. My memory's hopeless. Damn, where's my pencil?"

Alleyn opened his notebook and produced a small rule from his pocket. He measured the floor space, made a tiny plan and marked the positions of the two tables, and, as Thoms instructed him, those of the surgeons and nurses.

"Sir John would be here, about half-way along the table, isn't it? I stood opposite there. Marigold hovered round here, and the other two moved about a bit."

"Yes. Well, where, as near as you can give it, would they all be for the operation?"

"The surgeons and anæsthetist where I have shown you. Marigold on Sir John's right and the other two somewhere in the background."

"And for the camphor injection?"

"As before, except for the Bolshie, who gave it. She would be here, by the patient's arm, you see."

"Did you watch Nurse Banks give this injection?"

"Don't think so. I wouldn't notice. Probably wouldn't see her hands—they'd be hidden by the little screen across the patient's chest."

"Oh. I'll take a look at that afterwards if I may. Now the anti-gas injection."

"That was after Sir John had sewed him up. I dressed the wound and asked for the serum. I damned that girl to heaps for keeping me waiting—felt rather a brute when she hit the floor two minutes later—what? I stood here, on the inside of the table; Sir John was opposite; Marigold had moved round to my side. Roberts and Banks, if that's her name, were fussing round over the patient, and Roberts kept bleating about the pulse and so on. They were both at the patient's head."

"Wait a bit. I'll fix those positions. Perhaps I'll get you to help me to reconstruct the operation later on. You have no doubts, I suppose, about it being the correct syringe—the one you used, I mean?"

"None. It seemed to be perfectly in order."

"Was there any marked change in the patient's condition after this injection?"

"Roberts is the man to ask about that. My own idea is that he was worried about the patient for some time before I gave the injection. He asked for camphor, remember. Naturally, you'll think, I want to stress that point. Well, Inspector, so I do. I suppose the serum injection is the dangerous corner as far as I'm concerned. Still, I did *not* prepare the syringe and I could hardly palm it and produce another from behind my left ear. Could I? What? Ha ha ha!"

"Let's have a look at it," said Alleyn imperturbably, "and we'll see."

Thoms went to one of the shelves and returned with a syringe at the sight of which the inspector gave a little shout of horror.

"Good God, Mr. Thoms, are you a horse-coper? You don't mean to tell me you jabbed that horror into the poor man? It's the size of a fire extinguisher!"

Thoms stared at him and then roared with laughter. "He didn't feel it. Oh, yes, we plugged it into him. Well, now, I could hardly produce a thing like that by sleight of hand, could I?"

"Heavens, no! Put it away, do; it makes me feel quite sick. A disgusting, an indecent, a revolting implement."

Thoms made a playful pass at the inspector, who seized the syringe and bore it away. He examined it, uttering little noises of disgust.

"This is the type used for the other two injections," explained Thoms, who had been peering into the array of instruments. He showed Alleyn a hypodermic syringe of the sort familiar to the layman.

"Sufficiently alarming, but not so preposterous. This would be the kind of thing Dr. Roberts handled?"

"Yes—or rather, no. Roberts didn't give the camphor injection. The nurse gave it."

"Oh, yes. Is that usual?"

"It's quite in order. Generally speaking, that injection is given by the anæsthetist, but there's nothing in his asking the nurse to give it."

"This needle's a delicate-looking thing. I suppose you never carry a syringe about ready for use?"

"Lord, no! In the theatre, of course, they are laid out all complete."

"Would you mind filling this one for me?"

He gave Thoms a small syringe. The surgeon poured some water into a measuring-glass, inserted the needle and pulled back the piston.

"There you are. If a tablet's used, the usual procedure is to squirt the syringe half full into the glass, dissolve the tablet, and

98

then draw it up again."

"The whole business only takes a few seconds?"

"Well—the tablet has to dissolve. In the case of the serum and the camphor the stuff was there ready."

"Yes, I've got that. May I see the bottle the serum is kept in?"

"It's not kept in a bottle, but in ampoules which hold the exact amount and are then thrown away. There aren't any kicking about in the theatre. I'll beat some up for you to see if you like."

"Very good of you, Mr. Thoms. I'm being a crashing bore, I'm afraid."

Thoms protested his freedom from boredom and fussed away. Alleyn prowled meditatively round the theatre until the fat man returned.

"Here we are," said Thoms cheerfully. "Here are ampoules of oil and camphor. Here's the anti-gas serum and here's the hyoscine solution. All labelled, as you see. Tell you what I'll do: I'll set out the table as it would have been for the op. How will that do you?"

"Splendid!"

"Let's see now—ampoules here, serum there. Here's the bottle of hyoscine solution; thought you'd want to see that too. Old-fashioned idea—it should be in ampoules, but matron's a bit of a dug-out."

"The bottle's nearly full, I see."

"Yes. I believe one injection had been given." Alleyn noted mentally that this tallied with Nurse Harden's and the scally's impression that the bottle had been full before the operation and had since been used once.

"Can anyone have access to this bottle?" asked Alleyn suddenly.

"What? Oh, yes—any of the theatre staff."

"May I have a small amount—I may have to get it tested?"

He produced a tiny bottle from his pocket and Thoms, looking rather intrigued, filled it with the solution.

"There you are. Now—where were we? Oh! Along here, small syringe for the camphor, another small syringe for the hyoscine—they hold twenty-five minims each. That would be the one Sir John would use for his tablet. Now the whopper for the serum. It holds ten c.c.'s."

"Ten c.c.'s?"

"That's about a hundred and sixty minims," explained Thoms.

"What's that in gallons?"

Thoms looked at the inspector as if he had uttered something in Chinese and then burst out laughing.

"Not quite as solid as that," he said. "One hundred and sixty minims is equal to two and two-thirds drachms. That any better?"

"Not much," grumbled Alleyn. "The dawn may break later on. I'm talking like Nurse Banks. What's the strength of this hyoscine?"

"Quarter per cent."

"But—what does that mean? They'll have to get someone cleverer than me for this game."

"Cheer up. It's one grain in one point one ounces of water."

"That sounds as though it means something. I must look up those horrid little things at the end of an arithmetic-book. Wait a moment, now. Don't say a word, Mr. Thoms, if you please," begged Alleyn. "I'm doing sums."

He screwed up his face and did complicated things with his fingers. "Twenty-fives into ones, you can't. No, anyway you don't want to. Drat. Wait a bit." He opened his eyes suddenly and began to speak rapidly. "The twenty-five-minim syringe could hold a twentieth of a grain of hyoscine, and the vet's pump could hold eleven thirty-seconds of a grain. There!" he added proudly.

"Quite correct—good for you!" shouted Thoms, clapping the inspector on the back.

"There's more to come. I can do better than that. Eleven thirty-seconds is three thirty-seconds more than a quarter, which is only eight thirty-seconds. How's that?"

"Brilliant, but I don't see the application?"

"Don't you?" asked Alleyn anxiously. "And yet I know I thought it rather important a moment ago. Ah, well—it's gone now. I'll just write the others down."

Mr. Thoms moved to his elbow and looked curiously at his tiny hieroglyphics.

"I can't see," complained Alleyn and walked over to the light.

Mr. Thoms didn't follow and so did not see the last of his minute entries, which read:

"The large syringe could hold a little over the amount found at the P.M."

He shut his little book tenderly and put it in his pocket.

"Thank you a thousand times, Mr. Thoms," he said. "You've made it very easy for me. Now there's only one more person I've got to see to-day and that's Dr. Roberts. Can you tell me where I'll find him?"

"Well, he's not the usual anæsthetist here, you know. He does a lot of Dr. Grey's work for him. Hasn't been in since this affair. I should think at this time you'd find him at his private address. I'll ring up his house if you like."

"That's very good of you. Where does he live?"

"Not sure. His name's Theodore. I know that because I heard Grey calling him Dora. Dora!" Mr. Thoms laughed extensively and led the way to a black hole with a telephone inside it.

He switched on a light and consulted the directory.

"Here we are. Roberts, Roberts, Roberts. Dr. Theodore. Wigmore Street. That's your man."

He dialled the number. Alleyn leant patiently against the door.

"Hallo. Dr. Roberts's house? Is he in? Ask him if he can see Inspector——" He paused and put his hand over the receiver. "Alleyn, isn't it? Yes—ask him if he can see Inspector Alleyn if he comes along now."

Thoms turned towards Alleyn. "He's in—that'll be all right, I expect. Hallo, is that you, Roberts? It's Thoms here. Inspector Alleyn has just been over the O'Callaghan business with me. They've found hyoscine—quarter of a grain. That makes you sit up. What? I don't know. Yes of course it is. Well, don't get all agitated. They're not going to arrest you. Ha ha ha! What! All right—in about twenty minutes, I should think. Look out, my boy—don't give yourself away—what!"

He hung up, and taking Alleyn by the elbow, walked with him to the front door.

"Poor old Roberts is in an awful hum about it, spluttering away down the telephone like I don't know what. Well, let me know if there's anything more I can do."

"I will indeed. Thank you so much. Good night."

"Good night. Got a pair of handcuffs for Roberts? Ha ha ha!"

"Ha ha ha!" said Alleyn. "Good night."

CHAPTER XI

The Anæsthetist

Tuesday, the sixteenth. Afternoon and evening.

Dr. Roberts lived in a nice little house in Wigmore Street. It was a narrow house with two windows on the first floor, and on the street level was a large vermilion front door that occupied a fair proportion of the wall.

A man-servant, small and cheerful to suit the house, showed Alleyn into a pleasant drawing-room-study with apple-green walls and bookshelves, glazed chintz curtains, and comfortable chairs. Above the fireplace hung an excellent painting of lots of little people skating on a lake surrounded by Christmas trees. A wood fire crackled on the hearth. On a table near the bookcase was a sheaf of manuscript weighted down by the old wooden stethoscope that Mr. Thoms had found so funny.

After an appreciative glance at the picture, Alleyn walked over to the bookcase, where he found a beguiling collection of modern novels, a Variorum Shakespeare that aroused his envy, and a number of works on heredity, eugenics and psycho-analysis. Among these was a respectable-looking volume entitled *Debased Currency*, by Theodore Roberts. Alleyn took it out and looked at the contents. They proved to be a series of papers on hereditary taints. Roberts evidently had read them at meetings of the International Congress on Eugenics and Sex Reform.

Alleyn was still absorbed in this evidence of Roberts's industry when the author himself came in.

"Inspector Alleyn, I believe," said Roberts.

With a slight effort Alleyn refrained from answerlng "Dr. Roberts, I presume." He closed the book over his thumb and

102

came forward to meet the anæsthetist. Roberts blinked apprehensively and then glanced at the volume in the inspector's hand.

"Yes, Dr. Roberts," said Alleyn, "you've caught me redhanded. I never can resist plucking from bookshelves and I was so interested to see that you yourself wrote."

"Oh," answered Roberts vaguely, "the subject interests me. Will you sit down, Inspector?"

"Thank you. Yes, the problems of heredity have an extraordinary fascination, even for a layman like myself. However, I haven't come here to air my ignorance of your country, but to try and fill out some of the blanks in my own. About this O'Callaghan business——"

"I am extremely sorry to hear of the result of the autopsy," said Roberts formally. "It is terribly distressing, shocking, an irreplaceable loss." He moved his hands nervously, gulped, and then added hurriedly: "I am also exceedingly distressed for more personal reasons. As anæsthetist for the operation I feel that I may be held responsible, that perhaps I should have noticed earlier that all was not well. I *was* worried, almost from the start, about his condition. I said so to Sir John and to Thoms."

"What did they answer?"

"Sir John was very properly concerned with his own work. He simply left me to deal with mine, after, I think, commenting in some way on my report. I do not remember that Thoms replied at all. Inspector Alleyn, I sincerely hope you are able to free Sir John from any possibility of the slightest breath of suspicion. Any doubt in that direction is quite unthinkable."

"I hope to be able to clear up his part in the business as soon as the usual inquiries have been made. Perhaps you can help me there, Dr. Roberts?"

"I should be glad to do so. I will not attempt to deny that I am also very selfishly nervous on my own account."

"You gave no injection, did you?"

"No. I am thankful to say, no."

"How was that? I should have imagined the anæsthetist would have given the camphor and the hyoscine injections."

Roberts did not speak for a moment, but sat gazing at Alleyn with a curiously helpless expression on his sensitive face. Alleyn noticed that whenever he spoke to Roberts the doctor seemed to suppress a sort of wince. He did this now, tightening his lips and drawing himself rigidly upright in his chair.

103

"I—I never give injections," he said. "I have a personal and very painful reason for not doing so."

"Would you care to tell me what it is? You see, the fact that you did not give an injection is very important from your point of view. You did not see the patient while he was conscious and so—to be frank—could hardly have poured hyoscine down his throat without someone noticing what you were up to."

"Yes. I see. I will tell you. Many years ago I gave an overdose of morphia and the patient died as the result of my carelessness. I—I have never been able to bring myself to give an injection since. Psychologically my behaviour has been weak and unsound. I should have overcome this repulsion, but I have been unable to do so. For some time I even lost my nerve as an anæsthetist. Then I was called in for an urgent case with heart disease and the operation was successful." He showed Alleyn his stethoscope and told him its history. "This instrument represents an interesting experiment in psychology. I began to mark on it all my successful cases of heart disease. It helped enormously but I have never been able to face an injection. Perhaps some day I may. Sir John is aware of this—peculiarity. I told him of it the first time I gave an anæsthetic for him. It was some time ago in a private house. He very thoughtfully remembered. I believe that in any case he prefers to give the hyoscine injection himself."

He turned very white as he made his unhappy confession, and it was curious to see how, in spite of his obvious distress, he did not lose his trick of formal phraseology.

"Thank you so much, Dr. Roberts," said Alleyn gently. "We need not trouble any more about that. Now, you say you were worried almost from the start about Sir Derek's condition. Would you describe this condition as consistent with hyoscine poisoning?"

"Ever since Thoms rang up I have been considering that point. Yes, I think I should. In the light of the autopsy, of course, one is tempted to correlate the two without further consideration."

"Did you notice any definite change in the patient's condition, or did the same symptoms simply get more and more acute, if that's the right way of putting it?"

"The pulse was remarkably slow when I first examined him in the anæsthetising-room. The condition grew steadily more disquieting throughout the operation."

"But, to stress my point, there was no decided change at any time, only a more or less gradual progression?"

"Yes. There was perhaps a rather marked increase in the symptoms after Sir John made the first incision."

"That would be after he had given the hyoscine injection, wouldn't it?"

Roberts glanced at him sharply.

"Yes, that is true," he said quickly, "but do you not see, the small amount Sir John injected—a hundredth of a grain, I think it was—would naturally aggravate the condition if hyoscine had already been given?"

"That's perfectly true," agreed Alleyn. "It's an important point, too. Look here, Dr. Roberts, may I take it that it's your opinion that hyoscine—a fatal amount—was somehow or other got into the man before the operation?"

"I think so," Roberts blinked nervously. He had that trick of blinking hard, twice—it reminded Alleyn of a highly strung boy. "Of course," he added uneasily, "I realise, Inspector, that it would probably be to my advantage if I said that I thought the lethal dose was given when the patient was on the table. That, however, is, in my opinion, most improbable."

"I must here trot out my customary cliché that it is always to an innocent person's advantage to tell the truth," Alleyn assured him. "Do you know, it's my opinion that at least two-thirds of the difficulties in homicidal cases are caused by innocent asses lying for all they're worth."

"Indeed? I suppose there is no possibility of suicide in this instance?"

"It seems very unlikely so far. Why? How? Where's the motive?"

"There need not necessarily be any usual motive." Roberts hesitated and then spoke with more assurance than he had shown so far. "In suggesting this," he said, "I may be accused of mounting my special hobby-horse. As you have seen I am greatly interested in hereditary taints. In Sir Derek O'Callaghan's family there is such a taint. In his father, Sir Blake O'Callaghan, it appeared. I believe he suffered at times from suicidal mania. There has been a great deal of injudicious inbreeding. Mark you, I am perfectly well aware that the usual whole-hearted condemnation of inbreeding is to be revised in the light——"

He had lost all his nervousness. He lectured Alleyn roundly for ten minutes, getting highly excited. He quoted his own works and other authorities. He scolded the British public in the person of one of their most distinguished policemen for their criminal neglect of racial problems. Alleyn listened, meek and greatly interested. He asked questions. Roberts got books from his shelves, read long passages in a high-pitched voice, and left the volumes on the hearthrug. He told Alleyn he should pay more attention to such things, and finally, to the inspector's secret amusement, asked him flatly if he knew, if he had taken the trouble to find out, whether he himself was free from all traces of hereditary insanity.

"I had a great-aunt who left all her money to a muffin-man with coloured blood," said Alleyn. "She was undoubtedly bats. Otherwise I have nothing to tell you, Dr. Roberts."

Roberts listened to this gravely and continued his harangue. By the time it was over Alleyn felt that he had heard most of the theories propounded at the International Congress on Sex Reform and then some more. They were interrupted by the man-servant, who came in to announce dinner.

"Inspector Alleyn will dine," said Roberts impatiently.

"No—really," said Alleyn. "Thank you so much, but I must go. I'd love to, but I can't." The man went out.

"Why not?" asked Roberts rather huffily.

"Because I've got a murder to solve."

"Oh," he said, rather nonplussed and vexed. Then as this remark sank in, his former manner returned to him. He eyed Alleyn nervously, blinked, and got to his feet.

"I am sorry. I become somewhat absorbed when my pet subject is under discussion."

"I too have been absorbed," Alleyn told him. You must forgive me for staying so long. I may have to reconstruct the operation—perhaps if I do you will be very kind and help me by coming along?"

"I—yes, if it is necessary. It will be very distasteful."

"I know. It may not be necessary, but if it is——"

"I shall do my part, certainly."

"Right, I must bolt. This has been an unpropitious sort of introduction, Dr. Roberts, but I hope I may be allowed to renew our talk without prejudice some time. The average bloke's ignorance of racial problems is deplorable."

"It's worse than that," said Roberts crisply. "It's lamentable—criminal. I should have thought in your profession it was essential

106

to understand at least the rudiments of the hereditary problem. How can you expect——" He scolded on for some time. The servant looked in, cast up his eyes in pious resignation and waited. Roberts gave Alleyn his book. "It's the soundest popular work on the subject, though I do not pretend to cover a fraction of the ground. You'd better come back here when you've read it."

"I will. Thank you a thousand times," murmured the inspector and made for the door. He waited until the servant had gone into the hall and then turned back.

"Look here," he said quietly. "Can I take it you think the man committed suicide?"

Again Roberts turned into a rather frightened little man.

"I can't say—I—sincerely hope so. In view of his history, I think it's quite possible—but, of course, the drug—hyoscine— it's very unusual." He stopped and seemed to think deeply for a moment. Then he gave Alleyn a very earnest and somewhat pathetic look. "I hope very much indeed that it may be found to be suicide," he said quietly. "The alternative is quite unthinkable. It would cast the most terrible slur conceivable upon a profession of which I am an insignificant unit, but which I deeply revere. I would hold myself in part responsible. Self-interest is at the bottom of most motives, they say, but something more than self-interest, I think, prompts me to beg most earnestly that you explore the possibility of suicide to its utmost limit. I have kept you too long. Good night, Inspector Alleyn."

"Good night, Dr. Roberts."

Alleyn walked slowly down Wigmore Street. He reflected that in some ways his last interview had been one of the oddest in his experience. What a curious little man! There had been no affectation in that scientific outburst. The inspector could recognise genuine enthusiasm when he met it. Roberts was in a blue funk over the O'Callaghan business, yet the mere mention of his pet subject could drive any feeling of personal danger clean out of his head. "He's very worried about something, though," thought Alleyn, "and it rather looks as though it's Phillips. Phillips! Damn. I want my Boswell. Also, I want my dinner."

He walked to Frascati's and dined alone, staring so fixedly at the tablecloth that his waiter grew quite nervous about it. Then he rang up Fox and gave him certain instructions, after which he took a taxi to Chester Terrace to call on his Boswell.

"And I suppose the young ass will be out," thought Alleyn bitterly.

But Nigel Bathgate was at home. When the front door opened Alleyn heard the brisk patter of a typewriter. He walked sedately upstairs, pushed open the sitting-room door and looked in. There was Nigel, seated gloomily at his machine, with a pile of copy-paper in a basket beside it.

"Hello, Bathgate," said Alleyn. "Busy?"

Nigel jumped, turned in his chair, and then grinned.

"You!" he said happily. "I'm glad to see you, Inspector. Take a pew."

He pushed forward a comfortable chair and clapped down a cigarette-box on the broad arm. The telephone rang. Nigel cursed and answered it. "Hallo!" A beatific change came over him. "Good evening, darling." Alleyn smiled. "Who do you imagine I've got here? An old friend of yours. Inspector Alleyn. Yes. Why not hop into a taxi and pay us a visit? You will? Splendid. He's probably in difficulties and wants our help. Yes. Right." He hung up the receiver and turned, beaming, to Alleyn.

"It's Angela," he said. Miss Angela North was Nigel's betrothed.

"So I imagined," remarked the inspector. "I shall be delighted to see the minx again."

"She's thrilled at the prospect herself," Nigel declared. He made up the fire, glanced anxiously at his desk and made an effort to tidy it.

"I've just been writing you up," he informed Alleyn.

"What the devil do you mean? What have I got to do with your perverted rag?"

"We're hard up for a story and you've got a certain news value, you know. 'The case is in the hands of Chief Detective-Inspector Roderick Alleyn, the most famous crime expert of the C.I.D. Inspector Alleyn is confident——' Are you confident, by the way?"

"Change it to 'inscrutable'. When I'm boxed I fall back on inscrutability."

"Are you boxed?" asked Nigel. "That, of course, is why you've come to me. What can I do for you, Inspector?"

"You can take that inordinately conceited look off your face and compose it into its customary mould of startled incredulity. I want to talk and I can think of no one who would really like to

108

listen to me. Possibly you yourself are too busy?"

"I've finished, but wait until Angela comes."

"Is she to be trusted? All right, all right."

Nigel spent the next ten minutes telling Alleyn how deeply Miss Angela North was to be trusted. He was still in full swing when the young woman herself arrived. She greeted Alleyn as an old friend, lit a cigarette, sat on the hearth, and said:

"Now—what have you both been talking about?"

"Bathgate has talked about you, Miss Angela. I have not talked."

"But you will. You were going to, and I can guess what about. Pretend I'm not here."

"Can Bathgate manage that?"

"He'll have to."

"I won't look at her," said Nigel.

"You'd better not," said Angela. "Please begin, Inspector Alleyn."

"Speak!" said Nigel.

"I will. List, list, oh list."

"I will."

"Don't keep interrupting. I am engaged on a murder case in which the victim is not a relation of yours, nor yet, as far as I know, is the murderer your friend. In view of our past experiences, this is very striking [see *Enter a Murderer* and *A Man Lay Dead*] and remarkable."

"Come off the rocks. I suppose you mean the O'Callaghan business?"

"I do. The man was murdered. At least three persons assisting at his operation had sufficient motive. Two of them had actually threatened him. No, that is not for publication. No, don't argue. I'll let you know when it is. I have reached that stage in the proceedings when, like heroines in French dramas, I must have my confidante. You are she. You may occasionally roll up your eyes and exclaim "*Hélas, quelle horreur!*" or, if you prefer it, "Merciful Heaven, can I believe my ears?" Otherwise, beyond making sympathetic noises, don't interrupt."

"Right ho."

Alleyn smiled amiably at him.

"You're a patient cove, Bathgate, and I get much too facetious. It's an infirmity—a disease. I do it when I'm bothered and this is a bothering case. Here's the cast of characters, and, look here, the

109

whole conversation is confidential."

"Oh murder!" said Nigel. This was a favourite ejaculation of his. "It hurts, but again—Right you are."

"Thank you. As you know, O'Callaghan either took or was given an overdose of hyoscine. At least a quarter of a grain. He never recovered consciousness after his operation. As far as the experts can tell us, the stuff must have been given within the four hours preceding his death, but I'm not fully informed on that point. Now—*dramatis personae*. You'll know most of them from the inquest. Wife—the ice-maiden type. Knew her husband occasionally kicked over the traces. Too proud to fight. Urged inquest. Sister—rum to a degree and I think has gone goofy on a chemist who supplied her with patent medicines. Urged patent medicines on brother Derek on bedder-sickness in hospital prior to operation. Now very jumpy and nervous. Private secretary—one of the new young men. Semi-diplomatic aroma. All charm and engaging manners. Friend of Mr. Bathgate, so may be murderer. Name, Ronald Jameson. Any comment?"

"Young Ronald? Gosh, yes. I'd forgotten he'd nailed that job. You've described him. He's all right, really."

"I can't bear the little creature," said Angela vigorously. "Sorry!" she added hurriedly.

"Surgeon—Sir John Phillips. Distinguished gent. Friend of victim till victim took his girl away for a week-end and then dropped her. Severed friendship. Visited victim and scolded him. In hearing of butler expressed burning desire to kill victim, who then died. That makes you blanch, I see. Injected hyoscine which he prepared himself. Very unusual in surgeons, but he always does it. No real proof he didn't give overdose. No proof he did. Assistant surgeon—Thoms. Comedian. Solemn warning to Inspector Alleyn not to be facetious. Injected serum with thing like a pump. Was in the theatre alone before operation, but said he wasn't. This may be forgetfulness. Could have doctored serum-pump, but no known reason why he should. Anæsthetist—Dr. Roberts. Funny little man. Writes books about heredity and will talk on same for hours. Good taste in books, pictures and house decoration. Nervous. Very scared when murder is mentioned. In past killed patient with overdose of morphia, so won't give any injections now. Matron of hospital—Sister Marigold. Genteel. Horrified. Could have doctored serum, but imagination boggles at thought. First theatre nurse—Banks, a Bolshie. Expressed

110

delight at death of O'Callaghan, whom she considered enemy of proletariat. Attends meetings held by militant Communists who had threatened O'Callaghan. Gave camphor injection. Second theatre nurse—Jane Harden. Girl friend mentioned above. Spent week-end with deceased and cut up rough when he ended affair. Very good-looking. Threatened deceased in letter. Brought anti-gas syringe to Thoms. Delayed over it. Subsequently fainted. You may well look startled. It's a rich field, isn't it?"

"Is that all—not that it isn't enough?"

"There's his special nurse. A nice sensible girl who could easily have given him poison. She found out about Miss O'Callaghan handing out the patent medicine."

"Perhaps she lied."

"Oh, do you think so? Surely not."

"Don't be facetious," said Nigel.

"Thank you, Bathgate. No, but I don't think Nurse Graham lied. Jane Harden did over her letters. Well, there they all are. Have one of your celebrated lucky dips and see if you can spot the winner."

"For a win," Nigel pronounced at last, "the special nurse. For a place the funny little man."

"Why?"

"Oh, the crime-fiction line of reasoning. The two outsiders. The nurse looks very fishy. And funny little men are rather a favourite line in villains nowadays. He might turn out to be Sir Derek's illegitimate brother and that's why he's so interested in heredity. I'm thinking of writing detective fiction."

"You should do well at it."

"Of course," said Nigel slowly, "there's the other school in which the obvious man is always the murderer. That's the one you favour at the Yard, isn't it?"

"Yes, I suppose it is," agreed Alleyn.

"Do you read crime fiction?"

"I dote on it. It's such a relief to escape from one's work into an entirely different atmosphere."

"It's not as bad as that," Nigel protested.

"Perhaps not quite as bad as that. Any faithful account of police investigations, in even the most spectacular homicide case, would be abysmally dull. I should have thought you'd seen enough of the game to realise that. The files are a plethora of drab details, most of them entirely irrelevant. Your crime novelist gets

111

over all that by writing grandly about routine work and then selecting the essentials. Quite rightly. He'd be the world's worst bore if he did otherwise."

"May I speak?" inquired Angela.

"Do," said Alleyn.

"I'm afraid I guess it's Sir John Phillips."

"I've heard you say yourself that the obvious man is usually the ace," ruminated Nigel after a pause.

"Yes. Usually," said Alleyn.

"I suppose, in this case, the obvious man *is* Phillips."

"That's what old Fox will say," conceded Alleyn with a curious reluctance.

"I suppose it's hopeless to ask, but have you made up your mind yet, Inspector?"

Alleyn got up, walked to the fireplace, and then swung round and stared at his friend.

"I regret to say," he said, "that I haven't the foggiest notion who killed Cock Robin."

CHAPTER XII

The Lenin Hall Lot

Tuesday, the sixteenth. Night.

"Of course," said Angela suddenly, "it may be the matron. I always suspect gentility. Or, of course——" She stopped.

"Yes?" asked Alleyn. "There's still some of the field left."

"I knew you'd say that. But I *do* mistrust people who laugh too much."

Alleyn glanced at her sharply.

"Do you? I must moderate my mirth. Well, there's the case, and I'm glad to have taken it out and aired it. Shall we go to the Palladium?"

"Why!" asked Nigel, astonished.

"There's a sketch on the programme that I am anxious to see. Will you both come? We'll only miss the first two numbers."

"We'd love to," said Angela. "Are you up to one of your tricks?" she added suspiciously.

"I don't know what you mean, Miss Angela. Bathgate, will you ring up for seats?"

They went to the Palladium and enjoyed themselves. Thoms's sketch was the third number in the second half. It had not run three minutes before Nigel and Angela turned and stared owlishly at the inspector. The sketch was well cast and the actor who played the surgeon was particularly clever. Alleyn sensed a strange feeling of alertness in the audience. Here and there people murmured together. Behind them a man's voice asked: "Wonder if Sir John Phillips goes to the Palladium?" "Ssh," whispered a woman.

"The great British public twitching its nose," thought Alleyn

113

distastefully. The sketch drew to a close. The surgeon came back from the operating theatre, realistically bloody. A long-drawn "Ooooo" from the audience. He pulled off his mask, stood and stared at his gloved hands. He shuddered. A nurse entered upstage. He turned to face her: "Well, Nurse?"

"He's gone." The surgeon walked across to a practical basin and began to wash his hands as a drop curtain, emblazoned with an enormous question-mark, was drawn down like a blind over the scene.

"So that's why we came?" said Angela, and remained very quiet until the end of the show.

They had supper at Alleyn's flat, where Angela was made a fuss of by Vassily.

"Curious coincidence, that little play, didn't you think?" asked Alleyn.

"Very rum," agreed Nigel. "When did you hear about it?"

"Thoms told me that he and Phillips discussed it before the operation. Thoms seemed so anxious not to talk about it I thought it might be worth seeing. I can't help wondering if he meant to convey precisely that suggestion."

"Had Sir John seen it?" inquired Angela.

"No. Thoms told him about it."

"I say," said Nigel. "Do you think that could have given Phillips the big idea?"

"It might be that."

"Or it might be—something quite different," added Angela, watching him.

"I congratulate you, Miss Angela," said Alleyn.

"Did Mr. Thoms tell you quite frankly about their conversation?"

"No, child, he didn't. He flustered like an old hen."

"And what did you deduce from that?" asked Angela innocently.

"Perhaps he was afraid of incriminating his distinguished colleague and senior."

"Oh," she said flatly. "What's he like in other ways?"

"Besides being a bit of a buffoon? Well, I should say either rather forgetful or a bit of a liar. He says he came out of the theatre with Phillips after the latter had prepared the hyoscine injection. Phillips, Matron and Banks say he didn't."

"Oh," said Angela, "they do, do they?"

"I haven't the least idea what you're driving at, Angela," complained Nigel. "I should like to hear more about the funny little man. Didn't he behave at all queerly?"

"He behaved very queerly indeed," said Alleyn. "He was as scary as a rabbit whenever the murder was mentioned. He's obviously very frightened whenever he thinks of it. And yet I don't think his alarm is purely selfish. He said it was, I believe. Thoms, in that asinine way of his, made very merry over Roberts's alarm when he rang up."

Alleyn looked steadily at Angela.

"Roberts is the man, depend upon it," pronounced Nigel. "I'll back him with you for a quid."

"I won't," said Angela. "I'll back——"

"I'm afraid the official conscience won't allow me to join in this cold-blooded gamble," said Alleyn. He looked at them both curiously. "The attitude of the intelligent layman is very rum," he observed.

"I lay you two to one the field, bar Roberts, Angela," said Nigel.

"Done," said Angela. "In guineas," she added grandly. "And what were you saying, Inspector?"

"I was only reflecting. Does the decision rest with the judge?"

"What do you mean?"

"Well—if it does, you are betting on a man or woman who, if you're right, will presumably be hanged. I can't imagine you doing this over any other form of death. That's what I mean about the attitude of the layman."

Angela turned red.

"That's the second time in our acquaintanceship you've made me feel a pig," she said. "The first was because I was too sensitive. The bet's off, Nigel."

"You can be pretty cold-blooded yourself, Alleyn," said Nigel indignantly.

"Oh, yes," said Alleyn, "but I'm an official."

"Anyway," argued Angela, "I was betting on Dr. Roberts's innocence."

"So you were."

"And, anyway," said Nigel, "I think he did it."

"How?"

"Er—well—somehow. With an injection."

"He gave no injections."

"Who *could* have done it?" asked Angela. "I mean who had the opportunity?"

"Phillips, who prepared and gave an injection. The special, who was alone with the patient. Ruth, ditto. Banks, who prepared and gave an injection. Thoms gave an injection, but did not prepare it. He was alone in the theatre for a few minutes if Phillips and the matron are telling the truth. He used the big syringe, and as he quite frankly pointed out, he could hardly have palmed another. Jane Harden had time to empty and refill with hyoscine."

"Which of them do you say were alone in the theatre before the operation?"

"All the nurses. Thoms and Phillips had the chance to be there, I suppose."

"Not Roberts?" asked Nigel.

"I think not. He went straight to the anæsthetic-room, where he was joined by the special with the patient."

"Bad luck, darling," said Angela. "It really looks as though he's the only man who couldn't have murdered Sir Derek."

"Then he's a certainty," declared Nigel. "Isn't it true that when there's a cast-iron alibi the police always prick up their ears?"

"Personally, I let mine flop with a thankful purr," said Alleyn. "But you may be right. This is scarcely an alibi. Roberts was there; he merely had no hypodermic to give and no syringe to use."

"And no motive," added Angela.

"Look for the motive," said Nigel.

"I will," said Alleyn. "There's precious little else to look for. Has it occurred to you, if the lethal injection *was* given during the operation, how extraordinarily favourable the *mise en scène* was for the murderer? As soon as a patient is wheeled away they set to work, and as far as I can see, they literally scour out the theatre. Nothing is left—everything is washed, sterilised, polished. The syringes—the dishes—the instruments—the floor—the tables. Even the ampoules that held the injections are cast into outer darkness. If you wanted to think of a perfect place to get rid of your tracks, you couldn't choose a likelier spot." He got up and looked at his watch.

"He wants us to go," remarked Angela calmly.

"It's only eleven o'clock," murmured Alleyn. "I wondered if

you'd both care to do a job of work for me?"

"What sort of job?" they asked.

"Attend a Bolshevik meeting at midnight."

"To-night?"

"I'd adore to," said Angela quickly. "Where is it? What's the time? What do we do?"

"It'll be a bit of copy for you, Bathgate," said Alleyn. "Mr. Nicholas Kakaroff, agent of a certain advanced section of Soviet propagandists, is holding a meeting at Lenin Hall, Saltarrow Street, Blackfriars. Lenin Hall is a converted warehouse. Mr. Kakaroff is a converted minor official, originally from Krakov. I feel sure Kakaroff is a made-up name. 'Kakaroff of Krakov'—it's too good to be really true, don't you feel? There's an air of unreality about his whole gang. As far as we know, they are not officially recognised by Russia or any other self-respecting country. Your genuine Soviet citizen is an honest-to-God sort of chap in his own way, once you get past his prejudices. But these fellows are grotesques—illegitimate offsprings of the I.W.W. You'll see. Nurse Banks attends the meeting. So do we. Myself disguised and feeling silly. Banks might penetrate my disguise, which would not be in the great tradition, so you sit next to her and get her confidence. You have been given your tickets by one Mr. Marcus Barker, who will not be there. He's an English sympathiser at present in custody for selling prohibited literature. He has a bookshop in Long Acre. Don't talk about him; you'd get into a mess if you did. I want you to pump the lady. You are enthusiastic converts. Let her hear that from your conversation together and leave it to her to make friends. If you can do it artistically, rejoice over O'Callaghan's death. Now wait a moment—I want to ring Fox up. Here, read this pamphlet and see if you can get down some of the line of chat."

He looked in his desk, produced a pamphlet bound in a vermilion folder, entitled "The Soviet Movement in Britain, by Marcus Barker." Angela and Nigel sat side by side and began to read it.

Alleyn rang up Fox, who was at the Yard.

"Hallo, Brer Fox. Any news?"

"Hallo, sir. Well, I don't know that I've got anything much for you. Inspector Boys checked up on that heredity business. It seems to be quite O.K. Sir Derek's father was what you might call a bit wanting, very queer old gentleman he seems to have been. There's a great-uncle who fancied he was related to the Royal Family and did himself in in a very peculiar manner with a hedger's knife, and a great-aunt who started some religious affair and had to be shut up over it. She was always undressing herself, it seems."

"Really? What about Ruth?"

"Well, as soon as you rang off I called at Miss O'Callaghan's house to inspect the hot-water cistern and I had a cup of tea with the cook and the housemaid. They were both rather talkative ladies and full of *l'affaire O'Callaghan*," said Fox with one of his excursions into French. "They like Miss O'Callaghan all right, but they think she's a bit eccentric. It seems she was very much attached to her brother and it seems she's very thick with this chemist affair—Mr. Harold Sage. It seems he visits her a great deal. The housemaid gave it as her opinion that they were courting. Miss O'Callaghan takes a lot of his medicines."

"Say it with soda-mints? Anything more?"

"One useful bit of information, sir. Mr. Sage is a Communist."

"The devil he is! Bless me, Fox, that's a plum. Sure?"

"Oh, yes—quite certain, I should say. He's always leaving his literature about. Cook showed me a pamphlet. One of the Marcus Barker lot, it was.

Alleyn glanced through the study door at Nigel and Angela sitting very close together, their heads bent over the vermilion leaflet.

"Did you gather if Miss O'Callaghan sympathised with these views?" he asked.

At the other end of the telephone Fox blew his nose thoughtfully.

"Well, no; it seems not. Nina, that's the housemaid, said she thought the lady was trying to influence him the other way. She gave it as her opinion that Sir Derek would have had a fit if he'd known what was going on."

"Highly probable. You've done a good bit of work there, Fox. What a success you are with the ladies!"

"I'm more at home below-stairs," said Fox simply, "and the cook was a very nice sort of woman, Is that all, sir?"

"Unless you've any more gossip. See you later."

"That's right, sir. *Au revoir*."

"Bung-oh, you old devil."

Alleyn returned to the study and repeated the gist of Fox's

118

information. "See if you can hear anything of this Sage who is Miss O'Callaghan's soul-mate," he said. "He may be there tonight. Bathgate, I'm just going to change. Won't be five minutes. Ask Vassily to call a taxi and give yourself a drink."

He vanished into his tiny dressing-room, where they heard him whistling very sweetly in a high key.

"Darling," said Nigel, "this is like old times. You and I on the warpath."

"I won't have you getting into trouble," said Angela. "You did last time, you know."

"That was because I was so much in love I couldn't think."

"Indeed? And I suppose that no longer applies?"

"Do you? Do you?"

"Nigel—darling, this is no moment for dalliance."

"Yes, it is."

Alleyn's whistling drifted into the silent room. "Hey, Robin, jolly Robin, tell me how thy lady does," whistled the inspector. In a very short time he was back again, incredibly changed by a dirty chin, a very ill-cut shoddy suit, a cheap-smart overcoat, a cap, a dreadful scarf, and pointed shoes. His hair was combed forward under the cap.

"Oh!" exclaimed Angela, "I can't bear it—you always look so frightfully well turned out and handsome."

To Nigel's amusement Inspector Alleyn turned red in the face, and for the first time in their acquaintance seemed at a loss for an answer.

"Has no one ever told you you are handsome, Inspector?" pursued Angela innocently.

"Fox raves over me," said Alleyn. "What are you standing there for, Bathgate, with that silly grin on your face? Have you ordered the taxi? Have you had a drink?"

Nigel had done neither of these things. However, this was soon remedied and a couple of minutes later they were in a taxi, heading for the Embankment.

"We'll walk the last part of the way," said Alleyn. "Here are your tickets. We got these three with a good deal of difficulty. The brethren are becoming rather exclusive. Now do be careful. Remember *The Times* criticised me for employing Bright Young People in the Frantock case. Repeat your lesson."

They did this, interrupting each other a good deal, but giving the gist of his instructions.

"Right. Now it's only eleven-twenty. We're early, but there will be plenty of people there already. With any luck I'll spot Banks and you may get near her. If not, drift in her direction afterwards. I'll be near the door. As you come out brush up against me, and if you've been shown the Sage, point him out to each other so that I can hear you. See? Good. Here's where we get out, for fear of seeming proud."

He stopped the taxi. They were still down by the river. The air felt chilly and dank, but exciting. The river, busy with its night traffic, had an air of being apart and profoundly absorbed. There were the wet black shadows, broken lights, and the dark, hurried flow of the Thames towards the sea. London's water-world was about its nightly business. The roar of the streets became unimportant and remote down here, within sound of shipping sirens and the cold lap of deep water against stone.

Alleyn hurried them along the Embankment for a short way and then turned off somewhere near Blackfriars Underground Station. They went up a little dark street that resembled a perspective in a woodcut. A single street lamp, haloed in mist, gave accent to shadows as black as printer's ink. Beyond the lamp a flight of stone steps led dramatically downwards. They followed these steps, came out in a narrow alley, took several more turns and fetched up at last by an iron stairway.

"Up you go," said Alleyn. "We've arrived."

The stairs ended in an iron landing which rang coldly under their feet. Here, by a closed door, stood a solitary man, who struck his hands together and blew on his fingers. Alleyn showed him his ticket, which he inspected by the light of an electric torch. Nigel and Angela followed. The man flashed his torch on their faces, a disconcerting business.

"New, aren't you?" he said to Nigel.

"Yes," said Angela quickly, "and terribly excited. Will it be a good meeting?"

"Should be," he answered, and opened the door behind him. They went through and found themselves in a narrow passage lit by a solitary globe at the far end. Under this lamp stood another man, who watched them steadily as they came towards him. Angela took Nigel's arm.

" 'Evening," said Alleyn.

" 'Evening, comrade," said the man self-consciously. "You're early to-night."

120

"That's right. Many here?"

"Not many yet. Show your tickets, please." He turned to the others. "You newcomers?"

"Yes," said Nigel.

"I'll have to take your names, comrades."

"That's new," remarked Alleyn.

"Instructions from headquarters. We've got to be more careful."

"Just as well. I'm bringing Miss Northgate and Mr. Batherston. Friends of Comrade Marcus Barker." He spelt the names while the man wrote them down. "They come from Clearminster-Storton, Dorset, and are both right-minded."

"Anything doing in your part of the world?" asked the man.

"Gosh, no!" said Nigel. "All landed gentry, bourgeoisie and wage-slaves."

"Bone from the eyes up," added Angela perkily.

The man laughed loudly.

"You've said it! Just sign these cards, will you?"

With an effort they remembered their new names and wrote them at the foot of two pieces of pasteboard that seemed to be inscribed with some sort of profession of secrecy. Angela felt rather guilty. While they did this someone came in at the outside door and walked along the passage. The man took their cards, pulled open the door and turned to the newcomer. Led by Alleyn, they all walked through the door, which immediately was shut behind them.

They found themselves in a large room that still looked like a warehouse. Six office lamps with china shades hung from the ceiling. The walls were unpapered plaster in bad condition. A few Soviet propagandist posters, excellent in design, had been pasted on the walls. The Russian characters looked strange and out of place. At the far end a rough platform had been run up. On the wall behind it was an enlarged photograph of Lenin draped in a grubby festoon of scarlet muslin. There were some thirty people in the room. They stood about in small groups, talking quietly together. One or two had seated themselves among the chairs and benches that faced the platform. Nigel, who prided himself on this sort of thing, tried to place some of them. He thought he detected a possible newsagent, two undergraduates, three Government school teachers, compositors, shopkeepers, a writing bloke or two, and several nondescripts who might be anything from artists to itinerant hawkers. There were one or two women of the student type, but as Alleyn made no sign, Nigel concluded that none of these was Nurse Banks. Evidently the inspector had been to former meetings. He went up to a middle-aged, vehement-looking man with no teeth, who greeted him gloomily and in a little while began to talk very excitedly about the shortcomings of someone called Sage. "He's got no guts," he repeated angrily, "no guts at all."

More people came in at intervals; a few looked like manual labourers, but the majority seemed to belong to that class abhorred of Communists, the bourgeoisie. Nigel and Angela saw Alleyn point them both out to his gloomy friend, who stared morosely at them for a moment and then burst into an offensive guffaw. Presently Alleyn rejoined them.

"My friend has just come in," he said quietly. "She's that tall woman in a red hat."

They looked towards the door and saw the tall woman. Her face, as well as her hat, was red, and was garnished with pince nez and an expression of general truculence. Banks was as formidable out of uniform as she was in it, Alleyn reflected. She glanced round the room and then marched firmly towards the second row of chairs.

"Off you go," murmured Alleyn. "Remember, you come from O'Callaghan's county, but are not of it."

They walked down the centre aisle and seated themselves alongside Nurse Banks.

She produced an uncompromising mass of wool, grey in colour, and began to knit.

"Don't you feel ever so excited, Claude?" asked Angela loudly in a very second-rate voice.

Nigel suppressed a slight start and checked an indignant glance.

"It's a wonderful experience, Pippin," he replied.

He felt Angela quiver.

"I wish I knew who everyone was," she said. "We're so out of touch. These are the people who are really getting things done and we don't know their names. If only Mr. Barker had been here."

"Ye gods, it makes me wild!" apostrophised Nigel. "And they call this a free country. Free!"

Angela, who was next to Banks, dared not look at her. Banks's needles clicked resolutely.

"Do you think," ventured Angela after a pause, "do you think we could ever make any headway down in the dear old village?"

"The dear old village, so quaint and old-world," gibed Nigel. "So typically English, don't you know. No, I don't. The only headway you could make there would be with a charge of dynamite. God, I'd like to see it done!"

"They'll all be in heavy mourning now, of course."

"Yes—for Sir Derek Bloody O'Callaghan."

They both laughed uproariously and then Angela said: "Ssh—be careful," and glanced apprehensively at Banks. She was smiling.

"I wonder if he's here yet?" whispered Angela.

"Who?"

"Kakaroff."

"There's someone going on to the platform now."

"Claude! Can it be he?"

This exclamation sounded so incredible that she instantly regretted it and was infinitely relieved to hear Miss Banks remark in a firm baritone:

"Comrade Kakaroff isn't here yet. That's Comrade Robinson."

"Thanks ever so," said Angela brightly. "We're strangers ourselves and don't know anybody, but we're terribly keen."

Banks smiled.

"You see," continued Angela, "we come from the backwoods of Dorset, where everything died about the time Anne did."

"The counties," said Banks, "are moribund, but in the North there are signs of rebirth."

"That's right!" ejaculated Nigel fervently. "I believe it will come from the North."

"I hope you were not very shocked at what my gentleman-friend said just now about O'Callaghan?" Angela ventured.

"Shocked!" said Banks. "Scarcely!" She laughed shortly.

"Because, you see, we come from the same place as his family and we're about fed to the back teeth with the mere name. It's absolutely feudal—you can't imagine."

"And every election time," said Nigel, "they all trot along like good little kids and vote for dear Sir Derek once again."

"They won't do that any more."

The other seats in their row filled up with a party of people engaged in an earnest and rather bloodthirsty conversation. They paid no attention to anyone but themselves. Nigel continued the approach of Banks.

"What did you think about the inquest?" he asked blandly.

She turned her head slowly and looked at him. "I don't know," she said. "What did you?"

"I thought it rather peculiar myself. Looks as if the police know something. Whoever had the guts to fix O'Callaghan I reckon was a national hero. I don't care who knows it either," said Nigel defiantly.

"You're right," cried Banks, "you're right. You can't heal a dog-bite without a cautery." She produced this professional analogy so slickly that Nigel guessed it was a standardised argument. "All the same," added Banks with a slight change of voice, "I don't believe anyone could, if they would, claim the honour of striking this blow for freedom. It was an accident—a glorious accident."

Her hands trembled and the knitting-needles chattered together. Her eyes were wide open and the pupils dilated.

"Why, she's demented," thought Angela in alarm.

"Hyoscine," murmured Nigel. "Wasn't that the drug Crippen used?"

"I believe it was," said Angela. "Isn't that the same as Twilight Sleep?"

She paused hopefully. Banks made no answer. A young man came and sat in front of them. He looked intelligent and would have been rather a handsome fellow if his blond curls had been shorter and his teeth less aggressively false.

"I don't know," said Nigel; "I'm no chemist. Oh! Talking of chemists, we must see if we can find that chap Harold Sage here. I'd like to meet him."

"Well, it's so difficult. They never said what he was like. Perhaps—er——" Angela turned towards Miss Banks. "Perhaps you could help us. There's a gentleman here who knows a friend of ours." She wondered if this was risky. "His name's Harold Sage. He's a chemist, and we thought if we could see him——"

The young man with the blond curls turned round and flashed a golden smile at her.

"Pardon," he fluted throatily. "That won't be very difficult. May neem's Hawrold Seege."

CHAPTER XIII

Surprising Antics of a Chemist

Tuesday to Wednesday. The small hours

To say that Nigel and Angela were flabbergasted by this announcement is to give not the slightest indication of their derangement. Their mouths fell open and their eyes protruded. Their stomachs, as the saying is, turned over. Mr. Sage continued the while to smile falsely upon them. It seemed as if they took at least three minutes to recover. Actually about five seconds elapsed before Angela, in a small voice that she did not recognise, said:

"Oh—fancy! What fun!"

"Oh," echoed Nigel, "fancy! What luck! Yes."

"Yes," said Angela.

"I thought I heard someone taking my name in vain," continued Mr. Sage playfully. It would be tedious to attempt a phonetic reproduction of Mr. Sage's utterances. Enough to say that they were genteel to a fantastic degree.

"Aye thot Aye heeard somewon teeking may neem in veen," may give some idea of his rendering of the above sentence. Let it go at that.

"I was just going to make you known to each other," said Nurse Banks. So great was their dilemma they had actually forgotten Nurse Banks.

Mr. Sage cast a peculiarly reluctant glance upon her and then turned to his quarry. "And who," he asked gaily, "is the mutual friend?"

Frantic alternatives chased each other through Angela's and Nigel's brains. Suppose they risked naming Marcus Barker again—he of the vermilion pamphlet. He had a shop. He was in prison. That was all they knew of Comrade Barker. Suppose——

Nigel drew a deep breath and leant forward.

"It is——" he began.

"Comrades!" shouted a terrific voice. "We will commence by singing the Internationale."

They turned, startled, to the platform. A gigantic bearded man, wearing a Russian blouse, confronted the audience. Comrade Kakaroff had arrived.

The comrades, led by the platform, instantly burst into a deafening rumpus. Nigel and Angela, pink with relief, made grimaces indicative of thwarted communication at Mr. Sage, who made a suitable face in return and then stood to attention and, with a piercing headnote, cut into the Internationale.

When they talked the affair over afterwards with Inspector Alleyn they could not remember one utterance of Comrade Kakaroff during the first half of his speech. He was a large Slav with a beautiful voice and upright hair. That was all they took in. When the beautiful voice rose to an emotional bellow they managed to exchange a panicky whisper.

"Shall we slip away?"

"We *can't*. Not now."

"Afterwards?"

"Yes—perhaps too fishy."

"What do you mean?"

"Ssh! I'm going to——"

"Ssh!"

They glared at each other. To his horror, Nigel saw that Angela was about to get the giggles. He frowned at her majestically and then folded his arms and stared, with an air of interest, at Comrade Kakaroff. This unfortunately struck Angela, who was no doubt hysterical, as being intolerably funny. Her blood ran cold, her heart sank, she was panic-stricken, but she felt she must laugh.

"Shut up," breathed Nigel out of the corner of his mouth. He was foolish enough to kick her. Her chair quivered. She looked round wildly to the four corners of the room. In the fourth corner, between a diagonal vista of rapt faces, she saw someone who watched her. It was the man to whom Alleyn had spoken when they first arrived. Her throat quivered no longer. It went dry. Suddenly nothing seemed funny. Perhaps no one had noticed her. Banks, uttering an occasional "Hear! hear! in a tone of magisterial approval, gazed only at Nicholas Kakaroff. Mr. Sage's back was towards them. Angela was herself again and greatly ashamed. She began to think coherently and presently she formed a plan. Alleyn had talked at some length about Ruth O'Callaghan. He had a vivid trick of description and Angela felt she knew exactly what Miss O'Callaghan was like. Suppose——? She stared like an attentive angel at Comrade Kakaroff and as she stared she made up her mind. As if in echo of her thoughts, she suddenly became aware of his utterances.

"The death of the late Home Secretary—Derek O'Callaghan," boomed Comrade Kakaroff. Jerked out of their unhappy meditation, they began to listen with a will.

"——not for us the sickly sentiment of an effete and decadent civilisation. Not for us the disgusting tears of the wage-slave hypocrite. It was in a good hour that man died. Had he lived he would have worked us great evil. He was struck down with the words of tyranny on his lips. I say it was in a good hour he died. We know it. Let us boldly declare it. He was the enemy of the people, a festering sore that drained the vitality of the proletariat. Listen to me, all of you. If he was deliberately exterminated and I knew the man who had done it, I would greet that man with the outstretched hand of brotherhood. I would hail that man as—Comrade."

He sat down amidst loud noises of encouragement. Mr. Sage had sprung excitedly to his feet.

"Comrade!" he shouted excitedly. It was as if he had touched a spring. The age-old yeast of mob-hysteria was at work. Half of them were on their feet yelling. Miss Banks cast down her knitting and made curious staccato gestures with her hands. "Up the anarchists!" someone screamed behind them. The uproar lasted for some minutes while Kakaroff gazed intently at his work. Then Comrade Robinson walked to the edge of the platform and held up his hands. It was not until the Russian, half contemptuously, had joined him that the din died away.

"Friends," said Kakaroff, "have patience. It will not be for long. In the meantime—be patient. It is with difficulty we manage to hold these meetings. Let us not arouse too much suspicion in the brilliant brains of those uniformed automatons who guard the interests of the capitalist—our wonderful police."

The comrades made merry. Angela distinctly heard the rare

laugh of Inspector Alleyn. The meeting broke up after a brief word from Comrade Robinson about outstanding subscriptions. Mr. Sage, a winning smile upon his face, turned eagerly towards them.

"Magnificent, wasn't it?" he cried.

"Marvellous!"

"Wonderful!"

"And now," continued Mr. Sage, looking admiringly upon Angela, "please tell me—who is our mutual friend?"

"Well, she's not exactly a *close* friend," said Angela, "although we both like her ever so much." She glanced round her and leant forward. Mr. Sage gallantly inclined his curls towards her.

"Miss Ruth O'Callaghan," said Angela, just loud enough for Nigel to hear. He instantly supposed she had gone crazy.

Mr. Sage must have tilted his chair too far backwards, for he suddenly clutched at the air in a very singular manner. His feet shot upwards and the next instant he was decanted over their feet.

"Murder!" ejaculated Nigel, and hurriedly bent over him. Mr. Sage fought him off with great violence, and after a galvanic struggle, regained his feet. "I say," said Angela, remembering her new voice, "I do hope you haven't hurt yourself. I'm ever so sorry."

Mr. Sage gazed at Nigel in silence for some moments. At last he drew in his breath and said: "No, thanks. Aye'm quate O.K."

"But you've gone pale. It was an awful bump you came. Sit down for a moment."

"Thanks," he said, and sank into a chair. "Dear me, that was a very silly thing to do."

"Very painful, I should say," remarked Nigel solemnly.

Suddenly Angela began to laugh.

"Oh," she said, "I'm awfully sorry. It's just horrid of me, but I can't help it."

"Really, An—Pippin!" scolded Nigel.

"The instinct to laugh at bodily injury," said Mr. Sage, who had recovered his colour, "is a very old one. Possibly it goes back to the snarl of the animal about to engage an adversary. You can't help yourself."

"It's nice of you to take it like that," said Angela through her tears. "It was rather a funny introduction."

"Yes."

"I'd better explain," continued Angela. Nigel, who had

128

regarded the upsetting of Mr. Sage as a dispensation of Providence, listened in horror. "We come from Clearminster-Storton in Dorset, near the holy ancestral home of the O'Callaghans. We've no time for the others and let it be known frankly. But she's different, isn't she, Claude?"

"Quite different."

"Yes. We've seen her in London and tried to make her look at things in the enlightened way, and although she's hide-bound by the tradition of her class, she doesn't refuse to listen. She told us about you, Mr. Sage. She thinks you're awfully clever, doesn't she, Claude?"

"That's right," said poor Nigel.

"So that is the way of it?" said Mr. Sage. "I have too attempted to make Miss O'Callaghan think, to open her eyes. She is a customer of mine and is interested in my work. I accept patronage from nobody, mind. She has not offered patronage, but comradeship. I don't really know her well, and——" He paused and then, looking straight at Nigel, he added: "To be frank with you, I have not seen much of her since O'Callaghan introduced his infamous Bill. I felt the situation would be too severe a strain on our friendship. We have never discussed her brother. She knows my views and would understand. Er—quite."

"Oh, quite," murmured Angela.

"Just so," said Nigel.

"As a matter of fact," continued Mr. Sage, "I must own I don't go as far as Comrade Kakaroff in the matter of O'Callaghan's death. Undoubtedly it is well he is gone. I realise that theoretically there is such a thing as justifiable extermination, but murder—as this may have been—no."

"This *was* justifiable extermination," said Nigel fiercely.

"Then it should have been done openly for the Cause."

"No one fancies the rope."

"Claude, you are awful. I agree with Mr. Sage."

"Thank you Miss—er. Pardon, I'm afraid I don't know——"

"Pippin!" exclaimed Nigel suddenly. "We're keeping our pal waiting. He's hanging round outside the door there. Murder! It's half-past one and we swore we'd meet those other chaps before then."

"Ow, gracious, how awful!" said Angela. They grasped Mr. Sage's hand, said hurriedly they hoped they'd meet again, and scuttled away.

The comrades had broken up into groups. Many of them had gone. Nigel and Angela saw Alleyn at the door with his gloomy friend. A short, well-dressed man followed them out, passed them, walked quickly to the outer door, and ran noisily down the iron stairs. Alleyn stood and stared after him. He and the truculent man exchanged a glance.

"Come on," said Alleyn.

As they all walked out Nigel and Angela kept up a rather feverish conversation in their assumed voices. Alleyn was completely silent and so was his friend. Angela felt rather frightened. Did this man suspect them?

"I thought it was a perfectly marvellous meeting," she said loudly as they walked down the empty street.

"Stimulating—that's what it was, stimulating," gushed Nigel. The man grunted. Alleyn was silent.

"I was so pleased to meet Comrade Sage," continued Angela with an air of the greatest enthusiasm.

"He's all right," conceded Nigel, "but I wouldn't say he was quite sound."

"You mean about O'Callaghan? Oh, I don't know. What did you think about O'Callaghan, comrade?" Angela turned desperately to Alleyn.

"Oh, I'm all for bloodshed," said Alleyn dryly. "Aren't you, comrade?" He turned to his friend.

The man uttered a short sinister laugh. Angela took Nigel's hand. "He was an ulcer," she said confusedly, but with energy. "When we find an ulcer we——we——"

"Poultice it?" suggested Alleyn.

"*Paw onzcorager les autres*," said the man in diabolical French.

"Oh," said Nigel, "not exactly that, comrade——er——?"

"Fox," said Alleyn. "You've met before."

"?!!"

"It's all right, sir," said Inspector Fox soothingly. "It's the removal of my dentures that did it. Rather confusing. You were getting on very nicely. It was quite a treat to listen to you."

"Stimulating—that's what it was, stimulating," added Alleyn.

"Inspector Alleyn," said Angela furiously, "I'll never forgive you for this—never."

"Hist!" said Alleyn. "The very walls have ears."

"Oh!" stormed Angela. "Oh! Oooo! Oh!"

"Murder!" said Nigel very quietly.

They walked on in silence until they came out by the river. A taxi drew up alongside them and they got in. Inspector Fox took a cardboard box from his pocket, turned delicately aside, and inserted his plates.

"Begging your pardon, miss," he said, "but it's pleasanter to have them."

"And now," said Alleyn, "just exactly what have you been up to?"

"I won't tell you."

"Won't you, Miss Angela? That's going to make it rather difficult."

"Oh, come on, Angela," said Nigel resignedly. "He'll have to know. Let's come clean."

They came clean. The two policeman listened in silence.

"Yes," said Alleyn when they had finished. "That's all very interesting. It's informative too. Let me get it straight. You say that when you quoted Miss O'Callaghan as your friend—a very dangerous trick, Miss Angela—Sage fell over backwards. Do you think he did this accidentally or deliberately? Do you think he got such a shock he over-balanced and crashed, or did you feel he used this painful ruse to distract your attention? Or were you both acting your socks off so enthusiastically that you did not notice?"

"Certainly not. At least——"

"I think he got a shock," said Nigel.

"Well, yes," agreed Angela, "so do I. But he seemed more upset, oddly enough, afterwards, when he was lying there. His face went pea-green. Oh dear, he *did* look dreadfully funny."

"No doubt. What did you say—did you say anything that would account for this diverting phenomenon?"

"I—no. Nigel said something. We both exclaimed, you know."

"I grabbed hold of him and he fairly fought me off."

"And then, you know, he got up and we asked if he was hurt and he said he was 'quate O.K.' and seemed to get better."

"What was it you said, Bathgate?"

"I dunno. 'Gosh!' or 'Help!' or 'Oh fie!' Something."

"Subsequently he said that he did not altogether respond to Comrade Kakaroff's wave of brotherly love for O'Callaghan's murderer—that it?"

"He seemed to think that was going a bit far."

"And yet"—Alleyn went on—"and yet I seem to remember that at the conclusion of Kakaroff's jolly little talk, Comrade Sage leapt to his feet and yelled 'Comrade'."

"Yes—he did," Nigel agreed, "but he may have been all carried away. He's not a bad little tick, really, I should say, once you've got past his frightful refinement."

"He spoke quite decently about Miss O'Callaghan," added Angela.

"So it appears. Did he and my girl-friend Banks have anything to say to each other?"

"Not a word."

"Well, Fox?"

"Well, sir?"

"I suppose I visit Mr. Sage at his shop to-morrow—oh, Lord, it's to-day, isn't it? What's the time?"

Inspector Fox drew his watch from the inside pocket of the threadbare coat he was wearing. He held it up in a large and filthy paw. "Just on two, I make it," he said. "Listen."

He lowered the window of the taxi. The lost, woe-begone voice of a siren sounded out on the river. Then Big Ben, up in the cold night air, tolled two.

Inspector Fox regarded his watch with grave approval, put it away, and laid his hands on his knees.

"Longing for your bed, Fox?" asked Alleyn.

"I am for mine," said Angela.

"Suppose we let Bathgate take the taxi on, and turn into the office for half an hour?"

"Right ho, sir."

"Here we are."

He tapped on the window and the taxi stopped. The two detectives got out. Their breath hung mistily on the frosty air. Alleyn spoke for a moment to the driver and then looked inside.

"Thank you so much for your help, both of you," he said.

"I say, Alleyn, I hope you don't think we've made awful mugs of ourselves?" said Nigel lugubriously.

Alleyn thought for a moment.

"It was a very spirited effort, I consider," he said at last.

"We shall have to get you both in the Force, sir," added Fox. His matter-of-fact voice sounded oddly remote out there in the cold.

"Ah, Inspector Fox," said Nigel suspiciously, "I've heard you say that before."

"Good night, Comrade Angela," said Alleyn, "sleep well."

"Good night, Inspector; I don't grudge you your joke."

"Bless you," answered Alleyn gently and slammed the door.

The taxi drove off. Farther along the Embankment men were hosing down the street surface. A great fan of water curved out and made all the sound there was except for the siren and the distant toot of the taxi. The two men stared at one another.

"I wonder just how much harm they've done," said Alleyn.

"None at all, sir, I should say."

"I hope you're right. My fault if they have. Come on, let's have a smoke."

In Alleyn's room they lit their pipes. Alleyn wrote at his desk for some time. Fox stared gravely at the opposite wall. They looked a queer couple with their dreadful clothes, grimy faces and blackened hands.

"She seems a very nice young lady," Fox said presently. "Is she Mr Bathgate's fiancée, sir, if I may ask?"

"She is."

"A very pleasant young couple."

Alleyn looked at him affectionately.

"You're a quaint old bag of nonsense." He laid down his pen. "I don't think, really, I took too big a risk with them. The little man was nowhere near them. You recognised him, of course?"

"Oh, yes—from the inquest. I didn't see who it was till he passed us in the doorway, but I'd noticed him earlier in the evening. He had his back towards us."

"Yes, I saw him, too. His clothes were good enough to shine out in that assembly. No attempt made to dress down to comrade level."

"No," said Fox. "Funny—that."

"It's altogether very rum. Passing strange. He walked straight past Sage and Nurse Banks. None of them batted an eyelash."

"That's so. If they are in collusion, it might be deliberate."

"You know, Fox, I can't think this Communist stuff is at the root of it. They're a bogus lot, holding their little meetings, printing little pamphlets, making their spot of trouble. A nuisance from our point of view, but not the stuff that assassins are made of. Of course, given one fanatic——" He stopped and shook his head.

"Well," said Fox, "that's so. They don't amount to much. Perhaps he's different, though. Perhaps he's the fanatic."

"Not that sort, I'd have thought. I'll go and see him again. To-morrow. To-day. I rather like the bloke. We'll have to get hold of the expert who's doing the Kakaroff bunch and find out if he's deep in. It's been a field day, this. It seems an age since we sat here and waited for the report on the post-mortem. Damn. I feel we are as one about to be had. I feel we are about to give tongue and run off on a false scent. I feel we are about to put two and two together and make a mess."

"That's a pity," said Fox.

"What's the time? Half-past two. Perhaps Bathgate will be back in his own flat by now, having dropped Miss Angela, who looked tired, at her uncle's house. I think I shall send him to bed happy."

He dialled a number on his telephone and waited.

"Hallo, Bathgate. How much are you betting on your funny little man?"

"Roberts?" quacked Nigel's voice clearly.

"Yes, Roberts."

"Two to one, wasn't it? Why? What's up?"

"Did you notice he was at the meeting to-night?"

"Robets!"

"Yes, Roberts. Good night."

He hung up the receiver.

"Come on," he said wearily. "Let's put two and two together and make a mess."

CHAPTER XIV

"Fulvitavolts"

Wednesday, the seventeenth. Morning and afternoon.
The following morning Chief Inspector Alleyn and Inspector Fox
reviewed their discussion.

"The Lenin Hall theory looks even shoddier by the light of
day," said Alleyn.

"Well, sir," said Fox, "I won't say it isn't weak in places, but
we can't ignore the thing, can we?"

"No. I suppose not. No."

"If there's nothing in it, it's a peculiar coincidence. Here's this
lady, deceased's sister——"

"Oh yes, Fox, and by the way, I'm expecting the family
solicitor. Mr. Rattisbon, of Knightley, Knightley and Rattisbon,
an uncle of Lady O'Callaghan's, I believe. Unusually come-toish
advance—rang up and suggested the visit himself. He mentioned
Miss O'Callaghan so guardedly that I can't help feeling she plays a
star part in the will. You were saying?"

"I was going to say here's this lady, deceased's sister, giving
him patent medicines. Here's the Sage affair, the chemist, a
member of the advanced party that threatened deceased, sup-
plying them. Here's the doctor that gave the anæsthetic turning
up at the same meeting as the chemist and the nurse that gave the
injection. The nurse knows the chemist; the chemist, so Mr.
Bathgate says, isn't so keen to know the nurse. The doctor,
seemingly, knows neither of them. Well now, that may be bluff
on the doctor's part. Suppose they were all working in collusion?
Sage wouldn't be very keen on associating himself with Nurse
Banks. Dr. Roberts might think it better to know neither of

135

them. Suppose Sage had supplied Miss O'Callaghan with a drug containing a certain amount of hyoscine, Nurse Banks had injected a bit more, and Dr. Roberts had made a job of it by injecting the rest?"

"All of them instructed by Comrade Kakaroff?"

"Well—yes."

"But why? Why involve three people when one might do the trick? And anyway, none of them knew O'Callaghan was going to throw a fit and lie-for-dead in the House of Commons and then be taken to Sir John Phillips's nursing-home."

"That's so, certainly, but Sage would know, through Miss O'Callaghan, that her brother intended having Sir John to look at him as soon as the Bill was read. It seems they knew it was appendix. Mightn't they even have said he'd better go to the hospital and have it out? The lady tells Mr. Sage about this. He reports. He and Nurse Banks and Dr. Roberts think they'll form a plan of action."

"And, lo and behold, it all comes to pass even as they had said. I don't like it, Fox. And anyway, my old one, how did Dr. Roberts give the injection with no syringe? Why didn't he take the golden opportunity of exercising his obvious right of giving the hypodermic? To establish his innocence, you will say. He gave it on the sly, all unbeknown. But how? You can't carry a syringe all ready for use, complete with lethal dose, in your trouser pocket. And anyway, his trousers, like all the rest of him, were covered with a white nightie. And he was never alone with the patient."

"That's so, and I admit it's a bit of a facer. Well—perhaps he simply arranged the matter with Miss Banks and she gave the injection, using hyoscine instead of camphor."

"Subsequently letting everyone know how delighted she was at the death. Do you think that was subtlety or stupidity?"

Fox shook his head solemnly.

"I don't say I support the theory, chief, but it *is* a theory."

"Oh, yes. There's another point about the hyoscine. It's kept in a bottle, which Thoms tells me is very out of date—it should be in an ampoule. Phillips, I suppose, doesn't object, as he always uses his own tablets. Now Jane Harden says that the bottle was full and that one injection has since been used. I've checked that. When I saw the bottle it was almost full. Thoms brought it to me."

"Thoms did?" repeated Fox in his slow way.

"Yes. I got a sample and am having it analysed. If anyone has added water, the solution will be below strength."

"Yes—but they might have managed to add more solution."

"I don't see how. Where would they get it from? It would have to be done there and then."

Alleyn got up and walked about the room. "You've never told me your views on intuition," he said.

"I can't say I've got any. No views, I mean—and no intuition either, for a matter of that. Very unimaginitive I've always been. I recollect at school I was a poor hand at writing compositions, as they called them. Still I wouldn't say," said Fox cautiously, "that there is no such thing as intuition. I've known you come out rather strong in that line yourself."

"Thank you, Fox. Well, the weird is upon me now, if that's the expression. By the pricking of my thumbs, something wicked this way comes. I've got a hunch that the Bolshie lot is not one of the principal factors. It's a secondary theme on the bloody cantata. And, yet, blast it, we'll have to follow it up."

"Oh well," Fox rose to his feet. "What's my job of work for to-day, sir?"

"Get hold of Boys or whoever has been watching the comrades and see if Roberts's connection with them can be traced. If there's anything in this we'll have to try and get evidence of collusion. Since the Krasinky-Tokareff affair Sumiloff has had to fade out, but there's Comrade Robinson. He seems to have wormed his way into the foreground. You'd better call him in. We pay the brute enough; let him earn it. Call him in, Fox, and tell him to ferret. He might tell the comrades we've been asking questions and see how they respond. And, talking about ferreting, I've been going through the reports on the medical gentlemen. It's the devil's own game beating it all up and there's a lot more to be done. So far there's nothing very much to excite us." He pulled forward a sheaf of papers. "Here you are. Phillips—Educated at Winchester and Cambridge. Medical training at Thomas's. Brilliant record. Distinguished war service. You can read it. Inspector Allison has spent days on this stuff. Thomas's was full of enthusiasm for one of its brightest boys. No bad marks anywhere. Here's Detective-Sergeant Bailey on Roberts. Educated at home. Delicate child. Medical training at Edinburgh and abroad, in Vienna. After qualifying went to Canada, Australia, and New Zealand, returning to England after war. Red Cross work, during war, in Belgium. Books on heredity—he lent me one and it seems damn' good. I suppose we'll have to go into the history abroad. I'll ring up Toronto to-night. We'll have to check up on that story about the overdose. Talk about routine! How long, O Lord, how long! Thoms—Educated St Bardolph's, Essex, and Guy's. I rang up a friend of mine at Guy's who was his contemporary. Very good assistant surgeon and never likely to get much farther than that. Undistinguished but blameless career, punctuated by mild scandals about women. Little devil! My friend was rather uncomplimentary about Thoms. He called him a 'lecherous little blight.' That's as far as we've got."

The telephone rang and Alleyn answered it.

"It's Mr. Rattisbon. Go down and make much of him, Fox. Bring him up tenderly, treat him with care. If he's anything like the rest of his family, he'll need warming. Use your celebrated charm."

"O.K." said Fox. "*Toojoor la politesse*. I'm on to the third record now, chief, but their peculiar ways of pronunciation give me a lot of trouble. Still, it's a sort of hobby, as you might say."

He sighed and went, returning to usher in Mr. James Rattisbon, of Knightley, Knightley and Rattisbon, uncle to Lady O'Callaghan and solicitor to the deceased and his family. Mr. Rattisbon was one of those elderly solicitors whose appearance explains why the expression 'dried-up' is so inevitably applied by novelists to men of law. He was desiccated. He was dressed in clothes of a dated type that looked rather shabby, but were actually in good repair. He wore a winged collar, rather high, and a dark tie, rather narrow. He was discreetly bald, somewhat blind, and a little tremulous. He had a kind of quick shuttering utterance, and a curious trick of thrusting out his pointed tongue and rattling it exceedingly rapidly between his thin lips. This may have served as an antidote to the stutter or it may have signified a kind of professional relish. His hands were bird-like claws with very large purplish veins. It was impossible to picture him in any sort of domestic surroundings.

As soon as the door had been closed behind him he came forward very nimbly and said with incredible speed:

"Chief Detective-Inspector Alleyn?"

"Good morning, sir," said Alleyn. He advanced a chair towards Mr. Rattisbon and offered to take his hat.

"Good morning, good morning," said Mr. Rattisbon.

"Thank—yer, thank—yer. No, thank—yer. Thank—yer."

He clung to his hat and took the chair.

"It's good of you to call. I would have been delighted to save you the trouble by coming to your office. I believe you want to see me about the O'Callaghan business?"

"That is the business—that is the reason—it is in connection with that matter that I have waited upon you, yes," rattled Mr. Rattisbon. He stopped short, darted a glance at Alleyn, and beat a finicky tattoo on the crown of his hat.

"Oh yes," said Alleyn.

"As no doubt you are aware, Inspector Alleyn, I was the late Sir Derek O'Callaghan's solicitor. I am also his sister's, Miss Catherine Ruth O'Callaghan's, solicitor, and of course his wife's—his wife's—ah, solicitor."

Alleyn waited.

"I understand from my clients that certain representations made by Lady O'Callaghan were instrumental in prompting you to take the course you have subsequently adopted."

"Yes."

"Yes. I understand that is the case. Inspector Alleyn, this is not, strictly speaking, a professional call. Lady O'Callaghan is my niece. Naturally I have a personal as well as a professional interest in the matter."

He looked, thought Alleyn, as though he was incapable of any interest that was not professional.

"Of course, sir," said Alleyn.

"My niece did not consult me before she took this step. I must confess that had she done so I should—I should have entertained grave doubts as to the advisability of her action. However, as matters have turned out, she was fully justified. I was of course present at the inquest. Since then I have had several interviews with both these ladies. The last took place yesterday afternoon and was—was of a somewhat disquieting nature."

"Really, sir?"

"Yes. It is a matter of some delicacy. I have hesitated—I have hesitated for some time before making this appointment. I learn that since the inquest Miss O'Callaghan has visited you and has—has suggested that you go no farther with your investigation."

"Miss O'Callaghan," said Alleyn, "was extremely distressed at the idea of the post-mortem."

"Quite. Quite so. It is at her request that I have come to see you myself."

"Is it, by Jove!" thought Alleyn.

"Miss O'Callaghan," continued Mr Rattisbon, "fears that in her distress she spoke foolishly. I found it difficult to get from her the actual gist of her conversation, but it seems that she mentioned a young protégé of hers, a Mr. Harold Sage, a promising chemist, she tells me."

"She did speak of a Mr. Sage."

"Yes." Mr. Rattisbon suddenly rubbed his nose very hard and then agitated his tongue. "She appears to think she used somewhat ambiguous phrasing as regards the young man, and she—in short, Inspector, the lady has got it into her head that she may have presented him in a doubtful light. Now I assured her that the police are not to be misled by casual words spoken at a time of emotional stress, but she implored me to come and see you, and though I was disinclined to do so, I could scarcely refuse."

"You were in a difficult position, Mr. Rattisbon."

"I *am* in a difficult position. Inspector Alleyn, I feel it my duty to warn you that Miss Ruth O'Callaghan, though by no means *non compos mentis*, is at the same time subject to what I can only call periods of hysterical enthusiasm and equally hysterical depression. She is a person of singularly naive intelligence. This is not the first occasion on which she has raised an alarm about a matter which subsequently proved to be of no importance whatever. Her imagination is apt to run riot. I think it would not be improper to attribute this idiosyncrasy to an unfortunate strain in her heredity."

"I quite appreciate that," Alleyn assured him. "I know something of this family trait. I believe her father——"

"Quite so. Quite," said Mr. Rattisbon, shooting a shrewd glance at him. "I see you take my point. Now, Inspector Alleyn, the only aspect of the matter that causes me disquietude is the possibility of her calling upon you again, actuated by further rather wild and, I'm afraid, foolish motives. I did think that perhaps it would be well to——"

"To put me wise, sir? I'm grateful to you for having done so. I should in any case have called on you, as I shall be obliged to make certain inquiries as regards the deceased's affairs."

Mr. Rattisbon appeared to tighten all over. He darted another glance at the inspector, took off his glasses, polished them, and in an exceedingly dry voice said:

"Oh, yes."

"We may as well get it over now. We have not yet got the terms of Sir Derek's will. Of course, sir, we shall have to know them."

"Oh, yes."

"Perhaps you will give me this information now. Just the round terms, you know."

It is perfectly true that people more often conform to type than depart from it. Mr. Rattisbon now completed his incredibly classical portrait of the family lawyer by placing together the tips of his fingers. He did this over the top of his bowler. He then regarded Alleyn steadily for about six seconds and said:

"There are four legacies of one thousand pounds each and two of five hundred. The residue is divided between his wife and his sister in the proportion of two-thirds to Lady O'Callaghan and one-third to Miss Catherine Ruth O'Callaghan."

"And the amount of the entire estate? Again in round terms?"

"Eighty-five thousand pounds."

"Thank you so much, Mr. Rattisbon. Perhaps later on I may see the will, but at the moment that is all we want. To whom do the legacies go?"

"To the funds of the Conservative Party, to the London Hospital, to his godchild, Henry Derek Samond, and to the Dorset Benevolent Fund, one thousand in each instance. To Mr. Ronald Jameson, his secretary, five hundred pounds. To be divided among his servants in equal portions of one hundred each, the sum of five hundred pounds."

Alleyn produced his notebook and took this down. Mr. Rattisbon got up.

"I must keep you no longer, Inspector Alleyn. This is an extremely distressing affair. I trust that the police may ultimately—um——"

"I trust so, sir," said Alleyn. He rose and opened the door.

"Oh, thank-yer, thank-yer," ejaculated Mr. Rattisbon. He shot across the room, paused, and darted a final look at Alleyn.

"My nephew tells me you were at school together," he said. "Henry Rattisbon, Lady O'Callaghan's brother."

"I believe we were," answered Alleyn politely.

"Yes. Interesting work here? Like it?"

"It's not a bad job."

"Um? Oh, quite. Well, wish you success," said Mr. Rattisbon, who had suddenly become startlingly human. "And don't let poor Miss Ruth mislead you."

"I'll try not to. Thank you so much, sir."

"Um? Not at all, not at all. Quite the reverse. Good morning. Good morning."

Alleyn closed the door and stood in a sort of trance for some minutes. Then he screwed his face up sideways, as though in doubt, appeared to come to a decision, consulted the telephone directory, and went to call upon Mr. Harold Sage.

Mr. Sage had a chemist's shop in Knightsbridge. Inspector Alleyn walked to Hyde Park Corner and then took a bus. Mr. Sage, behind his counter, served an elderly lady with dog powders designed, no doubt, for a dyspeptic pug which sat and groaned after the manner of his kind at her feet.

"These are our own, madam," said Mr. Sage. "I think you will find they give the little fellow immediate relief."

"I *hope* so," breathed the elderly lady. "And you *really* think there's no need to worry?"

The pug uttered a lamentable groan. Mr. Sage made reassuring noises and tenderly watched them out.

"Yes, sir?" he said briskly, turning to Alleyn.

"Mr. Harold Sage?" asked the inspector.

"Yes," agreed Mr. Sage, a little surprised.

"I'm from Scotland Yard. Inspector Alleyn."

Mr. Sage opened his eyes very wide, but said nothing. He was naturally a pale young man.

"There are one or two questions I should like to ask you, Mr. Sage," continued Alleyn. "Perhaps we could go somewhere a little more private? I shan't keep you more than a minute or two."

"Mr. Brayght," said Mr. Sage loudly.

A sleek youth darted out from behind a pharmaceutical display.

"Serve, please," said Mr. Sage. "Will you just walk this way?" he asked Alleyn and led him down a flight of dark steps into a storeroom which smelt of chemicals. He moved some packages off the only two chairs and stacked them up, very methodically, in a dark corner of the room. Then he turned to Alleyn.

"Will you take a chair?" he asked.

"Thank you. I've called to check up one or two points that have arisen in my department. I think you may be able to help us."

142

"In what connection?"

"Oh, minor details," said Alleyn vaguely. "Nothing very exciting, I'm afraid. I don't want to take up too much of your time. It's in connection with certain medicines at present on the market. I believe you sell a number of remedies made up from your own prescriptions—such as the pug's powders, for instance?" He smiled genially.

"Oh—quayte," said Mr. Sage.

"You do? Right. Now with reference to a certain prescription which you have made up for a Miss Ruth O'Callaghan."

"Pardon?"

"With reference to a certain prescription you made up for a Miss Ruth O'Callaghan."

"I know the lady you mean. She has been a customer for quite a while."

"Yes. This was one of your own prescriptions?"

"Speaking from memory, I think she has had several of my little lines—from tayme to tayme."

"Yes. Do you remember a drug you supplied three weeks ago?"

"I'm afraid I don't remember off-hand——"

"This is the one that contained hyoscine," said Alleyn. In the long silence that followed Alleyn heard the shop door buzzer go, heard footsteps and voices above his head, heard the sound of the Brompton Road train down beneath them and felt its vibration. He watched Harold Sage. If there was no hyoscine in any of the drugs, the chemist would say so, would protest, would be bewildered. If there was hyoscine, an innocuous amount, he might or might not be flustered. If there was hyoscine, a fatal amount—what would he say?

"Yes," said Mr. Sage.

"What was the name of this medicine?"

" 'Fulvitavolts.' "

"Ah, yes. Do you know if she used it herself or bought it for anyone else?"

"I reely can't say. For herself, I think."

"She did not tell you if she wanted it for her brother?"

"I reely don't remember, not for certain. I think she said something about her brother."

"May I see a packet of this medicine?"

Mr Sage turned to his shelves, ferreted for some time and finally produced an oblong package. Alleyn looked at the spirited picture of a nude gentleman against an electric shock.

"Oh, this is not the one, Mr. Sage," he said brightly. "I mean the stuff in the round box—so big—that you supplied afterwards. This has hyoscine in it as well, has it? What was the other?"

"It was simply a prescription. I—I made it up for Miss O'Callaghan."

"From a doctor's prescription, do you mean?"

"Yes."

"Who was the doctor?"

"I reely forget. The prescription was returned with the powder."

"Have you kept a record?"

"No."

"But surely you have a prescription-book or whatever it is called?"

"I—yes—but—er—an oversight—it should have been entered."

"How much hyoscine was there in this prescription?"

"May I ask," said Mr. Sage, "why you think it contained hyoscine at all?"

"You have made that quite clear yourself. How much?"

"I—think—about one two-hundreth—something very small."

"And in 'Fulvitavolts'?"

"Less. One two-hundred-and-fiftieth."

"Do you know that Sir Derek O'Callaghan was probably murdered?"

"My Gawd, yes."

"Yes … With hyoscine."

"My Gawd, yes."

"Yes. So you see we want to be sure of our facts."

"He 'ad no hoverdose of 'yoscine from 'ere," said Mr. Sage, incontinently casting his aitches all over the place.

"So it seems. But, you see, if he had taken hyoscine in the minutest quantity before the operation we want to trace it as closely as possible. If Miss O'Callaghan gave him 'Fulvitavolts' and this other medicine, that would account for some of the hyoscine found at the post-mortem. Hyoscine was also injected at the operation. That would account for more."

"You passed the remark that he was murdered," said Mr. Sage more collectedly.

"The coroner did," corrected Alleyn. "Still, we've got to explore the possibility of accident. If you could give me the name of the doctor who prescribed the powder, it would be a great help."

"I can't remember. I make up hundreds of prescriptions every week."

"Do you often forget to enter them?"

Mr. Sage was silent.

Alleyn took out a pencil and an envelope. On the envelope he wrote three names.

"Was it any of those?" he asked.

"No."

"Will you swear to that?"

"Yes. Yes, I would."

"Look here, Mr. Sage, are you sure it wasn't your own prescription that you gave Miss O'Callaghan?"

" 'Fulvitavolts' is my own invention. I told you that."

"But the other?"

"No, I tell you—no."

"Very well. Are you in sympathy with Comrade Kakaroff over the death of Sir Derek O'Callaghan?"

Mr. Sage opened his mouth and shut it again. He put his hands behind him and leant against a shelf.

"To what do you refer?" he said.

"You were at the meeting last night."

"I don't hold with the remarks passed at the meeting. I never 'ave. I've said so. I said so last night."

"Right. I don't think there's anything else."

Alleyn put the packet of 'Fulvitavolts' in his pocket.

"How much are these?"

"Three and nine."

Alleyn produced two half-crowns and handed them to Mr. Sage, who, without another word, walked out of the room and upstairs to the shop. Alleyn followed. Mr. Sage punched the cash register and conjured up the change. The sleek young man leant with an encouraging smile towards an incoming customer.

"Thank you very much, sir," said Mr. Sage, handing Alleyn one and threepence.

"Thank you. Good morning."

"Good morning, sir."

Alleyn went to the nearest telephone-booth and rang up the Yard.

"Anything come in for me?"

"Just a moment, sir ... Yes. Sir John Phillips is here and wants to see you."

"Oh. Is he in my room?"

"Yes."

"Ask him to speak to me, will you?"

A pause.

"Hallo."

"Hallo. Is that Sir John Phillips?"

"Yes. Inspector Alleyn—I want to see you. I want to make a clean breast of it."

"I'll be there in ten minutes," said Alleyn.

CHAPTER XV

The "Clean Breast" of Sir John Phillips

Wednesday to Thursday.

Phillips stared at Chief Inspector Alleyn's locked desk, at his chair, at the pattern of thick yellow sunlight on the floor of his room. He looked again at his watch. Ten minutes since Alleyn had rung up. He said he would be there in ten minutes. Phillips knew what he was going to say. There was no need to go over that again. He went over it again. A light footstep in the passage outside. The door handle turned. Alleyn came in.

"Good morning, sir," he said. "I'm afraid I've kept you waiting." He hung up his hat, pulled off his gloves and sat down at his desk. Phillips watched him without speaking. Alleyn unlocked the desk and then turned towards his visitor.

"What is it you want to tell me, Sir John?"

"I've come to make a statement. I'll write it down afterwards if you like. Sign it. That's what you have to do, isn't it?"

"Suppose I hear what it's all about first," suggested Alleyn.

"Ever since you went away yesterday I've been thinking about this case. It seems to me I must be suspected of the murder. It seems to me things look very black for me. You know what I wrote to O'Callaghan. You know I injected a lethal drug. I showed you the tablets—analysis will prove they only contain the normal dosage, but I can't prove the one I gave was the same as the ones you analysed. I can't prove I only gave one tablet. Can I?"

"So far as I know, you can't."

"I've thought of all that. I didn't kill O'Callaghan. I threatened to kill him. You've seen Thoms. Thoms is a decent little ass, but I can see he thinks you suspect me. He's probably told you I used a lot of water for the injection and then bit his head off because he said so. So I did. He drove me nearly crazy with his bloody facetiousness. Jane—Nurse Harden—told me what you'd said to her. You know a hell of a lot—I can see that. You possibly know what I'm going to tell you. I want her to marry me. She won't, because of the other business with O'Callaghan. I think she believes I killed him. I think she was afraid at the time. That's why she was so upset, why she hesitated over the serum, why she fainted. She was afraid I'd kill O'Callaghan. She heard Thoms tell me about that play. D'you know about the play?"

"Thoms mentioned that you discussed it."

"Silly ass. He's an intelligent surgeon, but in other matters he's got as much *savoir-faire* as a child. He'd swear his soul away I didn't do it and then blurt out something like that. What I want to make clear to you is this. Jane Harden's distress in the theatre was on my account. She thinks I murdered O'Callaghan. I know she does, because she won't ask me. Don't, for God's sake, put any other interpretation on it. She's got a preposterous idea that she's ruined my life. Her nerves are all to blazes. She's anaemic and she's hysterical. If you arrest me, she may come forward with some damn' statement calculated to drag a red herring across my trail. She's an idealist. It's a type I don't pretend to understand. She did nothing to the syringe containing the serum. When Thoms cursed her for delaying, I turned and looked at her. She simply stood there dazed and half fainting. She's as innocent as— I was going to say as I am, but that may not carry much weight. She's completely innocent."

He stopped abruptly. To Alleyn it had seemed a most remarkable little scene. The change in Phillips's manner alone was extraordinary. The smooth, guarded courtesy which had characterised it during their former interview had vanished completely. He had spoken rapidly, as if urged by some appalling necessity. He now sat glaring at Alleyn with a hint of resigned ferociousness.

"Is that all you came to tell me, Sir John?" asked Alleyn in his most non-committal voice.

"All? What do you mean?"

"Well, you see, you prepared me for a bombshell, I wondered what on earth was coming. You talked of making a clean breast of it, but, forgive me, you've told me little that we did not already know."

Phillips took his time over answering this. At last he said:

"I suppose that's true. Look here, Alleyn. Can you give me your assurance that you entertain no suspicions as regards Jane Harden?"

"I'm afraid I can't. I shall consider everything you have told me very carefully, but I cannot, at this stage, make a definite announcement of that sort. Miss Harden is in a very equivocal position. I hope she may be cleared, but I cannot put her aside simply because, to put it baldly, you tell me she is innocent."

Phillips was silent. After a moment he clasped his well-shaped, well-kept hands together, and looking at them attentively, began to speak again.

"There's something more. Has Thoms told you that I opened a new tube of tablets for the hyoscine injection?"

Alleyn did not move, but he seemed to come to attention.

"Oh yes," he said quietly.

"He has! Lord, what an ingenuous little creature it is! Did you attach any significance to this second tube?"

"I remembered it."

"Then listen. During the week before the operation I'd been pretty well at the end of my tether. I suppose when a man of my age gets it, he gets it badly—the psychologists say so—and—well, I could think of nothing but the ghastly position we were in— Jane and I. That Friday when I went to see O'Callaghan I was nearly driven crazy by his damned insufferable complacence. I *could* have murdered him then. I wasn't sleeping. I tried alcohol and I tried hypnotics. I was in a bad way, Alleyn. Then on top of it he came in, a sick man, and I had to operate. Thoms rubbed it in with his damn-fool story of some play or other. I scarcely knew what I did. I seemed to behave like an automaton." He stopped short and raised his eyes from the contemplation of his hands. "It's possible," he said, "that I may have made a mistake over the first tube. It may not have been empty."

"Even if the tube had been full," suggested Alleyn, "would that explain how the tablets got into the measure-glass?"

"I ... what do you say?"

"You say that the first tube may not have been empty, and you wish me to infer from this that you are responsible for Sir Derek's death?"

"I ... I ... That is my suggestion," stammered Phillips.

"Deliberately responsible or accidentally?"

149

"I am not a murderer," said Phillips angrily.

"Then how did the tablets get into the measure-glass?"

Phillips was silent.

The inspector waited for a moment and then, with an unusual inflexion in his deep voice, he said:

"So you don't understand the idealistic type?"

"What! No!"

"I don't believe you."

Phillips stared at him, flushed painfully and then shrugged his shoulders. "Do you want a written statement of all this?" he asked.

"I don't think so. Later, if it's necessary. You have been very frank. I appreciate both the honesty and the motive. Look here—what can you tell me to help yourself? It's an unusual question from a police officer, but—there it is."

"I don't know. I suppose the case against me, apart from the suggestion I have just made, is that I gave him an overdose of hyoscine. It looks fishy, my giving the injection at all, but it is my usual practice, especially when Roberts is the anæsthetist, as he dislikes the business. It looks still more suspicious using a lot of water. That, again, is my usual practice. I can prove it. I can prove that I suggested another surgeon to Lady O'Callaghan and that she urged me to operate. That's all. Except that I don't think—No, that's all."

"Have you any theories about other people?"

"Who did it, you mean? None. I imagine it was political. How it was done, I've no idea. I can't possibly suspect any of the people who worked with me. It's unthinkable. Besides—why? You said something about patent medicines. Is there anything there?"

"We're on that tack now. I don't know if there's anything in it. By the way, why does Dr. Roberts object to giving injections?"

"A private reason. Nothing that can have any bearing on the case."

"Is it because he once gave an overdose?"

"If you knew that, why did you ask me? Testing my veracity?"

"Put it like that. He was never alone with the patient?"

"No. No, never."

"Was any one of the nurses alone in the theatre before the operation?"

"The nurses? I don't know. I wouldn't notice what they did.

They'd been preparing for some time before we came on the scene."

"We?"

"Thoms, Roberts and myself."

"What about Mr. Thoms?"

"I can't remember. He may have dodged in to have a look round."

"Yes. I think I must have a reconstruction. Can you spare the time to-day or to-morrow?"

"You mean you want to go through the whole business in pantomime?"

"If I may. We can hardly do it actually, unless I discover a P.C. suffering from an acute abscess of the appendix."

Phillips smiled sardonically.

"I might give him too much hyoscine if you did," he said. "Do you want the whole pack of them?"

"If it's possible."

"Unless there's an urgent case, nothing happens in the afternoon. I hardly think there will be an urgent case. Business," added Phillips grimly, "will probably fall off. My last major operation is enjoying somewhat unfavourable publicity."

"Well—will you get the others for me for to-morrow afternoon?"

"I'll try. It'll be very unpleasant. Nurse Banks has left us, but she can be found."

"She's at the Nurses' Club in Chelsea."

Phillips glanced quickly at him.

"Is she?" he said shortly. "Very well. Will five o'clock suit you?"

"Admirably. Can we have it all as closely reproduced as possible—same impedimenta and so on?"

"I think it can be arranged. I'll let you know." Phillips went to the door.

"Good-bye for the moment," he said. "I've no idea whether or not you think I killed O'Callaghan, but you've been very polite."

"We are taught manners at the same time as point-duty," said Alleyn. Phillips went away and Alleyn sought out Detective-Inspector Fox, to whom he related the events of the morning. When he came to Phillips's visit Fox thrust out his under lip and looked at his boots.

"That's your disillusioned expression, Fox," said Alleyn.

"What's it in aid of?"

"Well, sir, I must say I have my doubts about this self-sacrifice business. It sounds very nice, but it isn't the stuff people hand out when they think it may be returned to them tied up with rope."

"I can't believe you were no good at composition. Do you mean you mistrust Phillips's motive in coming here, or Nurse Harden's hypothetical attempt to decoy my attention?"

"Both, but more particularly number one. To my way of thinking, we've got a better case against Sir John Phillips than any of the others. I believe you're right about the political side—it's not worth a great deal. Now Sir John knows how black it looks against him. What's he do? He comes here, says he wants to make a clean breast of it, and tells you nothing you don't know already. When you point this out to him he says he may have made a slip over the two tubes. Do you believe that, chief?"

"No—to do the job he'd have had to dissolve the contents of a full tube. However dopey he felt he couldn't do that by mistake."

"Just so. And he knows you'll think of that. You ask me, sir," said Fox oratorically: " 'What's the man's motive?' "

"What's the man's motive?" repeated Alleyn obediently.

"Spoof's his motive. He knows it's going to be a tricky business bringing it home to him and he wants to create a good impression. The young lady may or may not have been in collusion with him. She may or may not come forward with the same kind of tale. 'Oh, please don't arrest him; arrest me. I never did it, but spare the boy-friend,' " said Fox in a very singular falsetto and with dreadful scorn.

Alleyn's mouth twitched. Rather hurriedly he lit a cigarette. "You seem very determined all of a sudden," he observed mildly. "This morning you seduced me with tales of Sage, Banks, and Roberts."

"So I did, sir. It was an avenue that had to be explored. Boys is exploring, and as far as he's got it's a wash-out."

"Alack, what news are these! Discover them."

"Boys got hold of Robinson, and Robinson says it's all my eye. He says he's dead certain the Bolshie push hasn't an idea who killed O'Callaghan. He says if they'd had anything to do with it he'd have heard something. It was Kakaroff who told him about it and Kakaroff was knocked sideways at the news. Robinson says if there had been any organisation from that quarter they'd have kept quiet and we'd have had no rejoicing. They're as pleased as punch and as innocent as angels."

"Charming! All clapping their hands in childish glee. How about Dr. Roberts?"

"I asked him about the doctor. It seems they don't know anything much about him and look upon him as a bit of an outsider. They've even suspected him of being what they call 'unsound'. Robinson wondered if he was one of our men. You recollect Marcus Barker sent out a lot of pamphlets on the Sterilisation Bill. They took it up for a time. Well, the doctor is interested in the Bill."

"Yes, of course," agreed Alleyn thoughtfully. "It's in his territory."

"From the look of some of the sons of the Soviet," said Fox, "I'd say they'd be the first to suffer. The doctor saw one of these pamphlets and went to a meeting. He joined the Lenin Hall lot because he thought they'd push it. Robinson says he's always nagging at them to take it up again."

"So that's that. It sounds reasonable enough, Fox, and certainly consistent with Roberts's character. With his views on eugenics he'd be sure to support sterilisation. You don't need to be a Bolshie to see the sense of it, either. It looks as though Roberts had merely been thrown in to make it more difficult."

Fox looked profound.

"What about Miss Banks and little Harold?" asked Alleyn.

"Nothing much. The Banks party has been chucking her weight about ever since the operation, but she doesn't say anything useful. You might call it reflected glory."

"How like Banks. And Sage?"

"Robinson hasn't heard anything. Sage is not a prominent member."

"He was lying about the second dose Miss O'Callaghan gave O'Callaghan. He admitted he had provided it, that it was from a doctor's prescription, and that he had not noted it in his book. All my eye. We can sift that out easily enough by finding out her doctor, but of course Sage may simply be scared and as innocent as a babe. Well, there we are. Back again face to face with the clean breast of Sir John Phillips."

"Not so clean, if you ask me."

"I wonder. I'm doing a reconstruction to-morrow afternoon. Phillips is arranging it for me. Would you say he was a great loss to the stage?"

"How do you mean, chief?"

"If he's our man, he's one of the best actors I've ever met. You come along to-morrow to the hospital, Fox, and see what you shall see. Five o'clock. And now I'm going to lunch. I want to see Lady O'Callaghan before the show, and Roberts too, if possible. I may as well get his version of the Lenin Hall lot. *Au revoir*, Fox."

"Do you mind repeating that, sir?"

"*Au revoir.*"

"*Au revoir*, monsieur," said Fox carefully.

"I'm coming to hear those records of yours one of these nights, if I may."

Fox became plum-coloured with suppressed pleasure.

"I'd take it very kindly," he said stiffly and went out.

Alleyn rang up the house in Catherine Street and learnt that Lady O'Callaghan would be pleased to receive him at ten to three the following afternoon. He spent half an hour on his file of the case. The analyst's report on Phillips's tablets and the hyoscine solution had come in. Both contained the usual dosage. He sent off the 'Fulvitavolts' and the scrap of paper that had enclosed Ruth O'Callaghan's second remedy. It was possible, but extremely unlikely, that there might be a trace of the drug spilt on the wrapper. At one o'clock he went home and lunched. At two o'clock he rang up the Yard and found there was a message from Sir John Phillips to the effect that the reconstruction could be held the following afternoon at the time suggested. He asked them to tell Fox and then rang Phillips up and thanked him.

Alleyn spent the rest of the day adding to the file on the case and in writing a sort of résumé for his own instruction. He sat over it until ten o'clock and then deliberately put it aside, read the second act of *Hamlet*, and wondered, not for the first time, what sort of a hash the Prince of Denmark would have made of a job at the Yard. Then, being very weary, he went to bed.

The next morning he reviewed his notes, particularly that part of them which referred to hyoscine.

"Possible sources of hyoscine," he had written:

"1. *The bottle of stock solution*.

"Probably Banks, Marigold, Harden, Thoms, Phillips, all had opportunity to get at this. All in theatre before operation. Each could have filled anti-gas syringe with hyoscine. If this was done, someone had since filled up bottle with 10 c.c.'s of the correct solution. No one could have done this during the operation.

Could it have been done later? No good looking for prints.

"2. *The tablets.*

"Phillips could have given an overdose when he prepared the syringe. May have to trace his purchases of h.

"3. *The patent medicines.*

"(a) '*Fulvitavolts.*' Negligible quantity unless Sage had doctored packet supplied to Ruth. Check up.

"(b) *The second p.m.* (more p.m.'s!) supplied to Ruth. May have been lethal dose concocted by Sage, hoping to do in O'Callaghan, marry Ruth and the money, and strike a blow for Lenin, Love and Liberty."

After contemplating these remarks with some disgust Alleyn went to the hospital, made further arrangements for the reconstruction at five and after a good deal of trouble succeeded in getting no farther with the matter of the stock solution. He then visited the firm that supplied Sir John Phillips with drugs and learnt nothing that was of the remotest help. He then lunched and went to call on Lady O'Callaghan. Nash received him with that particular nuance of condescension that hitherto he had reserved for politicians. He was shown into the drawing-room, an apartment of great elegance and no character. Above the mantelpiece hung a portrait in pastel of Cicely O'Callaghan. The artist had dealt competently with the shining texture of the dress and hair, and had made a conscientious map of the face. Alleyn felt he would get about as much change from the original as he would from the picture. She came in, gave him a colourless greeting, and asked him to sit down.

"I'm so sorry to worry you again," Alleyn began. 'It's a small matter, one of those loose ends that probably mean nothing, but have to be tidied up."

"Yes. I shall be pleased to give you any help. I hope everything is quite satisfactory?" she said. She might have been talking about a new hot-water system.

"I hope it will be," rejoined Alleyn. "At the moment we are investigating any possible sources of hyoscine. Lady O'Callaghan, can you tell me if Sir Derek had taken any drugs of any sort at all before the operation?" As she did not answer immediately, he added quickly: "You see, if he had taken any medicine containing hyoscine, it would be necesary to try and arrive at the amount in order to allow for it."

"Yes," she said, "I see."

155

"Had he, do you know, taken any medicine? Perhaps when the pain was very bad?"

"My husband disliked drugs of all kinds."

"Then Miss Ruth O'Callaghan's suggestion about a remedy she was interested in would not appeal to him?"

"No. He thought it rather a foolish suggestion."

"I'm sorry to hammer away at it like this, but do you think there'a a remote possibility that he did take a dose? I believe Miss O'Callaghan did actually leave some medicine here—something called 'Fulvitavolts,' I think she said it was?"

"Yes. She left a packet here."

"Was it lying about where he might see it?"

"I'm afraid I don't remember. The servants, perhaps——" Her voice trailed away. "If it's at all important——" she said vaguely.

"It is rather."

"I am afraid I don't quite understand why. Obviously my husband was killed at the hospital."

"That," said Alleyn, "is one of the theories. The 'Fulvitavolts' are of some importance because they contain a small amount of hyoscine. You will understand that we must account for any hyoscine—even the smallest amount—that was given?"

"Yes," said Lady O'Callaghan. She looked serenely over his head for a few seconds and then added: "I'm afraid I cannot help you. I hope my sister-in-law, who is already upset by what has happened, will not be unnecessarily distressed by suggestions that she was responsible in any way."

"I hope not," echoed Alleyn blandly. "Probably, as you say, he did not touch the 'Fulvitavolts'. When did Miss O'Callaghan bring them?"

"I believe one night before the operation."

"Was it the night Sir John Phillips called?"

"That was on the Friday."

"Yes—was it then, do you remember?"

"I think perhaps it was."

"Can you tell me exactly what happened?"

"No, about Miss O'Callaghan."

She took a cigarette from a box by her chair. Alleyn jumped up and lit it for her. It rather surprised him to find that she smoked. It gave her an uncanny resemblance to something human.

"Can you remember at all?" he said.

"My sister-in-law often came in after dinner. At times my

husband found these visits a little trying. He liked to be quiet in the evenings. I believe on that night he suggested that she should be told he was out. However, she came in. We were in the study."

"You both saw her, then?"

"Yes."

"What happened?"

"She urged him to try this medicine. He put her off. I told her he expected Sir John Phillips and that we ought to leave them alone. I remember she and I met Sir John in the hall. I thought his manner very odd, as I believe I told you."

"So you went out, leaving the medicine in the study?"

"I suppose so—yes."

"Did you come across it again?"

"I don't think so."

"May I speak to your butler—Nash, isn't it?"

"If you think it is any help." She rang the bell.

Nash came in and waited.

"Mr. Alleyn wants to speak to you, Nash," said Lady O"Callaghan. Nash turned a respectful eye towards him.

"I want you to think back to the Friday evening before Sir Derek's operation," Alleyn began. "Do you remember that evening?"

"Yes, sir."

"There were visitors?"

"Yes, sir. Miss O'Callaghan and Sir John Phillips."

"Exactly. Do you remember noticing a chemist's parcel anywhere in the study?"

"Yes, sir. Miss O'Callaghan brought it with her, I believe."

"That's the one. What happened to it?"

"I had it removed to a cupboard in Sir Derek's bathroom the following morning, sir."

"I see. Had it been opened?"

"Oh, yes, sir."

"Can you find it now, Nash, do you think?"

"I will ascertain, sir."

"Do you mind, Lady O'Callaghan?" asked Alleyn apologetically.

"Of course not."

Nash inclined his head solemnly and left the room. While he was away there was a rather uncomfortable silence. Alleyn, looking very remote and polite, made no effort to break it. Nash returned after a few minutes with the now familiar carton, on a silver salver. Alleyn took it and thanked him. Nash departed.

"Here it is," said the inspector cheerfully. "Oh, yes, Nash was quite right; it has been opened and—let me see—one powder has been taken. That doesn't amount to much." He put the carton in his pocket and turned to Lady O'Callaghan. "It seems ridiculous, I know, to worry about so small a matter, but it's part of our job to pick up every thread, however unimportant. This, I suppose, was the last effort Miss O'Callaghan made to interest Sir Derek in any remedy?"

Again she waited for a few seconds.

"Yes," she murmured at last. "I believe so."

"She did not mention another remedy to you after he had been taken to the hospital?"

"Really, Inspector Alleyn, I cannot possibly remember. My sister-in-law talks a great deal about patent medicines. She tries to persuade everyone she knows to take them. I believe my uncle, Mr. James Rattisbon, has already explained this to you. He tells me that he made it quite clear that we did not wish the matter to be pursued."

"I am afraid I cannot help pursuing it."

"But Mr. Rattisbon definitely instructed you."

"Please forgive me," said Alleyn very quietly, "if I seem to be unduly officious." He paused. She looked at him with a kind of cold huffiness. After a moment he went on. "I wonder if you have ever seen or read a play called *Justice*, by Galsworthy? It is no doubt very dated, but there is an idea in it that I think explains far better than I can the position of people who become involved, whether voluntarily or involuntarily, with the law. Galsworthy made one of his characters—a lawyer, I think—say that once you have set in motion the chariot wheels of Justice, you can do nothing at all to arrest or deflect their progress. Lady O'Callaghan, that is the exact truth. You, very properly, decided to place this tragic case in the hands of the police. In doing so you switched on a piece of complicated and automatic machinery which, once started, you cannot switch off. As the police officer in charge of this case I am simply a wheel in the machine. I must complete my revolutions. Please do not think I am impertinent if I say that neither you nor any other lay person, however much involved, has the power to stop the machine of justice or indeed to influence it in any way whatever." He stopped abruptly. "I am

158

afraid you *will* think me impertinent—I have no business to talk like this. If you will excuse me——"

He bowed and turned away.

"Yes," said Lady O'Callaghan, "I quite understand. Good afternoon."

"There's one other thing." said Alleyn. "I had nearly forgotten it. It's something that you can do, if you will, to help us as regards the hospital side of the problem."

She listened, apparently without any particular surprise or agitation, to his request, and agreed at once to do as he suggested.

"Thank you very much indeed, Lady O'Callaghan. You understand that we should like Miss O'Callaghan to be with you?"

"Yes," she said after a long pause.

"Shall I see her, or—perhaps you would rather ask her yourself?"

"Perhaps that would be better. I would much prefer her to be spared this unnecessary ordeal."

"I assure you," said Alleyn dryly, "that it may save her a more unpleasant one."

"I'm afraid I do not understand you. However, I shall ask her."

In the hall he walked straight into Miss Ruth O'Callaghan. When she saw him she uttered a noise that was something between a whoop of alarm and a cry of supplication, and bolted incontinently into the drawing-room. Nash, who had evidently just admitted her, looked scandalised.

"Is Mr. Jameson in, Nash?" asked Alleyn.

"Mr. Jameson has left us, sir."

"Really?"

"Yes, sir. His duties, as you might say, have drawn to a close."

"Yes," said Alleyn, unconsciously echoing Lady O'Callaghan. "I quite understand. Good afternoon."

CHAPTER XVI

Reconstruction Begun

Thursday, the eighteenth. Afternoon.

Alleyn found he still had over an hour to wait before the reconstruction. He had tea and then rang up Dr. Roberts, found he was at home, and made his way once more to the little house in Wigmore Street. He wanted, if possible, to surprise Roberts with an unexpected reference to the Lenin Hall meeting. The diminutive man-servant admitted him and showed him into the pleasant sitting-room, where he found Roberts awaiting him.

"I hope I'm not a great nuisance," said Alleyn. "You did ask me to come back some time, you know."

"Certainly," said Roberts, shaking hands. "I am delighted to see you. Have you read my book?" He swept a sheaf of papers off a chair and pulled it forward. Alleyn sat down.

"I've dipped into it—no time really to tackle it yet, but I'm enormously interested. At Lord knows what hour this morning I read the chapter in which you refer to the Sterilisation Bill. You put the case for sterilisation better than any other sponsor I have heard."

"You think so?" said Roberts acidly. "Then you will be surprised to hear that although I have urged that matter with all the force and determination I could command, I have made not one inch of headway—not an inch! I am forced to the conclusion that most of the people who attempt to administer the government of this country are themselves certifiable." He gave a short falsetto laugh and glared indignantly at Alleyn, who contented himself with making an incredulous and sympathetic noise.

"I have done everything—everything," continued Roberts. "I

joined a group of people professing enlightened views on the matter. They assured me they would stick at nothing to force this Bill through Parliament. They professed the greatest enthusiasm. *Have* they done anything?" He paused oratorically and then in a voice of indescribable disgust he said: "They merely asked me to wait in patience till the Dawn of the Proletariat Day in Britain."

Chief Inspector Alleyn felt himself to be in the foolish position of one who sets a match to the dead stick of a rocket. Dr. Roberts had most effectively stolen his fireworks. He had a private laugh at himself. Roberts continued angrily:

"They call themselves Communists. They have no interest in the welfare of the community—none. Last night I attended one of their meetings, and I was disgusted. All they did was to rejoice for no constructive or intelligent reason over the death of the late Home Secretary."

He stopped abruptly, glanced at Alleyn, and then with that curious return to nervousness which the inspector had noticed before he said: "But, of course, I had forgotten. That is very much your business. Thoms rang me up just now to ask me if I could attend at the hospital this afternoon."

"*Thoms* rang you up?"

"Yes. Sir John had asked him to, I believe. I don't know why," said Dr. Roberts, suddenly looking surprised and rather bewildered, "but I sometimes find Thoms's manner rather aggravating."

"Do you?" murmured Alleyn, smiling. "He is rather facetious."

"Facetious! Exactly. And this afternoon I found his facetiousness in bad taste."

"What did he say?"

"He said something to the effect that if I wished to make my get-away he would be pleased to lend me a pair of ginger-coloured whiskers and a false nose. I thought it in bad taste."

"Certainly," said Alleyn, hurriedly blowing his own nose.

"Of course," continued Dr. Roberts, "Mr. Thoms knows himself to be in an impregnable position, since he could not have given any injection without being observed, and had no hand in preparing the injection which he did give. I felt inclined to point out to him that I myself am somewhat similarly situated, but do not feel, on that account, free to indulge in buffoonery."

"I suppose Mr. Thoms was in the anteroom all the time until you went into the theatre?"

"I've no idea," said Roberts stiffly. "I myself merely went to the anteroom with Sir John, said what was necessary, and joined my patient in the anæsthetic-room."

"Ah, well—we shall get a better idea of all your movements from the reconstruction."

"I suppose so," agreed Roberts, looking perturbed. "It will be a distressing experience for all of us. Except, no doubt, Mr. Thoms."

He waited a moment and then said nervously:

"Perhaps this is a question that I should not ask, Inspector Alleyn, but I cannot help wondering if the police have a definite theory as regards this crime?"

Alleyn was used to this question.

"We've got several theories, Dr. Roberts, and all of them more or less fit. That's the devil of it."

"Have you explored the possibility of suicide?" asked Roberts wistfully.

"I have considered it."

"Remember his heredity."

"I have remembered it. After he had the attack in the House his physical condition would have rendered suicide impossible, and he could hardly have taken hyoscine while making his speech."

"Again remember his heredity. He might have carried hyoscine tablets with him for some time and under the emotional stimulus of the occasion suffered a sudden ungovernable impulse. In the study of suicidal psychology one comes across many such cases. Did his hand go to his mouth while he was speaking? I see you look incredulous, Inspector Alleyn. Perhaps you even think it suspicious that I should urge the point. I—I—*have* a reason for hoping you find that O'Callaghan killed himself, but it does not spring from a sense of guilt."

A strangely exalted look came into the little doctor's eyes as he spoke. Alleyn regarded him intently.

"Dr. Roberts," he said at last, "why not tell me what is in your mind?"

"No," said Robert's emphatically, "no—not unless—unless the worst happens."

"Well," said Alleyn, "as you know, I can't force you to give me your theory, but it's a dangerous business, withholding information in a capital charge."

"It may not be a capital charge," cried Roberts in a hurry.

162

"Even suppose your suicide theory is possible, it seems to me that a man of Sir Derek's stamp would not have done it in such a way as to cast suspicion upon other people."

"No," agreed Roberts. "No. That is undoubtedly a strong argument—and yet inherited suicidal mania sometimes manifests itself very abruptly and strangely. I have known instances——"

He went to his bookcase and took down several volumes, from which he read in a rapid, dry and didactic manner, rather as though Alleyn was a collection of students. This went on for some time. The servant brought in tea, and with an air of patient benevolence, poured it out himself. He placed Roberts's cup on a table under his nose, waited until the doctor closed the book with which he was at the moment engaged, took it firmly from him and directed his attention to the tea. He then moved the table between the two men and left the room.

"Thank you," said Roberts vaguely some time after he had gone.

Roberts, still delivering himself of his learning, completely forgot to drink his tea or to offer some to Alleyn, but occasionally stretched out a hand towards the toast. The time passed rapidly. Alleyn looked at his watch.

"Good Lord!" he exclaimed, "it's half-past four. We'll have to collect ourselves, I'm afraid."

"Tch!" said Roberts crossly.

"I'll call a taxi."

"No, no. I'll drive you there, Inspector. Wait a moment." He darted out into the hall and gave flurried orders to the little servant who silently insinuated him into his coat and gave him his hat. Roberts shot back into the sitting-room and fetched his stethoscope.

"What about your anæsthetising apparatus?" ventured Alleyn.

"Eh?" asked Roberts squinting round at him.

"Your anæsthetising apparatus."

"D'you want that?"

"Please—if it's not a great bore. Didn't Sir John tell you?"

"I'll get it," said Roberts. He darted off across the little hall.

"Can I assist you, sir?" asked the servant.

"No, no. Bring out the car."

He reappeared presently, wheeling the cruet-like apparatus with its enormous cylinders.

"You can't carry that down the steps by yourself," said Alleyn.

"Let me help."

"Thank you, thank you," said Roberts. He bent down and examined the nuts that fastened the frame at the bottom. "Wouldn't do for these nuts to come loose," he said. "You take the top, will you? Gently. Ease it down the steps."

With a good deal of bother they got the thing into Roberts's car and drove off to Brook Street, the little doctor talking most of the time.

As they drew near the hospital, however, he grew quieter, seemed to get nervous, and kept catching Alleyn's eye and hurriedly looking away again. After this had happened some three or four times Roberts laughed uncomfortably.

"I—I'm not looking forward to this experiment," he said. "One gets moderately case-hardened in our profession, I suppose, but there's something about this affair"—he blinked hard twice—"something profoundly disquieting. Perhaps it is the element of uncertainty."

"But you have got a theory, Dr. Roberts?"

"I? No. I did hope it might be suicide. No—I've no specific theory."

"Oh, well. If you won't tell me, you won't," rejoined Alleyn. Roberts looked at him in alarm, but said no more.

At Brook Street they found Fox placidly contemplating the marble woman in the waiting-room. He was accompanied by Inspector Boys, a large red-faced officer with a fruity voice and hands like hams. Boys kept a benevolent but shrewd eye on the activities of communistic societies, on near-treasonable propagandists, and on Soviet-minded booksellers. He was in the habit of alluding to such persons who came into these categories as though they were tiresome but harmless children.

"Hallo," said Alleyn. "Where are the star turns?"

"The nurses are getting the operating theatre ready," Fox told him. "Sir John Phillips asked me to let him know when we are ready. The other ladies are upstairs."

"Right. Mr. Thoms here?"

"Is that the funny gentleman, sir?" asked Boys.

"It is."

"He's here."

"Then in that case we're complete. Dr. Roberts has gone up to the theatre. Let us follow him. Fox, let Sir John know, will you?"

Fox went away and Alleyn and Boys took the lift up to the

theatre landing, where they found the rest of the *dramatis personae* awaiting them. Mr. Thoms broke off in the middle of some anecdote with which he was apparently regaling the company.

"Hallo, 'allo, 'allo!" he shouted. "Here's the Big Noise itself. Now we shan't be long."

"Good evening, Mr. Thoms," said Alleyn. "Good evening, Matron. I hope I haven't kept you all waiting."

"Not at all," said Sister Marigold.

Fox appeared with Sir John Phillips. Alleyn spoke a word to him and then turned and surveyed the group. They eyed him uneasily and perhaps inimically. It was a little as though they drew together, moved by a common impulse of self-preservation. He thought they looked rather like sheep, bunched together, their heads turned watchfully towards their protective enemy, the sheep-dog.

"I'd better give a warning bark or two," thought Alleyn and addressed them collectively.

"I'm quite sure," he began, "that you all realise why we have asked you to meet us here. It is, of course, in order to enlist your help. We are faced with a difficult problem in this case and feel that a reconstruction of the operation may go far towards clearing any suspicion of guilt from innocent individuals. As you know, Sir Derek O'Callaghan died from hyoscine poisoning. He was a man with many political enemies, and from the outset the affair has been a complicated and bewildering problem. The fact that he, in the course of the operation, was given a legitimate injection of hyoscine has added to the complications. I am sure you are all as anxious as we are to clear up this aspect of the case. I ask you to look upon the reconstruction as an opportunity to free yourselves of any imputation of guilt. As a medium in detection the reconstruction has much to commend it. The chief argument against it is that sometimes innocent persons are moved, through nervousness or other motives, to defeat the whole object of the thing by changing the original circumstances. Under the shadow of tragedy it is not unusual for innocent individuals to imagine that the police suspect them. I am sure that you are not likely to do anything so foolish as this. I am sure you realise that this is an opportunity, not a trap. Let me beg you to repeat as closely as you can your actions during the operation on the deceased. If you do this, there is not the faintest cause for alarm." He looked at his watch.

"Now then," he said. "You are to imagine that time has gone back seven days. It is twenty-five minutes to four on the afternoon of Thursday February 4th. Sir Derek O'Callaghan is upstairs in his room, awaiting his operation. Matron, when you get word will you and the nurses who are to help you begin your preparations in the anteroom and the theatre? Any dialogue you remember you will please repeat. Inspector Fox will be in the anteroom and Inspector Boys in the theatre. Please treat them as pieces of sterile machinery." He allowed himself a faint smile and turned to Phillips and Nurse Graham, the special.

"We'll go upstairs."

They went up to the next landing. Outside the door of the first room Alleyn turned to the others. Phillips was very white, but quite composed. Little Nurse Graham looked unhappy, but sensibly determined.

"Now, Nurse, we'll go in. If you'll just wait a moment, sir. Actually you are just coming upstairs."

"I see," said Phillips.

Alleyn swung open the door and followed Nurse Graham into the bedroom.

Cicely and Ruth O'Callaghan were at the window. He got the impression that Ruth had been sitting there, perhaps crouched in that arm-chair, and had sprung up when the door opened. Cicely O'Callaghan stood erect, very *grande dame* and statuesque, a gloved hand resting lightly on the window-sill.

"Good evening, Inspector Alleyn," she said. Ruth gave a loud sob and gasped "Good evening."

Alleyn felt that his only hope of avoiding a scene was to hurry things along at a business-like canter.

"It was extremely kind of you both to come," he said briskly. "I shan't keep you more than a few minutes. As you know, we are to go over the events of the operation, and I thought it better to start from here." He glanced cheerfully at Ruth.

"Certainly," said Lady O'Callaghan.

"Now." Alleyn turned towards the bed, immaculate with its smooth linen and tower of rounded pillows. "Now, Nurse Graham has brought you here. When you come in you sit—where? On each side of the bed? Is that how it was, Nurse?"

"Yes. Lady O'Callaghan was here," answered the special quietly.

"Then if you wouldn't mind taking up those positions——"

With an air of stooping to the level of a rather vulgar farce, Lady O'Callaghan sat in the chair on the right-hand side of the bed.

"Come along, Ruth," she said tranquilly.

"But why? Inspector Alleyn—it's so dreadful—so horribly cold-blooded—unnecessary. I don't understand ... You were so kind ..." She boggled over her words, turned her head towards him with a gesture of complete wretchedness. Alleyn walked quickly towards her.

"I'm so sorry," he said. "I know it's beastly. Take courage—your brother would understand, I think."

She gazed miserably at him. With her large unlovely face blotched with tears, and her pale eyes staring doubtfully up into his, she seemed dreadfully vulnerable. Something in his manner may have given her a little help. Like an obedient and unwieldy animal she got up and blundered across to the other chair.

"What now, Nurse?"

"The patient half regained consciousness soon after we came in. I heard Sir John and went out."

"Will you do that, please?"

She went away quietly.

"And now," Alleyn went on, "what happened? Did the patient speak?"

"I believe he said the pain was severe. Nothing else," murmured Lady O'Callaghan.

"What did you say to each other?"

"I—I told him it was his appendix and that the doctor would soon be here—something of that sort. He seemed to lose consciousness again, I thought."

"Did you speak to each other?"

"I don't remember."

Alleyn made a shot in the dark.

"Did you discuss his pain?"

"I do not think so," she said composedly.

Ruth turned her head and gazed with a sort of damp surprise at her sister-in-law.

"You remember doing so, do you, Miss O'Callaghan?" said Alleyn.

"I think—yes—oh, Cicely!"

"What is it?" asked Alleyn gently.

"I said something—about—how I wished—oh, Cicely!"

167

The door opened and Nurse Graham came in again.

"I think I came back about now to say Sir John would like to see Lady O'Callaghan," she said with a troubled glance at Ruth.

"Very well. Will you go out with her, please, Lady O'Callaghan?" They went out and Ruth and the inspector looked at each other across the smug little bed. Suddenly Ruth uttered a veritable howl and flung herself face-down among the appliqué-work on the counterpane.

"Listen," said Alleyn, "and tell me if I'm wrong. Mr. Sage had given you a little box of powders that he said would relieve the pain. Now the others have left the room, you feel you must give your brother one of these powders. There is the water and the glass on the table by your side. You unwrap the box, drop the paper on the floor, shake out one of the powders and give it to him in a glass of water. It seems to relieve the pain and when they return he's easier? Am I right?"

"Oh," wailed Ruth, raising her head. "Oh, how did you know? Cicely said I'd better not say. I told her. Oh, what shall I do?"

"Have you kept the box with the other powders?"

"Yes. He—they told me not to, but—but I thought if they were poison and I'd killed him——" Her voice rose with a shrill note of horror. "I thought I'd take them—myself. Kill myself. Lots of us do, you know. Great-Uncle Eustace did, and Cousin Olive Casebeck, and——"

"You're not going to do anything so cowardly. What would he have thought of you? You're going to do the brave thing and help us to find the truth. Come along," said Alleyn, for all the world as if she were a child, "come along. Where are these terrible powders? In that bag still, I don't mind betting."

"Yes," whispered Ruth, opening her eyes very wide. "They are in that bag. You're quite right. You're quite right. You're very clever to think of that. I thought if you arrested me——" She made a very strange gesture with her clenched hand, jerking it up across her mouth.

"Give them to me," said Alleyn.

She began obediently to scuffle in the vast bag. All sorts of things came shooting out. He was in a fever of impatience lest the others should return, and moved to the door. At last the round cardboard box appeared. He gathered up the rest of Ruth's junk and bundled it back as the door opened. Nurse Graham stood aside to let Phillips in.

"I think it was about now," she said.

"Right," said Alleyn. "Now, Sir John, I believe Miss O'Callaghan left the room while you examined the patient, diagnosed the trouble, and decided on an immediate operation."

"Yes. When Lady O'Callaghan returned I suggested that Somerset Black should operate."

"Quite so. Lady O'Callaghan urged you to do it yourself. Everyone agree to that?"

"Yes," said Nurse Graham quietly. Ruth merely sat and gaped. Lady O'Callaghan turned with an unusual abruptness and walked to the window.

"Then you, Sir John, went away to prepare for the operation?"

"Yes."

"That finishes this part of the business, then."

"No!"

Cicely O'Callaghan's voice rang out so fiercely that they all jumped. She had faced round and stood with her eyes fixed on Phillips. She looked magnificent. It was as if a colourless façade had been flood-lit.

"No! Why do you deliberately ignore what we all heard, what I myself have told you? Ask Sir John what my husband said when he saw who it was we had brought here to help him." She turned deliberately to Phillips. "What did Derek say to you—what did he say?"

Phillips looked at her as though he saw her for the first time. His face expressed nothing but a profound astonishment. When he answered it was with a kind of reasonableness and with no suggestion of heroics.

"He was frightened," he said.

"He cried out to us: 'Don't let——' You remember"—she appealed with assurance to Nurse Graham—"you remember what he looked like—you understood what he meant?"

"I said then," said Nurse Graham with spirit, "and I say now, that Sir Derek did not know what he was saying."

"Well," remarked Alleyn mildly, "as we all know about it I think you and I, Sir John, will go downstairs." He turned to the O'Callaghans.

"Actually, I believe you both stayed on in the hospital during the operation, but, of course, there is no need for you to do so now. Lady O'Callaghan, shall I ask for your car to take you back to Catherine Street? If you will forgive me, I must go to the theatre."

Suddenly he realised that she was in such a fury that she could not answer. He took Phillips by the elbow and propelled him through the door.

"We will leave Nurse Graham," he said, "alone with her patient."

CHAPTER XVII

Reconstruction Concluded

Thursday, the eighteenth. Late afternoon.

The "theatre party" appeared to have entered heartily into the spirit of the thing. A most convincing activity was displayed in the anteroom, where Sister Marigold, Jane Harden and a very glum-faced Banks washed and clattered while Inspector Fox, his massive form wedged into a corner, looked on with an expressionless countenance and a general air of benignity. A faint bass drone from beyond the swing-door informed Alleyn of the presence in the theatre of Inspector Boys.

"All ready, Matron?" asked Alleyn.

"Quite ready, Inspector."

"Well, here we all are." He stood aside and Phillips, Thoms and Roberts walked in.

"Are you at about the same stage as you were when the doctors came in?"

"At exactly the same stage."

"Good. What happens now?" He turned to the men. No one spoke for a moment. Roberts turned deferentially towards Phillips, who had moved across to Jane Harden. Jane and Phillips did not look at each other. Phillips appeared not to have heard Alleyn's question. Thoms cleared his throat importantly.

"Well now, let's see. If I'm not speaking out of my turn, I should say we got down to the job straight away. Roberts said he'd go along to the anæsthetic-room and Sir John, I believe, went into the theatre? That correct, sir?"

"Did you go into the theatre immediately, Sir John?" asked Alleyn.

"What? I? Yes, I believe so."

"Before you washed?"

"Naturally."

"Well, let's start, shall we? Dr. Roberts, did you go alone to the anæsthetic-room?"

"No. Nurse—er——?" Roberts blinked at Banks. "Nurse Banks went with me. I looked at the anæsthetising apparatus and asked Nurse Banks to let Sir Derek's nurse know when we were ready."

"Will you go along, then? Fox, you take over with Dr. Roberts. Now, please, Sir John."

Phillips at once went through into the theatre, followed by Alleyn. Boys broke off his subterranean humming and at a word from Alleyn took his place in the anteroom. Phillips, without speaking, crossed to the side table, which was set out as before with the three syringes in dishes of water. The surgeon took his hypodermic case from his pocket, looked at the first tube, appeared to find it empty, took out the second, and having squirted a syringeful of water into a measure-glass, dropped in a single tablet.

"That is what—what I believe I did," he said.

"And then? You returned to the anteroom? No. What about Mr. Thoms?"

"Yes. Thoms should be here now."

"Mr. Thoms, please!" shouted Alleyn.

The doors swung open and Thoms came in.

"Hallo, hallo. Want me?"

"I understood you watched Sir John take up the hyoscine solution into the syringe."

"Oh! Yes, b'lieve I did," said Thoms, rather less boisterously.

"You commented on the amount of water."

"Yes, I know, but—look here, you don't want me to go thinking——"

"I simply want a reconstruction without comment, Mr. Thoms."

"Oh, quite, quite."

Phillips stood with the syringe in his hand. He looked gravely and rather abstractedly at his assistant. At a nod from Alleyn he filled the syringe.

"It is now that Thoms remarks on the quantity of water," he said quietly. "I snub him and go back into the anæsthetic-room,

172

where I give the injection. The patient is there with the special nurse."

He took up the syringe and walked away. Thoms moved away with a grimace at Alleyn, who said abruptly:

"Just a moment, Mr. Thoms. I think you stayed behind in the theatre for a minute or two."

"No, I didn't—beg your pardon, Inspector. I thought I went out to the anteroom before Sir John moved."

"Sir John thought not, and the nurses had the impression you came in a little later."

"Maybe," said Thoms. "I really can't remember."

"Have you no idea what you did during the two or three minutes?"

"None."

"Oh. In that case I'll leave you. Boys!"

Inspector Boys returned to the theatre and Alleyn went out. In about a minute Thoms joined him.

Sir John appeared in the anteroom and washed up, assisted by Jane Harden and the matron, who afterwards helped the surgeons to dress up.

"I feel rather an ass," said Thoms brightly. Nobody answered him.

"It is now," said Phillips in the same grave, detached manner, "that Mr. Thoms tells me about the play at the Palladium."

"All agreed?" Alleyn asked the others. The women murmured an assent.

"Now what happens?"

"Pardon me, but I remember Mr. Thoms went into the theatre and then called me in to him," murmured Sister Marigold.

"Thank you, Matron. Away you go, then," Alleyn waited until the doors had swung to and then turned to where Phillips, now wearing his gown and mask, stood silently beside Jane Harden.

"So you were left alone together at this juncture?" he said, without stressing it.

"Yes," said Phillips.

"Do you mind telling me what was said?"

"Oh, please," whispered Jane. "Please, please!" It was the first time she had spoken.

"Can't you let her off this?" said Phillips. There was a sort of urgency in his voice now.

"I'm sorry—I would if I could."

173

"I'll tell him, Jane. We said it was a strange situation. I again asked her to marry me. She said no—that she felt she belonged to O'Callaghan. Something to that effect. She tried to explain her point of view."

"You've left something out—you're not thinking of yourself." She stood in front of him, for all the world as though she was prepared to keep Alleyn off. "He said then that he didn't want to operate and that he'd give anything to be out of it. His very words. He told me he'd tried to persuade—her—*his* wife—to get another surgeon. He hated the idea of operating. Does that look as though he meant any harm? Does it? He never thinks of himself—he only wants to help me, and I'm not worth it. I've told him so a hundred times——"

"Jane, my dear, don't."

There was a tap on the outer door and Roberts looked in. "I think it's time I came and washed up," he said.

"Come in, Dr. Roberts."

Roberts glanced at the others.

"Forgive me, Sir John," he began with the deference that he always used when he spoke to Phillips, "but as I remember it, Mr. Thoms came in with me at this juncture."

"You're quite right, Roberts," agreed Phillips courteously.

"Mr. Thoms, please," called Alleyn again.

Thoms shot back into the room.

"Late again, am I?" he remarked. "Truth of the matter is I can't for the life of me remember all the ins and outs of it. I suppose I wash up now? What?

"If you please," said Alleyn sedately.

At last they were ready and Roberts returned to Inspector Fox and the anæsthetic-room. The others, accompanied by Alleyn, went to the theatre.

The cluster of lights above the table had been turned up and Alleyn again felt that sense of expectancy in the theatre. Phillips went immediately to the window end of the table and waited with his gloved hands held out in front of him. Thoms stood at the foot of the table. Sister Marigold and Jane were farther away.

There was a slight vibratory, rattling noise. The door into the anæsthetic-room opened and a trolley appeared, propelled by Banks. Dr. Roberts and Nurse Graham walked behind it. His hands were stretched out over the head of the trolley. On it was a sort of elongated bundle made of pillows and blankets. He and

Banks lifted this on the table and Banks put a screen, about two feet high, across the place that represented the patient's chest. The others drew nearer. Banks pushed the trolley away.

Now that they had all closed round the table the illusion was complete. The conical glare poured itself down between the white figures, bathing their masked faces and the fronts of their gowns in a violence of light, and leaving their backs in sharp shadow, so that between shadow and light there was a kind of shimmering border that ran round their outlines. Boys and Fox had come in from their posts and stood impassive in the doorways. Alleyn walked round the theatre to a position about two yards behind the head of the table.

Roberts wheeled forward the anæsthetising apparatus. Suddenly, entirely without warning, one of the white figures gave a sharp exclamation, something between a cry and a protest.

"It's too horrible—really—I can't——!"

It was the matron, the impeccable Sister Marigold. She had raised her hands in front of her face as if shutting off some shocking spectacle. Now she backed away from the table and collided with the anæsthetising apparatus. She stumbled, kicked it so that it moved, and half fell, clutching at it as she did so.

There was a moment's silence and then a portly little figure in white suddenly screamed out an oath.

"What the bloody hell are you doing? Do you want to kill——"

"What's the matter?" said Alleyn sharply. His voice had an incisive edge that made all the white heads turn. "What is it, Mr Thoms?"

Thoms was down on his knees, an absurd figure, frantically reaching out to the apparatus. Roberts, who had stooped down to the lower framework of the cruet-like stand and had rapidly inspected it, thrust the little fat man aside. He tested the nuts that held the frame together. His hands shook a little and his face, the only one unmasked, was very pale.

"It's perfectly secure, Thoms," he said. "None of the nuts are loose. Matron, please stand away."

"I didn't mean—I'm sorry," began Sister Marigold.

"Do you realise——" said Thoms in a voice that was scarcely recognisable——"do you realise that if one of those cylinders had fallen out and burst, we'd none of us be alive. Do you know that?"

"Nonsense, Thoms," said Roberts in an unsteady voice. "It's

most unlikely that anything of the sort could occur. It would take more than that to burst a cylinder, I assure you."

"I'm sure I'm very sorry, Mr. Thoms," said Matron sulkily. "Accidents will happen."

"Accidents mustn't happen," barked Thoms. He squatted down and tested the nuts.

"Please leave it alone, Mr. Thoms," said Roberts crisply. "I assure you it's perfectly safe."

Thoms did not answer. He got to his feet and turned back to the table.

"And now what happens?" asked Alleyn. His deep voice sounded like a tonic note. Phillips spoke quietly.

"I made the incision and carried on with the operation. I found peritonitis and a ruptured abscess of the appendix. I proceeded in the usual way. At this stage, I think, Dr. Roberts began to be uneasy about the pulse and the general condition. Am I right, Roberts?"

"Quite right, sir. I asked for an injection of camphor."

Without waiting to be told, Nurse Banks went to the side table, took up the ampoule of camphor, went through the pantomime of filling a syringe and returned to the patient.

"I injected it," she said concisely.

Through Alleyn's head ran the old jingle: "A made an apple pie, B bit it, C cut it—I injected it," he added mentally.

"And then?" he asked.

"After completing the operation I asked for the anti-gas serum."

"I got it," said Jane bravely.

She walked to the table.

"I stood, hesitating. I felt faint. I—I couldn't focus things properly."

"Did anybody notice this?"

"I looked round and saw something was wrong," said Phillips. "She simply stood there swaying a little."

"You notice this, Mr. Thoms?"

"Well, I'm afraid, Inspector, I rather disgraced myself by kicking up a rumpus. What, nurse? Bit hard on you, what? Didn't know how the land lay. Too bad, wasn't it?"

"When you had finished, Nurse Harden brought the large syringe?"

"Yes."

Jane came back with the syringe on a tray. "Thoms took it," went the jingle in Alleyn's head.

"I injected it," said Thoms.

"Mr. Thoms then asked about the condition," added Roberts. "I said it was disquieting. I remember Sir John remarked that although he knew the patient personally he had had no idea he was ill. Nurse Banks and I lifted the patient on to the trolley and he was taken away."

They did this with the dummy.

"Then I fainted," said Jane.

"A dramatic finish—what?" shouted Thoms, who seemed to have quite recovered his equilibrium.

"The end," said Alleyn, "came later. The patient was then taken back to his room, where you attended him, Dr. Roberts. Was anyone with you?"

"Nurse Graham was there throughout. I left her in the room when I returned here to report on the general condition, which I considered markedly worse."

"And in the meantime Sir John and Mr. Thoms washed up in the anteroom?"

"Yes," said Phillips.

"What did you talk about?"

"I don't remember."

"Oh yes, sir, you do, surely," said Thoms. "We talked about Nurse Harden doing a faint, and I said I could see the operation had upset you, and you—" he grinned—"you first said it hadn't, you know, and then said it had. Very natural, really," he explained to Alleyn, who raised one eyebrow and turned to the nurses.

"And you cleaned up the theatre, and Miss Banks gave one of her well-known talks on the Dawn of the Proletariat Day?"

"I did," said Banks with a snap.

"Meanwhile Dr. Roberts came down and reported, and you and Mr. Thoms, Sir John, went up to the patient?"

"Yes. The matron, Sister Marigold, joined us. We found the patient's condition markedly worse. As you know, he died about half an hour later, without regaining consciousness."

"Thank you. That covers the ground. I am extremely grateful to all of you for helping us with this rather unpleasant business. I won't keep you any longer." He turned to Phillips. "You would like to get out of your uniforms, I'm sure."

"If you're finished," agreed Phillips. Fox opened the swing-door and he went through, followed by Thoms, Sister Marigold, Jane Harden, and Banks. Dr. Roberts crossed to the anæsthetising apparatus.

"I'll get this out of the way," he said.

"Oh—do you mind leaving it while you change?" said Alleyn. "I just want to make a plan of the floor."

"Certainly," said Roberts.

"Would you be very kind and see if you can beat me up a sheet of paper and a pencil, Dr. Roberts? Sorry to bother you, but I hardly like to send one of my own people hunting for it."

"Shall I ask?" suggested Roberts.

He put his head round the door into the anteroom and spoke to someone on the other side.

"Inspector Alleyn would like——"

Fox walked heavily across from the other end of the theatre.

"I can hear a telephone ringing its head off out there, sir," he said, looking fixedly at Alleyn.

"Really? I wonder if it's that call from the Yard? Go and see, will you, Fox? Sister Marigold won't mind, I'm sure."

Fox went out.

"Inspector Alleyn," ventured Roberts, "I do hope that the reconstruction has been satisfactory——" He broke off. Phillips's resonant voice could be heard in the anteroom. With a glance towards it Roberts ended wistfully:—"from every point of view."

Alleyn smiled at him, following his glance.

"From that point of view, Dr. Roberts, most satisfactory."

"I'm extremely glad."

Jane Harden came in with a sheet of paper and pencil which she gave Alleyn. She went out. Roberts watched Alleyn lay the paper on the side table and take out his steel tape measure. Fox returned.

"Telephone for Dr. Roberts, I believe, sir," he announced.

"Oh—for you, is it?" said Alleyn.

Roberts went out through the anæsthetic-room.

"Shut that door, quick," said Alleyn urgently.

Evidently he had changed his mind about making a plan. He darted like a cat across the room and bent over the frame of the anæsthetic apparatus. His fingers were busy with the nuts.

Boys stood in front of one door, Fox by the other.

"Hell's teeth, it's stiff," muttered Alleyn.

178

The double doors from the anteroom opened suddenly, banging Inspector Boys in the broad of his extensive back.

"Just a minute, sir, just a minute," he rumbled.

Under his extended arm appeared the face of Mr. Thoms. His eyes were fixed on Alleyn.

"What are you doing?" he said. "What are you doing?"

"Just a minute, if you please, sir," repeated Boys, and with an enormous but moderate paw he thrust Thoms back and closed the doors.

"Look at this!" whispered Alleyn.

Fox and Boys, for a split second, glimpsed what he held in his hand. Then he bent down again and worked feverishly.

"What'll we do?" asked Fox quietly. "Go right into it—now?"

For an instant Alleyn hesitated. Then he said:

"No—not here. Wait! Work it this way."

He had given his instructions when Roberts returned from the telephone.

"Nobody there," he told them. "I rang up my house, but there's no message. Whoever it was must have been cut off."

"Bore for you," said Alleyn.

Sister Marigold came in, followed by Thoms. Marigold saw the Yard men still in possession, and hesitated.

"Hallo, 'allo," shouted Thoms, "what's all this? Caught Roberts in the act?"

"Really, Mr. Thoms," said Roberts in a rage and went over to his apparatus. "All right, matron," said Alleyn, "I've done. You want to clear up, I expect."

"Oh, well—yes."

"Go ahead. We'll make ourselves scarce. Fox, you and Boys give Dr. Roberts a hand out with that cruet-stand."

"Thank you," said Roberts, "I'll manage."

"No trouble at all, sir," Fox assured him.

Alleyn left them there. He ran downstairs and out into Brook Street, where he hailed a taxi.

In forty minutes the same taxi put him down in Wigmore Street. This time he had two plain-clothes sergeants with him. Dr. Roberts's little butler opened the door. His face was terribly white. He looked at Alleyn without speaking and then stood aside. Alleyn, followed by his men, walked into the drawing-room. Roberts stood in front of the fireplace. Above him the picture of the little lake and the Christmas trees shone cheerfully in the lamplight. Fox stood inside the door and Boys near the window. The anæsthetic apparatus had been wheeled over by the desk.

When Roberts saw Alleyn he tried to speak, but at first could not. His lips moved as though he was speaking, but there were no words. Then at last they came.

"Inspector Alleyn—why—have you sent these men—after me?"

For a moment they looked at each other.

"I had to," said Alleyn. "Dr. Roberts, I have a warrant here for your arrest. I must warn you——"

"What do you mean!" screamed Roberts. "You've no grounds—no proof—you fool—what are you doing?"

Alleyn walked over to the thing like a cruet. He stooped down, unscrewed something that looked like a nut and drew it out. With it came a hypodermic syringe. The 'nut' was the top of the piston.

"Grounds enough," said Alleyn.

It took the four men to hold Roberts and they had to put handcuffs on him. The insane are sometimes physically very strong.

CHAPTER XVIII

Retrospective

Saturday, the twentieth. Evening.

Two evenings after the arrest Alleyn dined with Nigel and Angela. The inspector had already been badgered by Nigel for copy and had thrown him a few bones to gnaw. Angela, however, pined for first-hand information. During dinner the inspector was rather silent and withdrawn. Something prompted Angela to kick Nigel smartly on the shin when he broached the subject of the arrest. Nigel suppresed a cry of pain and glared at her. She shook her head slightly.

"Was it very painful, Bathgate?" asked Alleyn. "Er—oh—yes," said Nigel sheepishly.

"How did you know I kicked him?" Angela inquired. "You must be a detective."

"Not so that you would notice it, but perhaps I am about to strike form again."

"Hallo—all bitter, are you? Aren't you pleased with yourself over this case, Mr. Alleyn?" Angela ventured.

"One never gets a great deal of gratification from a fluke."

"A fluke!" exclaimed Nigel.

"Just that——"

He held his glass of port under his nose, glanced significantly at Nigel and sipped it.

"Go on," he said resignedly. "Go on. Ask me. I know perfectly well why I'm here and you don't produce a wine like this every evening. Bribery. Subtle corruption. Isn't it, now?"

"Yes," said Nigel simply.

"I won't have Mr. Alleyn bullied," said Angela.

"You would if *he* could," rejoined Alleyn cryptically. "I know your tricks and your manners."

The others were silent.

"As a matter of fact," Alleyn continued, "I have every intention of talking for hours."

They beamed.

"What an angel you are, to be sure," said Angela. "Bring that decanter next door. Don't dare sit over it in here. The ladies are about to leave the dining-room."

She got up; Alleyn opened the door for her, and she went through into Nigel's little sitting-room, where she hastily cast four logs on the fire, pulled up a low table between two armchairs, and sat down on the hearthrug.

"Come on!" she called sternly.

They came in. Alleyn put the decanter down reverently on the table, and in a moment they were all settled.

"Now," said Angela, "I do call this fun."

She looked from Nigel to Alleyn. Each had the contented air of the well-fed male. The fire blazed up with a roar and a crackle, lighting the inspector's dark head and his admirable hands. He settled himself back and, easing his chin, turned and smiled at her.

"You may begin," said Angela.

"But—where from?"

"From the beginning—well, from the operating theatre."

"Oh. The remark I invariably make about the theatre is that it afforded the ideal setting for a murder. The whole place was cleaned up scientifically—hygienically—completely—as soon as the body of the victim was removed. No chance of a fingerprint, so significant bits and pieces left on the floor. Nothing. As a matter of fact, of course, had it been exactly as it was, we should have found nothing that pointed to Roberts." Alleyn fell silent again.

"Begin from where you first suspected Roberts," suggested Nigel.

"From where *you* suspected him, rather. The funny little man, you know."

"By gum, yes. So I did."

"Did *you*?" Angela asked.

"I had no definite theory about him," said Alleyn. "That's why I talked about a fluke. I was uneasy about him. I had a hunch, and I hate hunches. The first day I saw him in his house I began to feel jumpy about him, and fantastic ideas kept dodging about at the back of my mind. He was, it seemed, a fanatic. That long, hectic harangue about hereditary taints—somehow it was too vehement. He was obviously nervous about the case and yet he couldn't keep off it. He very delicately urged the suicide theory and backed it up with a lecture on eugenics. He was certainly sincere, too sincere, terribly earnest. The whole atmosphere was unbalanced. I recognised the man with an *idée fixe*. Then he told me a long story about how he'd once given an overdose, and that was why he never gave injections. That made me uncomfortable, because it was such a handy proof of innocence. '*He* can't have done the job, because he never gives an injection.' Then I saw his stethoscope with rows of notches on the stem and again there was a perfect explanation. He said it was a sort of tally for every anæsthetic he gave successfully to patients with heart disease. I was reminded of Indian tomahawks and Edward S. Ellis, and more particularly of a catapult I had as a boy and the notches I cut in the handle for every bird I killed. The fantastic notion that the stethoscope was *that* sort of tally-stick nagged and nagged at me. When we found he was one of the Lenin Hall lot I wondered if he could possibly be their agent, and yet I didn't somehow think there was anything in the Lenin Hall lot. When we discovered he had hoped to egg them on over the Sterilisation Bill I felt that accounted perfectly for his association with them. Next time I saw him I meant to surprise him with a sudden question about them. He completely defeated me by talking about them of his own accord. That might have been a subtle move, but I didn't think so. He lent me his book and here again I found the fanatic. I don't know why it is that pursuit of any branch of scientific thought which is greatly concerned with sex so often leads to morbid obsession. Not always, by any means—but very often. I've met it over and over again. It's an interesting point and I'd like to know the explanation. Roberts's book is a sound, a well-written plea for rational breeding. It is not in the least hysterical, and yet, behind it, in the personality of the writer, I smelt hysteria. There was one chapter where he said that a future civilisation might avoid the expense and trouble of supporting its a-ments and de-ments by eliminating them altogether. 'Sterilisation,' he wrote, 'might in time be replaced by extermination.' After reading that I forced myself to face up to that uneasy idea that had worried me ever since I first spoke to him. O'Callaghan came of what Roberts would regard as tainted stock. Suppose—suppose, thought I, blushing at my own credulity, suppose Roberts had got the bright idea of starting the good work by destroying such people every time he got the opportunity? Suppose he had brought if off several times before, and that every time he'd had a success he ticked it up on his stethoscope?"

"Oh, murder!" Nigel apostrophised.

"You may say so."

"Have some port."

"Thank you. It sounded so incredibly far-fetched that I simply hadn't the nerve to confide in Fox. I carried on with all the others—Mr. Sage and his remedies, Phillips and his girl, Banks and the Bolshies. Well, the patent medicine Sage provided through Miss O'Callaghan—'Fulvitavolts,' he calls it—has an infinitesimal amount of hyoscine. The second lot that Miss O'Callaghan administered in the hospital was an unknown quantity until I got the remnant from her. Of course, the fact that he had been responsible for O'Callaghan taking any hyoscine at all threw our Harold into a fearful terror, especially as he was one of the Lenin Hall lot. He tried to get me to believe the second concoction was a doctor's prescription, and very nearly led himself into real trouble. We have since found that this drug, too, only contained a very small amount of hyoscine. Exit Mr. Sage. Banks might have substituted hyoscine for camphor when she prepared the syringe, but I found that the stock solution of hyoscine contained the full amount minus one dose that was accounted for. She might have smuggled in another somehow, or she might have filled up the jar afterwards, but it didn't seem likely. Phillips remained and Phillips worried me terribly. He loomed so large with his threats, his opportunity, his motive. Roberts paled beside him. I caught myself continually opposing these two men. After all, as far as one could see, Roberts had had no chance of giving a hypodermic injection, whereas Phillips, poor devil, had had every opportunity. I staged the reconstruction partly to see if there *was* any way in which Roberts could have done it. I called for him at his house. Now, although I had asked Phillips specifically to have the anæsthetic appliance, Roberts was coming away without it. When I reminded him, he went and got it. I noticed that he wasn't keen on my handling it, and that several times he touched the nuts. It was perfectly

184

reasonable, but it made me look at them and kept them in my mind. Remember I was by no means wedded to my fantastic idea—rather the reverse. I was ashamed of it and I still reasoned, though I did not feel, that Phillips was the principal suspect. We watched them all closely. Then came the fluke—the amazing, the incredible fluke. Old Marigold lost her nerve and did a trip over the cruet-thing that holds the gasometers. Thoms helped Roberts, in a way, by a spirited rendering of the jack-in-office. Thoms is a bit of a funk and he was scared. He made a rumpus. If it hadn't been for my 'idea,' I shouldn't have watched Roberts. As it was, he gave a magnificent performance. But he went green round the gills and he was most careful to let no one touch the nuts. As a matter of fact, I believe Thoms's funk was entirely superfluous—it is most unlikely that the cylinder would blow up. Think what a shock it must have been to Roberts. Suppose the syringe had fallen out! Practically an impossibility—but in the panic of the moment his imagination, his 'guilty knowledge' if you like, would play tricks with his reason. I rather felt I had allowed mine to do the same. My dears, my head was in a whirl, I promise you."

"But when," asked Angela, "did Dr. Roberts inject the hyoscine?"

"I think soon after the patient was put on the table. The screen over the chest would hide his hands."

"I see."

"After the reconstruction Roberts wouldn't leave us alone. He hung about in the theatre, intent, of course, on keeping me away from the cruet. Fox, bless his heart, rumbled this ruse and staged a bogus telephone call. He saw I wanted to be rid of Roberts. As soon as we were alone I fell on the cruet, and, after a nerve-racking fumble, unearthed the syringe. Eureka! Dénouement! Fox nearly had a fit of the vapours."

"So you arrested him there and then!" cried Angela.

"No. No, I didn't. For one thing I hadn't a warrant and for another—oh, well——"

Alleyn rested his nose on his clasped hands.

"Now what's coming?" asked Angela.

"I rather liked the little creature. It would have been an unpleasant business pulling him in there. Anyway, I went off and got a warrant and Fox and Boys accompanied him home. They watched him carefully in case he tried to give himself the *coup de grâce*, but he didn't. When I arrested him he had, I believe, a sudden and an appalling shock, a kind of dreadful moment of lucidity. He fought us so violently that he seemed like a sane man gone mad, but I believe he was a madman gone sane. It only lasted a few minutes. Now I don't think he cares at all. He has made a complete confession. He's batty. He'll have to stand his trial, but I think they'll find that the nut in the cruet-stand is not the only one loose. It may even be that Roberts, recognising the taint of madness in himself, felt the eugenic urge the more strongly and the need for eliminating the unfit. In that point of view there is precisely the kind of mad logic one would expect to find in such a case."

"If it hadn't been for the matron's trip, would you never have got him?" asked Nigel.

"I think we should—in the end. We should have got his history from Canada and Australasia. It's coming through now. When it's complete I am pretty certain we shall find a series of deaths after anæsthetics given by Roberts. They will all prove to be cases where there were signs of hereditary insanity. I shouldn't mind betting they correspond with the notches on the stethoscope—minus one."

"Minus one?" asked Nigel.

"He added a fresh notch, no doubt, on Thursday, the eleventh. The last one does look more recent, although he'd rubbed a bit of dirt into it. You may think, as judges say when they mean you ought to think, that it was an extremely rum thing for him to leave the syringe in the cruet after the job was done. Not so rum. It was really the safest place imaginable. Away from there it would have been a suspicious-looking object, with a nut, instead of the ordinary top, to the piston. I believe that extraordinary little man filled it up with hyoscine whenever he was called out to give an anæsthetic to someone he did not know, just on the off-chance the patient should turn out to be what I understand sheep-farmers call a 'cull'. It's a striking example of the logic of the lunatic."

"Oh," cried Angela, "I do hope they find him insane."

"Do you?"

"Don't you?"

"I hardly know. That means a criminal lunatic asylum. It's a pity we are not allowed to hand him one of his own hypodermics."

There was a short silence.

"Have some port?" said Nigel.

"Thank you," said Alleyn. He did not pour it out, however, but sat looking abstractedly into the fire.

"You see," he murmured at last, "he's done his job. From his point of view it's all a howling success. He does nothing but tell us how clever he's been. His one anxiety is lest he may not be appreciated. He's busy writing a monograph for which all your gods of Fleet Street, Bathgate, will offer fabulous prices. At least he is assured of competent defence."

"What about Sir John Phillips and Jane Harden?" asked Angela.

"What about them, Miss Angela?"

"Is she going to marry him now?"

"How should I know?"

"She'll be a fool if she doesn't," said Angela emphatically.

"I'm afraid you've got the movie-mind. You want a final close-up. 'John—I want you to know that—that—' Ecstatic glare at short distance into each other's faces. Sir John utters an amorous growl: 'You damned little fool,' and snatches her to his bosom. Slow fade-out."

"That's the stuff," said Angela. "I like a happy ending."

"We don't often see it in the Force," said Alleyn. "Have some port?"

"Thank you."

187

ALSO BY NGAIO MARSH

Vintage Murder

New Zealand theatrical manager Alfred Meyer wanted to celebrate his wife's birthday in style. The *pièce de résistance* would be
the jeroboam of champagne which would descend gently into a
nest of fern and coloured lights on the table, set up on stage
after the performance.

But something went horribly wrong. Chief Detective Inspector
Alleyn witnessed it himself. Was Meyer's death the product of
Maori superstitions? Or something much more down to earth?

'The theatre detail is engrossing.'   MARGARET LEWIS

'A far more ambitious novel than anything Marsh had
attempted before.'   *American Journal of Popular Culture*

'Her work is as nearly flawless as makes no odds. Character,
plot, wit, good writing, and sound technique.'   *Sunday Times*

ISBN: 0 00 651255 0

ALSO BY NGAIO MARSH

Death in a White Tie

The season had begun. Débutantes and chaperones were planning their luncheons, teas, dinners, balls. And the blackmailer was planning his strategies, stalking his next victim.

But Chief Detective Inspector Roderick Alleyn knew that something was up. He had already planted his friend Lord Robert Gospell at the scene.

But someone else got there first . . .

'The best detective story I have ever read'
DASHIELL HAMMETT

'[This book has] a distinction that puts the author in the front rank of crime story writers'   *Times Literary Supplement*

'A brilliant, vivacious teller of detective novels.'   *News Chronicle*

ISBN: 0 00 651257 7

ALSO BY NGAIO MARSH

Surfeit of Lampreys

The Lampreys had plenty of charm – but no cash. They all knew they were peculiar – and rather gloried in it. The double and triple charades, for instance, with which they would entertain their guests – like rich but awful Uncle Gabriel, who was always such a bore. The Lampreys thought if they jollied him up he would bail them out – yet again.

Instead, Uncle Gabriel met a violent end. And Chief Inspector Alleyn had to work our which of them killed him . . .

'Brilliantly readable . . . first class detection.'   *Observer*

'Ngaio Marsh transcended the detective genre by the power of her writing and the rich variety of characters who people her novels.'   P.D. JAMES

'Ngaio Marsh is among the most brilliant of those authors who are transforming the detective story from a mere puzzle into a novel with many other qualities.'   *Times Literary Supplement*

ISBN: 0 00 651236 4

ALSO BY NGAIO MARSH

Death and the Dancing Footman

It began as an entertainment: eight people, many of them enemies, gathered for a winter weekend by a host with a love for theatre. They would be the characters in a drama that he would devise.

It ended in snowbound disaster. Everyone had an alibi – and most a motive as well. But Chief Detective Inspector Roderick Alleyn, when he finally arrived, knew it all hung on Thomas, the dancing footman . . .

'On the plane of art.'

Tatler

'Nobody in her racket begins to touch her for writing grace and few possess her skill at creating potential corpses and suspects, building a puzzle and other essentials of grand and lofty detection. There hasn't been anyone like her since the palmiest days of Dorothy L. Sayers.'

New York Herald Tribune

'She is astoundingly good.'

Daily Express

ISBN: 0 00 651237 2

ALSO BY NGAIO MARSH

Colour Scheme

It was a horrible death – Maurice Questing was lured into a pool of boiling mud and left there to die.

Chief Inspector Roderick Alleyn, far from home on a wartime quest for German agents, knew that any number of people could have killed him: the English exiles he'd hated, the New Zealanders he'd despised or the Maoris he'd insulted. Even the spies he'd thwarted – if he was wasn't a spy himself. . .

'The queen of the straight crime novel – long may she reign!'
Sunday Times

'The brilliant New Zealander Ngaio Marsh claims a high level as to sheer writing and still more as a view of humanity.'
ELIZABETH BOWEN

'Nobody begins to touch Ngaio Marsh's skill at creating corpses and suspects . . . her dialogue is a continuius delight.'
New York Herald Tribune

ISBN: 0 00 651238 0

ALSO BY NGAIO MARSH

Scales of Justice

The lives of the inhabitants of Swevenings are disrupted only by a fierce competition to catch the Old Un, a monster trout known to dwell in a beautiful stream which winds past their homes.

Then one of their small community is found brutally murdered; beside him is the freshly killed trout. Both died by violence – but Chief Detective Inspector Roderick Alleyn's murder investigation seems to be much more interested in the fish . . .

Winner of a Crime Writers' Association 'Red Herring Award' in 1955.

'Excellently characterized, Miss Marsh's best yet.'   *Observer*

'The detection is first class. The whole affair is written with style and distinction.'   *BBC*

ISBN: 0 00 651242 9